TAKE A RISK

risqué one

SCARLETT FINN

ISBN: 9781914517365

www.scarlettfinn.com

Also by Scarlett Finn

GO NOVELS
GO WITH IT
GO IT ALONE
GO ALL OUT
GO ALL IN
GO FULL CIRCLE

MCDADE BROTHERS NOVELS
ALL. ONLY.
ONLY YOURS

WRECK & RUIN
RUIN ME
RUIN HIM

THE BRANDED SERIES
BRANDED
SCARRED
MARKED

EXILE
HIDE & SEEK
KISS CHASE

TO DIE FOR...
TO DIE FOR TRUTH
TO DIE FOR HONOR
TO DIE FOR VIRTUE
TO DIE FOR DUTY
TO DIE FOR LOVE

LOVE AGAINST THE ODDS STANDALONE COLLECTION
SWEET SEAS
HEIR'S AFFAIR
RESCUED
MAESTRO'S MUSE
GETTING TRICKY
THIRTEEN
REMEMBER WHEN...
RELUCTANT SUSPICION
XY FACTOR

NOTHING TO...
NOTHING TO HIDE
NOTHING TO LOSE
NOTHING TO DECLARE
NOTHING TO US
NOTHING TO SAY
NOTHING TO YOU

THE FORBIDDEN NOVELS
FORBIDDEN DESIRE
FORBIDDEN WANT
FORBIDDEN WISH
FORBIDDEN NEED

KINDRED SERIES
RAVEN
SWALLOW
CUCKOO
SWIFT
FALCON
FINCH

THE EXPLICIT SERIES
EXPLICIT INSTRUCTION
EXPLICIT DETAIL
EXPLICIT MEMORY

MISTAKE DUET
MISTAKE ME NOT
SLEIGHT MISTAKE

RISQUÉ & HARROW INTERTWINED
TAKE A RISK
FIGHTING FATE
RISK IT ALL
FIGHTING BACK
GAME OF RISK

LOST & FOUND
LOST
FOUND

ONE

"WITHOUT EVIDENCE that this person intends to do you harm, Doctor Cutler, there's nothing we can do."

To give him his due, Officer Ronson had been pleasant despite probably believing they were crazy. Sitting at his desk, Lyssa clutched her best friend's hand recognizing that Suzette was working herself into a lather. Appealing to the seasoned detective hadn't worked so far.

Ronson and his young partner, Miguel Chavez, had to be sick of the sight of her. At Suzette's prompting, she'd been in the precinct half a dozen times over the course of the last four months. With the lack of interest that always greeted her, Lyssa didn't see the point of reporting each incident, certainly not anymore.

"This is ridiculous," Suzette said. "My friend is being terrorized."

"With all due respect, Miss. Blossom, flowers on the back stairs don't rank high in the danger-to-life index."

The officer was doing his job and had a point.

Except her predicament was about so much more than flowers. "What about the phone calls?" Lyssa asked.

"You said it had been a couple of weeks since he called," Ronson said.

"Yes, but—"

"Maybe he's a secret admirer."

"He prowls around outside her house," Suzette exclaimed, slamming her hands to the table, thrusting onto her feet.

Hoping to soothe her friend, Lyssa stroked her arm. "It is disconcerting to know that someone was in my yard."

"You've called us out and we never find anyone," Ronson said, consulting the file in front of him. "Same as the suspicious cars you and your friend keep reporting. Everything checks out."

"You think I'm crazy," Lyssa muttered.

"She's a goddamn psychiatrist!" Suzette said, pointing at her. "If she was crazy, she'd be the first one to recognize the symptoms! You people are supposed to protect the innocent."

"Keep filling out your diary," Ronson said, pushing Lyssa's black notebook back to her. "And if you're threatened or attacked then please call nine-one-one."

"What use is that *after* she's been attacked?" Suzette asked.

Her best friend was fiercely protective but flipping out wouldn't get them anywhere.

Taking her purse from the floor, Lyssa slid the strap to her shoulder as she stood to put an arm around her friend. "Thank you for your time," she said, picking up the notebook and tucking it into her purse with one hand. "We'd appreciate you leaving a note in the file that we reported this."

"Sure thing," Ronson said, smiling for the first time, no doubt because the crazy people were leaving.

Chavez opened the door for them.

Even though Suzette kept her seething quiet, it was apparent with the red face and huffing impatience. Lyssa wound them through the precinct and got outside without them exchanging a word. Their car was parked around the block, so they cut down an alley at the side of the police building.

"We should report those guys," Suzette grumbled.

"Wait until we're in the car before you lose it, Suzie,"

Lyssa said. "We'll go somewhere nice for lunch."

Lunch would calm her friend down. Not that she'd say that out loud; Suzie had a short fuse at the best of times.

"Doctor Cutler?"

The voice from behind made both women turn. Miguel Chavez stood in a side doorway of the police building, alone. Before approaching them, he took the time to look up and down the alley.

"Come to belittle us some more, have you?" Suzette sniped.

"Ronson is old school," Chavez said. "He thinks stalking is a new fad."

"And you don't?" Lyssa asked.

"I know… something about it."

"Like what?"

"Like that you're not going to get very far here until you're hospitalized or dead. Short of coming up with concrete evidence that this lunatic is on your tail…"

It was nice to be believed if nothing else. "So you're here to tell me to stop wasting my time and yours?" Lyssa asked. "Forgive me, but if I don't report the prowler's actions then he's getting away with it. What else am I supposed to do?"

"Visit someone who can help," Chavez said, handing her a business card.

Black with curly red writing, it listed the address of something called "Risqué." If the outline of the woman draped along the side was anything to go by, it was a strip joint.

"A stripper?" Suzette asked. "You want us to go to a stripper?"

"No," Chavez said, moving in closer and lowering his voice. "Go there tomorrow night, eleven p.m., ask at the bar for Trapper."

"Trapper?" Lyssa said.

"Trust me; he'll be able to help. If anyone asks where you got this information don't use my name."

"Why not?" Suzette asked, getting excited. "Is he a superhero? A mercenary? Or a sniper, who will take this guy out with one shot? Pow!"

Trying not to laugh, Lyssa squeezed Suzette's hand. "I don't want to be the cause of anyone getting hurt."

"Trapper's not security," Chavez said. "But he will solve your problem."

"How will he do that?"

"Ask him."

Chavez walked backward toward the door and then disappeared inside, leaving Lyssa and Suzette staring at the card.

"What do you think?"

"Is it too early for a drink?" Suzette asked.

Taking her friend's lead, they went to the car and drove to their favorite restaurant only a block from the hospital Suzette worked at with her fiancé.

Once they'd ordered food and received their drinks, Lyssa took the card from her pocket and placed it on the table. "Is he setting us up?"

"For what?"

"I don't know. But I don't like the clandestine theatrics."

"He's a cop," Suzette said. "He's probably got all sorts of contacts. If this Trapper guy can help, then he's worth checking out."

"Are we there yet? I mean, are we really that desperate?"

"You're a prisoner in your own home. I want Lyssa back, my Lyssa, the real Lyssa. The Lyssa who wouldn't think twice about wandering the streets at three a.m. The Lyssa who would face off with bikers and boxers, who convinced an abusive husband to turn himself into the cops and be honest about his despicable deeds. Where is the Lyssa whose greatest aspiration was to write self-help books for us poor women clueless about the male mind?"

Lyssa smiled. "I haven't given up on that."

"No? You walked away from your marriage because your husband wouldn't support that dream."

"Archie didn't like to see me taking what he perceived as risks," Lyssa said. "He didn't have confidence that I knew what I was doing."

"Observing men in their natural habitat used to inspire you. When was the last time you went on one of your crazy crusades?"

"Studying male sexual behavior can be done at any time. I suppose I haven't been motivated recently."

"Because you think a stalker is studying you every minute," Suzette said, leaning back to let the server place their salads in front of them. When they were alone again, she took Lyssa's hand. "I don't blame you. It must be terrifying to know some nut is obsessed with you. But you've put your life on hold for him."

"I do find myself… concerned. But he's hardly a stalker, maybe he is just an admirer and doesn't mean any harm."

"After your divorce you bought that beautiful townhouse in the city and set up your practice. You promised me that taking on patients was a stopgap to help you pay the bills while you wrote your books. Writing was always your passion. The only reason you went to medical school was to appease your father."

"That's not entirely true," Lyssa said, used to her friend's rhetoric.

Her parents had scrimped and saved; they expected their only child to use her intelligence wisely. Seeing her graduate had been their greatest achievement. Though their happiest was probably watching her marry the rich plastic surgeon… shame that hadn't lasted. Telling them her marriage was over was the hardest thing she'd ever done.

Her intention had always been to study the mind, psychology fascinated her. She'd chosen to specialize in sexual dysfunction and never looked back. Her primary focus was male patients, but she worked with females and couples sometimes too. In her practice, she had a variety of patients ranging from those with simple marital issues, to victims of sexual abuse and assault.

"I want you to write your books," Suzette said. "Get inspired! Throw yourself into an assignment. Study your subjects up close, undercover, just like you used to."

If only it was that simple. With the admirer on her

tail, she'd become more aware of her movements, and her vulnerability. "I'm still writing and rewriting previous findings."

"But not studying anyone new, or putting yourself in new, exciting environments," Suzette said. "You're not going to do that until we get rid of this guy. I know you, Lyssa. You have to move on from this and find yourself again."

The only way to move forward was to free herself from the scrutiny of the obsessed person. But going to a stranger and asking for help didn't seem right. She liked to steer her own destiny. Playing the hapless or helpless victim wasn't in her nature. It was frustrating that this stalker had reduced her to that.

"Okay," she said to Suzette. "I'll think about it."

For now, that would have to do. Before making a decision, she liked to be absolutely sure. Once committed, Lyssa had a tendency towards jumping in at the deep end. The Risqué opportunity would play on her mind until the rendezvous time.

THAT EVENING, SITTING ALONE in the living room of her narrow townhouse, Lyssa read the latest instalment of her favorite fiction series under the light of a single floor lamp.

It played on her mind. The flowers, the precinct… Chavez's recommendation.

Until a few months ago, it hadn't bothered her that she didn't watch TV. Between med school and marriage, she'd never had time to sit down and absorb the banality of the latest sitcom. Without background noise, her home was eerily quiet, and she regretted never picking up the habit.

A sound. A snap outside… What was it? Was she being paranoid or was someone there?

Her house faced a city sidewalk. Most of the noise was ambient that she just filtered out. Occasionally, a sound or passing light would pique her attention.

The bedroom window seat was her favorite place to read. Showcasing her yard, sometimes she'd see wildlife in the trees that separated her property from the dog park behind it.

Since the whole stalker-admirer mess, she'd given up on reading there. The shadows out back convinced her things were there that weren't.

Given her profession, she could identify delusions and paranoid behavior. That was as much as her education could help. Sometimes she expected to look up and see the prowler in action, leaving roses on her back stairs or disappearing into the trees.

She never had.

Since buying her house after the divorce two years ago, she'd grown to love it more and more. Until the flowers and phone calls started, she'd been happy there. At first, the flowers were a surprise. The calls that followed unnerved her. Then, for no reason she could decipher, the admirer's actions stopped… only to start again the following week with flowers and a note. "*I see you.*" That was all it said.

From there, the harassment escalated in frequency, then abruptly stopped, and restarted to no discernable pattern. The assailant had no obvious goal, except to fixate on her, to scare and confuse her.

No one liked feeling helpless. Lyssa had fought to hold onto her confidence and maintain control while someone tried to take it away.

The predator wanted something. It was that unknown which scared her the most.

TWO

"I'M TELLING YOU, HONESTLY, Doctor Cutler, I'm so horny that purple statue thing over there is looking hot to me right now."

Displayed on a side dresser in her first-floor office, the steel statue was fashioned like a single teardrop flame with a similar shaped hole near the bulge at the base.

For a moment, both Lyssa and her patient focused on it. "Let's keep this in perspective," she said. "Your wife is still accommodating you. You said that you had sex twice last week and three times the week before."

"Yeah, but you don't understand." Her fidgety patient ran a hand through his hair. "When we got together, we were at it all the time, constantly, now it's like no big deal to her."

"You got together when you were eighteen," she said. "You've been together for twenty years and had three children. Relationships develop over time, they progress. We can't expect things to stay the same forever. You've had some success with my suggestions to entice Harriet."

"The thing is, there's this girl at work and man, oh, man. She's calling to me. We had lunch the other day and my leg brushed hers under the table. I had a boner the rest of the day."

Lyssa put her notebook on the circular table next to her leather armchair. "The first thing you told me when we started our sessions was that you loved your wife very much. You were determined to stay faithful. Has your stance changed?"

"No! I love Harriet and I do want to be with her, only her… she's just not meeting my needs."

Glancing at the clock she offered Lee Zucker a smile. "We'll pick up there next week, Lee," she said. "Just take it one day at a time. Try not to act on impulse and remember where your priorities lie."

She scheduled his next appointment, and they said goodbye. After he left, she went to her desk and updated patient notes on her laptop.

Her office and waiting room were on the first floor of the house. A basement beneath was storage and her home was laid over the second and third floors. There was attic space too, which she'd talked about converting, but hadn't acted on yet.

She didn't need more space. The two-bedroom house suited her. After enduring hectic med school and a marriage that didn't fit, enjoying her own space was a dream.

"Hello!"

Lyssa had just closed Lee's file when Suzette poked her head around the office door.

"Hey," Lyssa said. "I'm done, just let me get changed and we'll go."

"Dinner and drinks, then we hunt for your white knight."

Lyssa grabbed her purse while the computer shut down. "This Trapper guy could be a nut too, you know."

Her friend huffed. "I am not going to let you back out of this."

"We could be inviting trouble," Lyssa said, guiding Suzette out of the office.

They went upstairs to the main reception room at the front of the house. It encompassed her living room and kitchen. While Lyssa kicked off her shoes and wriggled out of her pantyhose, Suzette poured wine.

"Since when do you avoid trouble?"

"Trouble can be interesting," Lyssa conceded, wiggling her toes.

"Trouble is what you've been in for months," Suzette said. "This weirdo stalker is taking over your life and the police won't do a thing."

She went to the kitchen to accept the proffered wine. "Don't get upset again. The police can't do anything because there's no evidence. They can't pursue a person no one can identify."

"Which is why we're going to Risqué."

According to the internet, Risqué was a strip joint bordering the red-light district.

"All Chavez said was to go to the bar and ask for Trapper, doesn't that sound…"

Sinister. Ominous… Crazy?

"The cop chased us down with an off the record referral. We have to go, and it has to be tonight. What if there's no second chance? Aren't you curious?"

Yes, of course, but she was meant to be the sensible one. "The cops are powerless, maybe he felt bad about that. They can't stakeout my house for months waiting for this guy to show up."

"The cops can't do anything? Fine. Maybe this Trapper guy can. He could provide security. At least you'd get a decent night's sleep."

"Chavez said that Trapper wasn't security. He said he'd solve my problem."

"It's this or you come and stay with me. Pete and I would love to have you. If it would make you feel safer—"

"No," Lyssa said, taking her wine over to the living room couch. "I won't lead this potentially dangerous person to your place." Rubbing the back of her neck, she rolled her head. "I wish I knew who it was. Not knowing is the worst part."

"We're going to find out," Suzette said, sitting down to take her hand. "That's why we have to go. If we don't, anything could happen. Do you want the crazy stalker to catch up with you? Do you want to regret not giving this Trapper a shot? You'll regret it if the stalker rapes and guts you."

"Fine," Lyssa groaned, putting her wine in Suzette's hand. "I'll go and get ready… I'll need a few more glasses of wine to loosen me up."

"No argument here!" Suzette called.

Lyssa retreated to the bedroom to change out of her work clothes. Freeing herself of the stalker had to be a priority. The cops were clear that there was nothing they could do. She didn't blame them for their skepticism either. Evidence was sparse.

Even if pity was Officer Chavez's motivation, she shouldn't flout the opportunity. Suzette was right, passing up the possibility Trapper could help would be madness.

It could be a one-time deal.

Desperation was closer than she'd like. Some of her clients experienced that edge and it could escalate into dangerous territory quickly.

The tip had come from a cop. That gave confidence. It had to be legitimate. To sleep through the night again, she needed to have faith in her friend and in Officer Miguel Chavez.

THREE

WHEN THEY GOT OUT of the taxi on the blackened street, Lyssa looped her arm through Suzette's. "Oh yeah, this was a great idea," she whispered.

A group of men stood on the corner wearing baggy pants and bandanas or baseball caps. Some barely dressed women hung around on another. Either those girls worked in Risqué, or they worked the club's customers. Observing them for a few seconds, she deduced the women weren't on their way anywhere. The street corner was their workplace. She'd worked with hookers during her years of training. They taught her a lot.

"Come on, this is fun!" Suzette exclaimed. "Your sense of adventure has always been bigger than mine, you're fearless… Is this what your undercover assignments were like? I'm so excited."

An adrenaline high in such shady situations could be risky. Projecting confidence didn't mean being fearless. Still, in the name of science, pushing boundaries was exactly the point. While ensconced behind the façade of professional interest, misgivings were cast aside.

Suzette dragged her across the rain-soaked street. A flashing neon girl next to the illuminated red Risqué sign was the beacon calling to them.

Two bulky security guards, dressed in black, flanked the door.

"Hello, boys!" Suzette shrieked. "How does this work? Do we pay to get in? We're strip joint virgins."

She nudged her friend, rebuking the display of naivety, but the guards grinned. "No kidding," one of them said. The two giants separated to grant entry. "Women get in free."

Suzette squealed and rushed in, hurrying them toward the thumping music and flashing lights at the end of a dark corridor. Teeming with life, two clear types filled the massive space: leering men and near-naked women.

Most of the circular tables were occupied by those focused on the lit stage at the head of the room. Booths around the perimeter contained their own private podiums where topless women danced for the patrons' pleasure.

Fascinating.

Her intrigue could've kept her there all day. Thank God Suzette took charge and dragged her to the bar. Male bartenders handed trays of drinks to women in skin-tight, low-cut tops, and micro-mini skirts. This place kept Lycra in business for sure. Half a dozen men perched at the bar but features of faces and expressions were difficult to decipher in the low light.

A bartender came over. "Don't get many like you in here," the bartender called over the music coming from the stage. "Looking for a job?"

Squeezing her arm, Suzette urged her on. "We're looking for Trapper," Lyssa said.

Curiosity struck the bartender, shifting his expression from smiling to serious. "Wait here," he said and walked away.

No description or information, just a single instruction.

Suzette shoved Lyssa onto a stool. "Don't you feel better?" she asked. "This isn't so bad."

Someone else spoke before she could reply.

"What are you ladies drinking?" asked a grumbling voice from further along the bar.

"Oh!" Suzette said, beaming. "Are we being hit on?"

With a glare, Lyssa silenced her friend. Adrenaline was keeping Suzette on high. Lyssa tried to be more discerning. Her scientific curiosity was piqued by the mysterious male doused in shadow.

"You're surrounded by a host of semi-nude women," she said to him. "Why would you make a play for the only women not on offer here?"

"Those women are working and they're not hookers."

"Implying that we are?" Lyssa asked.

The broad man slid off his stool, three places away, and came to sit on the stool next to hers. Dark honey brown hair, rough stubble on his jaw… he was attractive. Very attractive. Would hookers be a hobby for this kind of guy?

He stretched his long legs toward her, his scrutiny sizing her up. "Can't figure why a woman would come into a place like this," he drawled. "Unless you two are together… and I wouldn't mind being the meat in that sandwich."

Suzette laughed. Lyssa wasn't so easily swayed and maintained eye contact with him. Flesh was on show, hot, sexy women were scattered around the room. Some were dancing, arousing their spectators. This guy didn't show a lick of interest. What a puzzle.

"Why would you come to a place like this and not watch the show?"

"I've seen their show," he said, his attention drifting down her body. "Yours is still a mystery."

"Which is the way it will stay," Lyssa said. "I'm here to talk to a friend."

"About what?"

"None of your business."

Suzette leaned past her. "She's being stalked," she hissed in a giggle.

Turned out wine and adrenaline were not a good combination for the beautiful blonde.

"Stalked, huh?" the man said, raising his brows. "Then you're looking for Trapper."

What? Hmm. How did he know that? Trapper must

have a reputation. With every word, the stranger's allure grew. Good thing she wasn't the type to be tempted by a handsome face… at least not until motives were clear.

"Do you know him?" she asked.

"Maybe," he said and shrugged. "Maybe if you'd been nicer and accepted that drink…"

"You'll give us information if we let you buy us drinks?" Suzette asked, then snorted. "That's a pretty good deal."

"He doesn't know anything," Lyssa said, less impressed. "He obviously heard me say Trapper's name to the bartender. He's trying to manipulate us into drinking with him. He'll probably spike the drinks."

The guy snickered. "Smart. You're smart… But Trapper doesn't let drugs in here."

"This is his club?" Lyssa asked.

"If you were his friends, you'd know his connection to Risqué… You're so full of shit."

He reached over to retrieve the drink he'd left at his previous seat, proving he wasn't worried about drugs or unattended drinks.

"We're not full of shit," Lyssa said.

"You're not friends of Trapper."

"We are!" Suzette asserted. "We are too his friends."

"Trapper doesn't have friends like either of you," he said after gulping from his glass.

Suspicion high, Lyssa peered closer. "How would you know that we're not his friends?"

"Because I've never had a conversation with you in my life, Doctor Cutler," he said, shoving his glass away, looking her in the eye. "I'd sure remember having a friend like you."

Suzette gasped. "You're Trapper?"

"Chavez gave me the story," he said. "I'm not interested."

Of that, Lyssa wasn't so sure. "Why go through the theatrics just to let me down?"

The bartender came over to pour wine for both women then left them alone with the bottle. It was the same wine they'd been drinking all night. Was that supposed to be impressive or creepy? Because it was leaning into the latter.

"You're not discreet," he said as though that explained the creepiness. "My methods are unusual, and I only take one case at a time. My time is valuable."

"You're worried that something better might come along?"

"She's a doctor," Suzette announced.

Even when her friend was intrusive, Lyssa and the guy remained fixated on each other.

"Yeah, a shrink," Trapper said. "Not exactly a lifesaver in your field, are you?"

"She could save dozens from the brink of suicide," Suzette said. "You don't know."

"You're a sex therapist," he said, ignoring her friend. "You contribute to dozens of chickens getting choked."

She was familiar with the snickers that accompanied opinions of her occupation. "You don't know what you're talking about. You know nothing about what I do."

"Ditto," he said. "I can help you. I could get rid of this guy for you and the mystery is maybe enough to keep me interested."

"So what's the problem?"

"I can't work with you. I don't like difficult clients. I *do* like clients who follow the rules."

"What are the rules?"

Looking past her to Suzette, Trapper put a palm on the bar, summoning the bartender over. "This is Suzette Blossom," he said, introducing the bartender to her friend. "Call her a cab, she needs to go home."

Affronted, the insult was made worse by concern. "You're not taking my friend anywhere," Lyssa said.

"Difficult," Trapper said to the bartender. "See, I knew it. Didn't I say it before she came in?"

"You have a way of reading people," the bartender said.

"I'll go," Suzette interjected, pouncing off her stool. "You need him. I'll call you when I get home."

"This is a power play," Lyssa said, turning to her

friend. "He's trying to assert dominance."

"And you're fighting him for it," Suzette murmured, coming closer to stroke her hair and rest a hand on her shoulder. "It's not a big deal. A cop knows you're here for goodness sake. You're safe."

The women embraced and said goodnight.

Anxiety stayed even after her friend was gone. They were relying on the word of a cop, one low on the hierarchy. Worrying was natural. Still, Suzette would be fine; she did self-defense and was going home to her fiancé.

Pete would be home in less than an hour and would expect the woman he loved to be there when he arrived. He was totally risk averse. Hence why they hadn't confessed the intended destination of the evening. He would never have let Suzette get involved. Maybe she should've followed that track too.

FOUR

SOMEONE TOOK HER HAND. As Lyssa turned to see who, her hair was swept from her shoulder. Trapper. Right there, brushing the back of his fingers down her cheek.

"What are you doing?" she asked.

The bar was at her back, stools boxed her in, so she couldn't remove herself from him.

"We're going back to my office."

"No! No way. I didn't come here for that kind of deal."

He smiled, like he was enamored. "I don't conduct business out here in public. I also protect the anonymity of my clients. Watching eyes need to think we have a personal connection."

Something in his countenance measured her. This was a test. Just like their conversation. Was everything a test?

"Okay then," she said, never one to pass up a challenge.

Wearing a smile, she drenched his body with hers, pressing herself up against him. He didn't recoil, even after her arm curved around to squeeze his ass.

"Nice," he said, splaying his hands on her back. "Ready to go?"

"After you."

Taking her hand, Trapper led her from the bar towards the stage. The whole way she watched his ass. Man, it had felt good, toned, hard and so much nicer than she'd expected. It had been a long time since she'd been that close to a male. Usually, they were opposite her on the patient's couch.

Weaving through tables and bodies, he took her past a security guard and through a door by the stage. In a corridor, they went upstairs to a long hallway with three doors. The middle one was their target. He unlocked it and flicked on a light while guiding her inside.

"Come in," he said, dropping her hand and closing the door.

A desk with a table and a couple of filers behind it. Reasonable office setup. No red flags. Beside the door was a three-seat sofa and love seat aimed at a widescreen TV.

"Sit down," he said, pointing at the guest chair of the desk while going around it to take his own.

"This is an odd set up, Trapper," she said, seating herself.

"Colt Warner," he said, leaning over to offer his hand. "Chavez always was a sucker for beautiful women."

"Lyssa Cutler," she said, shaking his hand, struck by the formal introduction in such an informal setting. "Why the alias?"

"I protect my anonymity too."

"What are we doing up here?"

"You want to know who this guy is," he said on an inhale. "Is that all?"

"I want him to stop. I assume once we know who he is, the cops can do their thing."

"So you don't know what you're talking about? Good to know… What you need is his identity and an evidence portfolio."

Clearly, he did know what he was talking about.

"Okay," she said.

"That will be a minimum of four to eight weeks, possibly longer depending on his frequency and severity."

"Okay."

"I have most of what I need to complete—"

"Wait, tell me what you do. You think you can identify this guy?"

"There are a number of candidates to consider. We'll look at the usual, boyfriends, ex-husband, neighbors, disgruntled colleagues, in your case your patients."

"You're going to investigate my clients? You can't do that. There's confidentiality and—"

"I don't investigate them, I investigate you." Her jaw fell. "Stalkers can be complete strangers or your best friend. I keep an open mind. Fixating on one person at a time takes too long, especially in a case like yours. You've seen hundreds of patients over the years, in education and practice. Any of them could be our candidate."

"You're going to investigate me? How do you plan to do that?"

Leaning over his desk, he smiled. "I'm going to stalk you."

"Excuse me?"

"This guy watches you sometimes, right? He comes to your house and calls you. Traditional stalkers enjoy watching their victim, monitoring them. If he's watching you, then I want to catch him at it."

"You're going to watch me like he does? I'm getting two stalkers for the price of one."

"I'm not really watching you. Think of it like a stakeout. I'll be further away than him. Taking in the bigger picture. It's my goal to stalk him. As soon as I identify him, I'll start monitoring his movements, that's how we compile the evidence portfolio. I'll assemble a file of evidence showing his activity in relation to you."

She smiled. "Then we turn it all over to the police."

"You've got it. It gets him off the street and out of your life, legitimately."

"Sounds like a perfect deal, what's the catch?"

"You have to follow my rules," he said. "There are four things I make clear to my clients. They are the main points of my contract which we'll sign before I start."

"Four? Which are?"

"Let's do them in descending order. Number four, my services aren't free. You will pay for all services and expenses as laid out in the contract. I don't care how attractive you are, I don't take barter."

"Okay, that's fair and expected. Three?"

"I'm not security or a hit man. I won't take this guy out for you and I'm not there to intervene if things get physical. If you're alone, or scared, or need reassurance, call a friend or boyfriend, that's not my job."

"I understand, number two?"

"My methods might not be what you expect, but they've proven effective. Through this, I could ask you to do a bunch of things, to participate in activities or take specific actions. No questions. You do it or I walk."

Suspicion flared. "What kind of activities or actions?"

"I don't need to see you naked," he said as though he could read her mind. "There will be a purpose to my request and if there's time and opportunity, I'll explain it."

"And if there's not?"

"You'll have to trust me," he said and must have seen her bristle. "Look, I'm going to be watching you day and night until we ID this guy. So I'm about to get to know you intimately. Chavez is my cousin; he's a good kid and wouldn't have sent you here if he didn't think I could solve this. He knows to give out my information in exceptional circumstances."

"What's the first rule?" she asked.

"Don't mention me to anyone. Ever. I understand why you brought your friend tonight; it was smart not to come alone. But when Suzette asks, you tell her it didn't work out. That we couldn't agree on a price, or I was a sleaze, whatever. I don't care. Do not relay our conversation."

"You're trusting me to keep your identity a secret?"

"Trust has to go both ways. I can give you your life back; it's up to you if you want to screw up your best chance for that."

"Why is your anonymity so important?"

"Because I can't do what I do if everyone knows what

I do. I don't need anyone looking for me."

For months, she'd lived in torment, wondering if the perpetrator was watching. Jumping at every creak in her house, convinced that shadows were monsters. This guy, Colt, was offering her a chance. At the very least, if he could ID the stalker, she'd have vindication.

"Okay," she said. "Do you have a card? A number where I can reach you?"

"No," he said. "We come to an arrangement tonight. Next time you see me, I'll be on the job."

Flummoxed, it took a moment to process. "I need time to think about this," she said, shaking her head. "You can't railroad me into handing you a check when we just met."

"Good, because I don't take checks. I deal in cash. You can give me the retainer next time we see each other. Soon. Once I have a better handle on things. I'll contact you when I'm ready."

Rolling his chair backward, he opened a filing cabinet to pull out a contract. He retrieved a pen from his desk drawer and pushed both toward her. "If you want my help, sign it."

Picking up the stack of sheets, she skim read all three pages. "I think I do want your help," she said, eyeing the signature page. "You're unconventional, but conventional hasn't worked for me. We hired a PI two months ago. All he came back with was my ex-husband's bio and pictures of patients coming in and out of my office."

A huff of a laugh accompanied his smile. "You'll get your money's worth from me. I will keep going until I figure out who this guy is. I'm a sucker for a mystery."

She pondered aloud. "You were referred by a police officer, that's a point in your favor. You're related to said cop, so I know something personal about you, which puts me more at ease…" There were also points against. "That your base is a seedy sex club—"

"We don't sell sex," he said. Her eyes narrowed on him. "What I mean is, our girls aren't hookers, though what they do on their own time is their business. But we don't let any of them deal out of here."

"We?"

"I have a financial stake in the club. I'm nothing to do with running it. The club belongs to my brother, Blaser. The bartender you met downstairs."

"Your folks liked guns, didn't they?"

"My little brother's name is Ruger," he said. "My father's former military."

"And you? How did you get into this line of work?"

"My skills lend themselves to this kind of work."

"From the military?"

"No, not me," he said, laying on amusement. "I'd say that's enough personal information for now, Doctor Cutler."

"What's the retainer?"

"Five grand," he said. "Paid in cash, it will be deducted from your final bill."

"Okay," she said, rising from the chair with the contract. "We have a deal."

He stood too. "Sign the papers and we'll shake on it."

"Good," she said and held out a hand, which he took his time to shake. "We have a deal. I'll sign the papers after I read them thoroughly. Providing there's nothing out of line, expect them to be ready when you get in touch for your retainer."

"That doesn't work for me," he said, frowning. "That contract shouldn't leave this room."

She smiled. "I don't like bullies, Mr. Warner. I won't put my name on something without reading it."

"You think I'm bullying you?"

"I think you're used to getting your way, but I'm not easily intimidated. These past few months I've learned that giving in to fear is what the bully wants."

"He hasn't broken you yet," Colt said as she tucked away the pen and contract in her purse. "Without me, he will break you eventually."

"Then it's a good thing we shook hands, Mr. Warner. Now we have a deal, I'm not without you, am I?"

Exuding as much confidence as possible, Lyssa whirled around and strode out of the office hoping the adrenaline shaking her limbs wasn't noticeable. She'd stood up to him, proving he didn't intimidate her. She was committed and hoped Colt was too.

FIVE

LUNCH WITH SUZETTE was a regular occurrence; lying to her best friend was not.

Since finding each other through a roommate service in college, they'd never kept secrets. Not big ones. Being there for each other was important. Suzette was her maid of honor, her shoulder to cry on as her marriage fell apart. She'd even lived with her between leaving Archie and buying her house.

At a lunch restaurant, not far from Lyssa's home, the conversation had been dominated by one thing.

"I should've stayed," Suzette said. "If I stayed, he would've helped. I'd have worked it out."

"It wasn't meant to be," Lyssa said, off her salad.

Her friend frowned. "Chavez was so sure he could help. This Trapper guy must be playing hardball. We should go back. Show we're committed. I could talk to Pete, once he's off work—"

"You want to ask your boyfriend to take us to a strip club? No. We're going to figure this out. I'm not ready to give up yet."

Last night, she'd left the club in a cab and arrived home in the dark. These days, being out at night was unsettling; entering her unilluminated home was worse.

Pepper spray was her newest companion. She held it tight while unlocking the door and checked every corner of her home before returning the deterrent to its spot with a sigh of relief.

Every time she told herself not to be paranoid. There was no evidence the stalker had been inside her home, but she didn't want to take any chances.

"It seems like a waste to go there and come out with nothing," Suzette said, biting into her sandwich.

"It was a fascinating experience, don't you think?" Lyssa asked, admitting her curiosity. "I wouldn't say we got nothing."

Suzette swallowed. "Oh," she said, perking up. "You have that look in your eye like before you start one of your crazy experiments."

"I take exception to that," Lyssa said, smirking. "None of my experiments are crazy. I wouldn't have chosen my particular field if human psyche and behavior didn't fascinate me."

The giddy smile on her friend's face was reminiscent of Risqué. "You're going to do it, aren't you? Launch yourself back into your book? It's about time! Will this be like the time you convinced that urologist to let you sit in on appointments? When you wore a Wonderbra and deliberately missed two buttons on your shirt?"

"That was a physiological experiment," she said, topping off their water glasses.

"And the free wedding night coaching?"

"To measure how pressure affected performance… those statistics were astounding by the way."

"And standing on street corners at three a.m. with sex workers interviewing them about clients?"

"You'd be surprised how many men open up to hookers. They're unlikely to see them again, so can be honest. Often performance issues present differently or disappear when pressure and identity are removed."

"You take it to a whole new level, you know? You actually enjoy delving into these intricacies, most people get a paycheck and go home to veg out, but you're always watching people and wondering. You love to get in amongst it, amongst your subjects."

"It's fun to be undercover. I've always been completely safe."

"Archie didn't think so. That hooker thing sent him over the edge."

"I never finished that study by the way," she said. The subject of her ex-husband always provoked a sigh. He was brilliant, intelligent, fastidious, he just didn't understand the buzz of satisfying curiosity. "He didn't object to that one out of concern for my safety. He thought I was making a spectacle of myself."

And by extension him.

"You didn't flaunt what you were doing," Suzette said. "I read your papers; they were amazing. You worked too hard to throw away incredible work like that. It's great to see you getting back to it."

"Being stalked sort of changed my perspective," Lyssa said, still not particularly hungry. "It's difficult to go undercover to explore people's sexual behavior when I may have a mad man on my tail."

"You love exploring sexual practice…" Suzette leaned in. "It's a shame you haven't had much practice yourself recently."

A quiet, tired laugh left her lips. "One step at a time. Let's find a way to get rid of the crazy stalker. After that, I can get back to my old ways and start thinking about men again."

Dealing with her admirer altered her perspective on so many things. She missed the freedom of her fearless days and was reminded of what she'd given up. Every situation bettered her knowledge of human interactions and motivations. Her studies made her better at her job. More than that, she loved being out among people. Her stalker prevented that. Hope held out that Colt was going to change things, and that lying to Suzette would be worth it in the end.

SIX

"JUST BY MAINTAINING this relationship you are making progress, Bobby," Lyssa said in her soothing doctor voice to the redhead on her patient couch. "We've known all along that this was going to be difficult."

"She's beautiful… I don't think she'll understand," Bobby said. "How do I explain…?"

"Don't feel like you have to rush. As the relationship develops, you'll grow closer. You don't have to feel pressured into revealing more of yourself than you're comfortable with."

He sighed. "You're so understanding… talking to her won't be like talking to you."

"No," she said. "We're all individuals and I'm your doctor, not your girlfriend." She paused. "You're seeing her on Saturday night. Take it one date at a time, Bobby. I'm very proud of all you've achieved so far."

Praise always pepped him up a little. "I couldn't have done any of this without you, doc. I can't thank you enough."

"You're welcome, Bobby," she said, checking her watch. "You've done all the hard work yourself, but I'm happy to help you in any way that I can. We'll carry on at your next session."

After saying goodbye to Bobby, she went through her

usual routine of updating the patient notes. He should've been the last of the day. With no plans and not relishing the idea of being alone all night, she'd jumped at the chance to take on a new patient. Staying on later than usual to treat him would be a distraction. Keeping busy, occupying her mind, was better than pondering when her stalker would next make himself known.

Each first session took a similar form. There was a raft of routine questions to go through. Most patients were referred by doctors who had eliminated physiological causes of dysfunction. The newbie had self-referred, so he'd require a full assessment.

Pulling together the usual packet given to new clients, she put it on the far side of her desk, within reaching distance of her chair.

"Nice setup you have here."

Lyssa hadn't heard anyone come in. Odd. A man crouched at the table by her door. At least he was until he stood up and turned around to reveal himself: Colt Warner.

Away from the seedy club, she tried to view him as a professional. It was difficult to be neutral when he was examining her furniture, her vents, her floor and ceiling.

"You're my next patient?"

He carried on with his exploration. "Yes, call me Joe."

Another name. "Okay, what are you doing, Joe?"

"Looking."

"For what?" she asked, leaving her desk when he ducked beneath it to run his hand along the underside.

"Just add paranoia to my list of symptoms."

Coming to her office as a legitimate patient wasn't likely to be Colt's motivation. More likely he wanted his money and the signed contract. Treatment was good cover for his true work… as long as it didn't take time away from her actual patients.

"What are your other symptoms?" she asked, seating herself in her listening chair while he continued his scrutiny.

"I saw that last guy leave, what was he in for?"

"I don't discuss patients with other patients."

"Who do you discuss them with?" he asked, moving every item from the dresser to examine it.

"My voice recorder," she said. "Does your paranoia link to your sexual dysfunction?"

As a perk, if he wasn't a real patient, she didn't have to treat him like one.

"No dysfunction with my anything sexual."

"You're posturing, strutting," she said. Now he was investigating her windows. The white roller blinds were down to limit distractions from the street. Privacy was always valued by clients. "Usually that means you're overcompensating. When was the last time you achieved an erection?"

Finally, a kink in his search. He put down the purple flame ornament and turned around, appearing amused and intrigued.

"This morning," he said. "You don't waste any time, do you? You get right to the good stuff."

"Identifying the issue is the first step to solving it," she said, reaching for her pad and pen to take notes. "Should I assume it was nocturnal penile tumescence?" His blank look said it all. "Morning glory. You woke up aroused?"

He strolled to the couch and sank down, his eyes trained on her. "Maybe."

"Did you wake up alone or with company?"

"Alone."

"And do you mind sharing your sexual orientation with me?"

"I'm heterosexual," he said with a twitch of a smile. "Straight down the line."

"Uh huh," she said, taking her time to make several notes. His smile grew. "Did you use the erection? Did you pleasure yourself to climax?"

"Man…" he said, pushing his hands down his thighs. "I love what you do. All those years it took to get an MD and you spend all day talking about cocks and jizz."

"I talk about the brain, Joe," she said remaining professional, despite the direct questions. "It's my goal to ensure my patients have satisfying, fulfilling, and healthy sex lives. I want you to be safe and happy."

"And how far will you go to achieve that?" Colt asked, letting his gaze slink to her crossed legs.

"You're not the first client to use sexual innuendo or make advances toward me. Please be assured, I have no physical contact with my patients. This has to be a safe space for both of us."

"Understood, doc, but if you're going to spend an hour talking to a guy about his junk…"

"Ah, issues with impulse control. Is that why you're here, Joe?"

"I came to find out if we could work together; trust takes time to establish."

"I agree," she said, using her notes to ensure the intensity didn't ramp up. "Do you have a girlfriend, long-term partner, wife?"

"None of the above."

"How would you identify your relationship with women?"

"All women?"

Usually, she wouldn't be so quickfire. "How do you view women?"

"You want to know if I respect them or just screw them and move on?"

"Is that what you do?" she asked, uncrossing her legs to cross them the other way.

The action heated his interest. "Sometimes," he said. "But I don't make a habit of one-night stands."

"Why not?"

Shrugging, he slid down to settle on the couch. "I don't know. They don't hold my interest, I guess. I'm not a teenager anymore."

"Sex has become less satisfying as you have gotten older?"

"Not less satisfying if you're doing it right," he said. "But it's not as important to have it every night. It's less about the physical as we age."

"What is it about?"

"Making a connection. Getting my rocks off is secondary to making sure my partner enjoys herself."

"Interesting," she said, discarding the pad to lean closer. "You have esteem issues; prioritize your mate and her pleasure over your own. Do you believe that you don't deserve gratification?"

"Oh, I deserve it, and I get it too, but if she doesn't get hers, why should I get mine?" he asked, meeting her eye. "It's about give and take, right?"

"That's important, but your mate must be of a similar mind. Have you ever been married?"

"Briefly."

Her surprise must have shown because his lips curled. "You were?" she asked. "What went wrong?"

"We wanted different things."

"What did you want?"

"I wanted her to give me a break."

"And what did she want?" Lyssa asked, retreating to use her pad as a disguise for her personal interest in his answer.

"Attention. I worked late a lot, sometimes nights. She couldn't handle that."

If he spent all his time at Risqué, his wife might have struggled with the nature of the venue.

"Were there women in your workplace that she disapproved of?"

"Disapproved of?" he asked. "No, other women weren't involved. She didn't like that I spent so much time with lowlifes instead of her."

"In bars?"

"I didn't work in bars; I was a cop in vice."

"A cop?"

"Briefly," he said, seeming to like that answer. "You've been on the divorce rollercoaster yourself."

"Yes," she replied when typically, she'd never reveal anything personal to a patient.

"And? How did that come about?"

"I took risks he disapproved of."

"Risks?" Sliding to the edge of the couch, he leaned closer. "I am intrigued. What kind of risks?"

"We're all students of life and I enjoy studying people

in various situations. I believe it makes me better at what I do."

"I can identify with that. Wanting to be effective is why I quit being a cop."

Getting to know her patient's history was important. As many as two or three sessions could be dedicated to talking about nothing except where they came from. Colt wasn't a genuine patient. Her subconscious caught onto that fast. She found herself admiring the angle of his jaw. The strength in his arms. A smatter of light brown hairs on his forearms left her wondering at the shade of hair on his chest.

A blush touched her cheeks. She lowered her attention to the notes, using them as a shield again. In her career, she'd never had inappropriate thoughts about a patient. Never. Good thing Colt wasn't a patient. Appreciating the bob of his Adam's apple wasn't unethical… Was it?

"You left because you felt you were ineffective at your job," she said.

"Yes."

He didn't elaborate.

She asked another question, "Do you feel ineffective with women?"

"In the sack? I've never had any complaints."

Fascinating. Why was she so intrigued? "Do you believe that women would complain?"

"I can tell when a woman isn't enjoying herself," he said.

"You mean that you think you can tell when your partner is faking her arousal?"

"Is this going to lead to a Meg Ryan scene replay?"

His joke made her smile. "Whether or not you know when a woman is faking orgasm is between you and your mate. Tell me what you hope to achieve from these sessions."

"Are you willing to work with me?" he asked, intent, his expression asking more than his question.

Setting her pad aside, she left her chair to retrieve the signed contract from her desk drawer. The envelope containing his retainer was there too. She took both to him.

"I'll accept you," she said, returning to her seat. "I'd

advise weekly sessions initially."

"Yes."

She took the new patient packet from the desk behind her and handed it over. "Read the literature. It discusses various conditions and what we can achieve together. It should prompt you to think about yourself and what you need. When you come back, we can talk about your conclusions."

"Lyssa," he said, tucking the contract and cash into the folder she'd given him to conceal it. "This is going to be a fruitful partnership."

"I'm glad you see it that way. This relationship is about give and take too. I'll work hard for you, but you're required to make a commitment to me as well."

Colt rose from the couch and held his hand out for hers. "That I can do, doc. Don't worry about a thing. Same time next week?"

She nodded.

He sauntered out of her office, closing the door behind him. Breathing out, the smile that spread on her face betrayed her relief. Odd that she hadn't been so relaxed in months. Knowing more about Colt helped her confidence in him. Somehow, things were going to change.

Berating her premature optimism, she stood, intending to sit at her desk. A small white rectangle on the couch caught her eye.

The envelope was blank. Inside was a single sheet of heavy writing paper.

I've planted a bug detection device. I'll check it back at base. If I get feedback, we'll know he's listening.

In the meantime, I'll be watching. Coming to your office as a patient gives us cover. Temporarily anyway. I'll let you train my wiener, doc, which is more than I let other clients do.

Your first task: change your routine. This guy knows what to expect. Shock him. Do something new that could draw him out. Throw him off. Get a new hobby. Take a second job or a class. Anything. We need to get you out of the house and on the move. I'll be on your tail.

The note wasn't signed but the sender was obvious, unlike ones sent by her stalker. Patient cover was great but meeting once a week wasn't enough. She wanted more regular updates. Waiting seven days was just too long. Being passive hadn't gotten her anywhere. It was time to regain control of her life.

Lyssa locked up and set out on a shopping mission. To accomplish her goal, she needed a good disguise. This was a role to nail. Colt wanted her to change her routine and shake this guy up? Her idea was perfect.

SEVEN

SHE WAITED THREE DAYS. Trying on outfits and flaunting her figure were more fun than she'd thought they would be. Not that she was shy, it just wasn't her usual behavior. Her form was taut and limber, she worked out at the gym and did yoga on at least five mornings. It would pass muster… she hoped.

At around nine thirty on the third night, she set out to grab a cab with Risqué in mind. A cop referred her to the club. The former cop she'd met there had a financial stake in it. The place had to be legitimate. Women couldn't be required to perform sex acts and drugs weren't allowed on the premises.

Risqué was the perfect location for her next social experiment. While still being a genuine experience, it was the closest to safe she could be given the stalker situation. Getting back on the horse was exciting. Truth was, a strip club presented too tempting an opportunity to ignore.

With her head held high, she strode past the bouncers, up the hallway and into the club. The pulsing music and mood fired her atoms. Ignoring the semi-nude women, she counted more men than before. But this time, there were none at the bar.

A few seconds after she propped herself on a stool, the bartender came around the corner at the other end. After being told they were related, Lyssa saw the family resemblance. This man, Blaser, was the same height as Colt, built with more muscle but the same dusty dark brown hair.

"Back again?" he asked, retrieving wine from the fridge.

"Thank you."

He filled a glass and put it in front of her. "No worries. It's left from the other night and is probably flat."

Smiling, she took a sip and shook her head. "It's good."

"Low maintenance. I like that."

"I don't imagine you serve much wine."

"No," he said. "Only when we're told to have it on the premises. Trapper isn't here."

"I know," she said. "I'm not looking for Colt. I came here to see you, Blaser."

"First name basis. It's like that, is it? So, you're intimate with my brother… rare for him… shame for me."

"Not exactly intimate, he works for me."

He laughed. "I'm not sure he'd like that description, even if it's accurate," Blaser said. "He doesn't give me details and I don't ask. If you're looking for information, you're—"

"I don't want information. I want a job. Here."

His brows rose. "A job?"

"Yes," she said, opening her jacket and leaning back to show the Lycra halter top that displayed her midriff. "I have no issues putting my body on show."

"I see that," Blaser said, spreading his hands on the bar. "You say you're not screwing my brother?"

"No. Why? Would that make a difference?"

He shrugged. "He's the monogamous type and gets protective of his girlfriends. If I hire you to shake your tail for my customers…"

Colt fit the bill as someone who'd have a problem with other men ogling his woman. "We're not romantically involved."

"Why do you want to work here?"

"I know Colt and Miguel Chavez," she said. "They're good guys. I trust this is a decent place. I know there are no drugs and no expectation for the women to deliver sexual services on-site."

"Or off-site," Blaser said. "We keep everything above board."

"Which I like." Until then, she'd been honest. A little lie was necessary to sell her request. "I need the money, Blaser. You'd be helping me out."

"Okay," he exhaled. "Dancers make the most money, but we never start girls there. You'll waitress: take orders, bring them to the bar, and deliver them to customers. You'll also arrange private dances. The more you flirt, the more tips you'll get. If you work out serving, we'll talk about a bump up the ladder. Waitressing is your probation."

Much as she didn't mind flirting and prancing around in her underwear, dancing was not on her agenda. She'd only make an idiot of herself. Blaser didn't need to know that.

"Okay," she said.

"We're open two p.m. until two thirty a.m. You're expected to be here ready for work by the time your shift starts, and waitresses stay to clean up when they're here at closing time. I can give you ten p.m. until close, Thursday to Sunday."

"That works for me," she said, thankful he hadn't asked her to do a dayshift.

"Come back tomorrow at eleven. One of the girls will give you a tour. You'll get three uniforms, but you're free to wear your own clothes so long as they fit requirements. You'll have to provide your own shoes, platform spikes."

"What are the uniform requirements?" she asked, seeking out waitresses in the slices of bright light spinning around the room.

"Micro-mini skirt and plunge halter bra, what are you? Thirty-four C?"

Impressed, she blinked at his indifferent observation. "Yes. How did you know that?"

"I'm good at my job," Blaser said. "Have you worked in a joint like this before?" She shook her head. "Cherry then."

"What?"

"We'll use your real name on your paperwork, but around here we'll call you Cherry."

"Okay," she said. "We'll do paperwork tomorrow?"

Someone approached the bar, attracting Blaser's focus. "See you then."

He went to the waitress to take care of the order.

Lyssa gulped down half of her wine. Having secured the job, she took the time to look around. The décor was tasteful. The T-shaped stage had three poles, one at each end point, shimmering white material served as the backdrop.

A security guard remained by the door Colt had used to take her backstage and upstairs to the offices. Her gaze snagged on a woman leading a man across the floor and through a door marked "private" at the other end of the bar. Maybe the private dances happened back there?

She'd find that out. That and so much more. Now the research could begin.

EIGHT

"IT'S OKAY," Lyssa said to her patient. "Take your time."

"I'm still struggling with the concept of this," Martin Schifford said. "Of therapy like this."

"You've had a few sessions now," she said. "We've discussed your childhood and your parents. You've told me about your work and your wife. But we do need to address the issue and the trigger point."

"The incident at my father-in-law's."

"Yes. You witnessed a horrendous event. It must have been traumatic," she said. "Were you physically injured?"

The hospital notes conveyed that Martin hadn't received any serious physical injuries, but she had to get him talking about the event somehow.

"Not badly," he said.

"But you and your wife haven't been intimate since it happened, have you?"

Shaking his head, she read embarrassment in his countenance. "Has your wife attempted to initiate—"

"Yes," he snapped. "But I don't understand how she can think about that!"

"Why not? Did what you witnessed influence your view of sexual behavior? Was there an assault on—"

"No, it was him!" Martin asserted, his frown laced with anger.

"Him, who?"

"My sister-in-law is flighty. She always has been, and… she had a disagreement with the family and was… she ran off."

"Your sister-in-law?" Lyssa asked, wondering what the sister-in-law had to do with this "*him.*"

"We didn't see her for months and when she came back, she had this… this man with her…"

Ah. "And this man is somehow connected to the event that took place at your father-in-law's?"

Martin shifted, squirming in his seat, refusing to make eye contact. "He's macho and overbearing, his chauvinism is ridiculous. Since my sister-in-law brought him into our lives… my wife won't stop talking about him."

"Do you think your wife desires this man?"

"How can she be impressed by him and still be satisfied with me?"

An inferiority complex was an easy fix, providing Martin was willing to do the work. "Do you question your own masculinity?"

"I never have," he barked. The abrupt form of speech was a classic defensive tell. "I work hard. I earn a lot of money. I do right by my wife. Women have always been impressed by me."

"And this different type of man introduced into your life has thrown up questions for you?"

He cleared his throat. "I suppose you could say that."

"We are all different, Martin," she said to reassure him. "Just as we are all attracted to different kinds of mates. You are not attracted to your sister-in-law, are you?"

"Of course not!"

"There is no reason to believe that your wife is attracted to your sister-in-law's partner. Perhaps she too is intrigued by this new kind of man."

"He's not in our lives anymore," Martin said. "He was very briefly, but we have not heard from him or my sister-in-law again."

"That chapter is closed?"

"It should be," he said. "But my wife insists on talking about it all the time, especially when we're alone with her parents."

"And that frustrates you… Have you told her that?" He shook his head. "At this point my advice would be to open communication with your wife. Ask her why she feels the need to bring up this individual. It is possible her answers will make things clearer for you. The conversation could be a springboard into improved communication."

"Do you think so?"

"Yes," she said. "Let's schedule another appointment for next week. You can tell me how it goes with your wife."

"Yes," he said. "Yes, okay then."

They scheduled the appointment and Martin departed. The case was nothing complex, but it was a shame to see him dejected by his wife's obsession with another man. Obsession didn't necessarily have to be sexual… Reminding herself of that seemed self-serving

Did her stalker have a family? Did they have any inclination about his unhinged fascination with her.

When Suzette called earlier to make plans for the weekend, Lyssa had to cut the conversation short. Eventually, she would tell Suzette about her new research project at Risqué. The project doubled as an opportunity to change her routine as per Colt's instructions. Those instructions also meant keeping her friend in the dark.

After cleaning up and getting into something Risqué suitable, she donned a calf length coat, and left home, wondering who was watching. Most people wouldn't think anything of heading out in the evening. If only she could be so oblivious. To prevent her course from being too obvious, and while keeping her eyes open, she traversed a few blocks to hail a cab to Risqué.

When she got there, Blaser was at the bar. Maybe he lived there, she'd never seen him anywhere else. With him was a towering blonde, at least five eleven in her heels. The beauty glowed, she wasn't too young, maybe in her late twenties. The red inserts in her platinum blonde hair suggested fun almost as much as her barely contained breasts. The white two-piece wet-look outfit had matching thigh-high boots. She loved it.

"This is Crystal," Blaser said to Lyssa with his attention on the waitresses approaching the bar. "She'll show you the ropes."

Blaser vanished to fill the new orders.

Crystal looped their arms together. "Cherry is a great pick. Blaser says he hired you as a favor to Colt. Are you friends?"

"I guess you could say that," Lyssa said.

Crystal directed her toward the door by the stage. "The other girls will notice if you're cozy with management. But Blaser is good to all his employees. I've been working here since day one, I know him pretty well."

A bassy tune blasted as two scantily clad women came onto the stage. That was as much as she saw before Crystal opened the backstage door to take her through it.

Crystal pointed to a curtain on their right. "That's the stairs to the stage. There's a corridor at the end that leads around to stairs for the other side."

"I won't be on stage."

"Not yet," Crystal said. "But it won't take long to get you up there. Blaser is a soft touch for his girls. If you don't already know, he and Colt don't always get along. My advice? Stay out of that sticky hot mess, if you can."

"Thanks."

"Those stairs you won't ever use," Crystal said, pointing to the stairs up to the three doors, to Colt's office. "Here's our office."

They went through a door beyond those stairs into an occupied communal changing room. Lockers, padded benches, mirrors and makeup, all expected. Rows and rows of hanging rails covered in underwear and costumes begged to be explored.

"Past the outfits are restrooms," Crystal said and produced a small key from her cleavage. "Your locker is number twelve."

She handed over the warm metal key.

Several women hung around the mirrors on stools

and lounging on a long couch. None of them paid much heed until Crystal shouted.

"Gals! This is Cherry. She's new around here, so y'all make her feel at home." Most of the women checked Lyssa out, but they quickly went back to their conversations. "They'll warm up to you soon enough," Crystal murmured, wearing a glittering grin. "Blaser won't hire anyone under twenty-five. We're mostly a good bunch. Bad apples get picked out quickly… That doesn't mean we don't enjoy a good gossip and a giggle." She took Lyssa to the clothes rail. "Do you need something to wear?"

Lyssa took the clip from her hair to flip and fluff it. Ready to rock, she removed her coat to show the baby-blue halter plunge bra and matching micro mini. Her outfit covered more than most of the others in the room, but she had complied with guidelines.

"Excellent."

"I don't expect preferential treatment," Lyssa said. "Because of my connection with Colt."

"You'll probably get it anyway because the brothers are big on family."

"Do you think the other girls will resent that?" Lyssa asked in a low volume.

"They won't say anything to your face," she said. "If you're nice to them and they like you, they'll get over it. They're used to mine and Blaser's friendship and like to use it to their advantage when they can."

"What does that mean?"

"If they want something, or they screw up, they come to me. That way, I can handle Blaser."

"Handle him?" Lyssa asked, wondering how Crystal did that and how close the pair were.

"Up until now no one has been able to handle Colt. He does things his way. Maybe you can change that."

"Don't put money on it," Lyssa said.

She and Colt weren't as close as Crystal obviously thought.

"We'll see. Put your purse and coat away. I'll show you the private dance area, you might have to take drinks in there sometimes."

Lyssa did as told. Crystal gave her a tour of the communal lap dance area and the six private rooms leading off it for the privileged private dances. Blaser approved her outfit, gave her a rundown of the routine, and she was shown the different zones of the room. Each night she'd be allocated a zone, which the girls organized on a rotational basis. After Crystal introduced her to some regulars, she was already feeling at home.

Not much more than an hour must have passed when she caught sight of a familiar figure at the bar. There he was, Colt Warner, back to the bar, scrutinizing her.

Her smile picked up on her return to the bar. She slid her tray to Blaser who took it and slunk off.

"Quite a change of routine," Colt said, having watched her every step.

"I did as I was told, rule number two."

"This wasn't what I meant. Why'd you choose this?"

"Research," she said. "I'm interested in what men who frequent these places get."

"What they get is a good time."

"But why?" she said, drumming her fingers on the bar as she surveyed the room. "Sexual behavior fascinates me."

Remaining on his stool, he leaned back against the bar to follow her line of vision. "Did you tell Blaser that?" Colt asked.

"No, he thinks I need the money. The research only works if the participants are unaware of it."

"So why are you telling me?" he asked.

"I'm here because of you and trust works both ways, right?"

"You want me to keep your secret from my own flesh and blood?"

"You and Blaser don't often get along for long," she admitted, continually checking the customers in her zone, but Crystal had taken to the stage so there was more drooling than drinking going on. "He hired me as a favor to you anyway."

"Who told you that?"

"Crystal," Lyssa said. "I came in last night and talked

to Blaser. Didn't he tell you about this?"

"I didn't come in last night or today. I've been watching you."

"And you didn't see me come in here last night?"

"I did, but I figured you were looking for me."

"Well, you did say that you would call," she said and smiled. "This works out better for both of us. You don't have to rely on coming in as a patient. Sometimes my clients run into Suzette. That could cause problems since you insist I lie to her. Also, my patients stay for a whole hour; they don't run out after ten minutes like you did. My admirer will see your departure as suspicious. And if he's bugged my place then we can't talk freely, I'm guessing you're confident he hasn't bugged Risqué."

"He hasn't bugged this place or yours. No one is listening in your office."

"In my office?" she said, turning to Colt, veering into concern. "What about the rest of my house?"

"I didn't go upstairs," he said. "But the stairs on the left, inside your front door, they go up to your residence, don't they?"

"Yes," she said. "My office door is just on the right of the lower floor, as soon as you come in the front door, you know that."

"Your front door is unlocked and unattended all day."

"My clients have to be able to come in."

"Anyone could wander upstairs," he said.

She trusted her clients not to go snooping. It had never occurred to her strangers might come in while she was in session.

"Are you trying to freak me out?" she asked.

He took a sip from his glass on the bar. "Not my job."

"Should you be drinking? While I'm here you're technically working."

"I would just love it if our stalker turned up here," he said, taking another drink. "If he does, all I have to do is recognize him. I'm not going to go ninja on his ass. I only work security for Blaser when it's absolutely necessary.

Anyway, it's just soda."

"Great," Lyssa said, noticing a table in need of service.

Taking his glass away from him, she drained the rest of the drink and went to work. Polite as could be, despite the inebriation of the customers, she took the order and relayed it to Blaser.

"You're doing good so far, do you need a break?" Blaser asked while filling the order.

"Maybe in a bit," she said, trying not to watch one of the podium girls cozying up to Colt.

"Don't mind them, him and Kitty have been over for a long time," Blaser said, putting the first drink on the tray.

"Sorry? Oh, what? No! Don't be stupid. I told you there was nothing between Colt and I."

Blaser kept working, his knowing smile crept higher. "He's been watching you since he came in. That outfit you're sporting made his eyes bug from his head. I can tell when my brother's interested. Comes from being twins I guess."

"Twins?"

"All our lives," he said. "Not identical." Obviously. "We've always butted heads, but we're there for each other when it counts."

"What about Ruger?"

"Colt's protective of the squirt, but he can hold his own. Tends to disappear without warning for periods of time, but he's alright."

"Why did Colt leave the police?"

"That he'll tell you when he's ready," Blaser said and pushed the tray towards her.

After delivering the order, she returned to the now alone Colt. Blaser was right, every time she checked, Colt was looking right at her.

"What has you so interested, Mr. Warner?"

"I'm an ass man, Doctor Cutler," he said. "And you have one worth looking at."

"Do you have no shame?" she asked.

"Turn around and let me see again."

The thrill that zipped through her prompted her to

do as asked.

She tipped her chin toward her shoulder. "Looked your fill?"

"If we weren't in public, I might be tempted to touch."

"Seeing your ex-girlfriend must have had an arousing effect," she said, resting back on the bar, interrupting his view.

"My ex?" he asked, propping his elbows on the bar.

"Blaser said you and Kitty used to—"

Colt laughed. "Miss. Lys, my brother is messing with you. I've never been with any of the girls in this place." His fingertip met her shoulder. "Question is, Miss. Lys… Why did you give a damn?"

The finger trailed down leaving goose bumps in their wake. "Cherry," she said, bringing her gaze to his. "In here, that's what they call me."

"I like it, you came here to pop it."

"I came here because I had confidence I'd be safe. You gave that to me. I used to embrace the experience of my behavior research projects. I relished compiling my book of observations. I looked forward to the day it would be published. I had a lust for life… but recently I've been putting my life, my confidence, on hold. You made me see that this guy is closer to breaking me than I realized. I need this. I need to get back to being me."

"You're relaxed. Less distracted. It's interesting to see you lighter."

"Thanks," she said. This guy spoke about her like he knew her. If he'd been researching, and watching, her then maybe he did. "You haven't answered the sixty-four-million-dollar question."

"I haven't?"

"Who is the guy? The crazy?"

"When are you due a break?" Colt asked.

"Soon," she said.

"Come up to my office and we'll talk."

He left the stool and took a step away.

She snagged his wrist. "Should I be worried?"

If he wouldn't reveal the identity of her stalker in

public, it was possible he was worried about her reaction.

"Yeah," he said. "You're being stalked, that would worry most rational people."

His arm slid out of her grip. He stalked through the ogling drinkers to the backstage door. It closed in the shadow, leaving her alone to speculate.

Blaser whistled. "Cherry!"

She turned to see him nodding towards patrons in need of service so hurried off to do her job.

NINE

HAVING THE BIG SCREEN TV in his office gave Colt a distraction when he needed a break from a case. Working from Risqué was easier and cheaper than renting office space. Most clients never saw the inside of his office. Privacy was the goal. A storefront declaring what he did was the last thing he needed.

But that night, waiting for Lyssa, he couldn't relax in front of the TV and working on her case was out. When he had followed her there last night, he'd believed it was a desperate attempt to get in touch with him, hence why he'd avoided Risqué. Such easy access for clients was something he discouraged.

Tonight, when she'd returned, he'd wondered if it was the same thing. For more than an hour, he sat outside waiting for her to exit. When she didn't, he went in and got the update from Blaser. Then he'd seen her.

And, whoa, boy. The tiny skirt was a second skin that just managed to cover her incredible ass. The smooth skin of her toned waist took his eyes to those voluptuous breasts. Usually, they were showcased in a white cotton shirt, that night, they looked ready to party.

Craving a client was against the rules. All the rules.

She'd given him trust and lit up in his company. He gave her hope. For the first time in his life, failure wasn't an option. Except so far that was where he was headed.

A tap on his door alerted him to her imminent entry, but it didn't diminish the effect of seeing that body again, this time in a quieter, lighter environment.

"Is this a good time?" she asked, helping herself to a seat on his couch and kicking off her shoes to lie her legs along his furniture. "How much extra do I have to pay you for a foot massage?"

"You'll get used to wearing the shoes… if you're here long enough."

"Did you get used to them?" she teased, spreading her hair over the arm of the couch behind her.

"That's what the girls say."

"How long have you guys had this place?"

Leaving the desk, he went over, choosing to sit on the arm of the couch beyond her feet. "A couple of years," he said.

"Do you enjoy it?"

"This is Blaser's bag," Colt said, admiring her legs while her eyes were closed. "Ruger and I just ponied up some cash to get him started. I help out when I'm needed and Blaser lets me work from here."

"Why don't you two get along? You seem friendly with each other."

"We're brothers, we'll always watch each other's back. We butt heads sometimes, that's all."

"I'm an only child," Lyssa said.

"I know."

"Of course you do," she said, smiling, her eyes parted to sleepy slits. "You've been learning about me, watching me."

"I have."

"And what have you found out?"

She sat up in the center of his couch, bending her knees to the side, tucking her feet by her ass.

"That you don't sleep well. That you toss and turn, then get up to make hot milk or read, which makes you feel guilty for being awake. You go back to bed only to endure your insomnia again. Because of your restless sleep, you struggle to wake up in the morning. But you always do your yoga and shower before being in your office at eight thirty sharp.

"You see your first patient at nine thirty and stay in the office until one. At that point, you either go to lunch with Suzette at the Wright Bite or have salad in your kitchen while talking to her on speakerphone. You're back in the office by two, your last patient leaves by six and you're upstairs after a brief stint on the computer. Updating records, I assume. After that, you change out of your work clothes, go to the gym, out with Suzette or you read, work and eat alone."

Had he said too much? The silent shock written all over her face sure seemed to suggest that. "You know all of that?"

"You asked. You'll always get the truth from me."

"Who is he?" she asked. "That's what I want to know."

"Your stalker? The man who brought us together."

"Stop vamping and tell me," she said, sliding closer to take his hand. "You're starting to worry me."

She and Suzette held hands regularly, or linked arms, so he took it that Lyssa was a tactile person. That knowledge didn't lessen the effect of her delicate digits between his clumsy ones.

"I haven't seen a soul," he said, dragging his mental focus from their physical link. "Whoever he is, he's not watching you, at least not pathologically."

"So he's gone? I've not had any calls or flowers this week."

"You told the cops that he's done this before, disappeared for a while. Maybe he works away or has other commitments."

"Thank you for not believing I'm just a nut."

"A nut who made up a stalker to get close to me?" he said and smiled. With wide, expectant eyes, she squeezed his hand. "You have no reason, that I've seen so far, to make this up."

"Thank you for not giving up on me."

"You're paying for a service, and I intend to deliver. It might just take us longer to get results. We'll have to wait for this guy to spring up again. He will eventually. They always do."

"You're committed," she said.

"We signed a contract. I intend to do my job."

She sighed. "This might be an everyday occurrence for you, but it's not for me. I've never met anyone with such patience and singular concentration. How do you do it?"

"I'm focused," he said, grazing her jaw with the back of his fingers. "I won't let you down."

"I believe that, Colt. I know you're capable and I'm glad that Chavez recommended you."

"What did you tell Suzette?"

"That it didn't work out. She wants to try a different PI, but I'm holding off for now."

"I'd appreciate not having a dick on my tail."

"Most men who identify as straight wouldn't," she said, and they shared a smile. "I don't like lying to my best friend."

"Keeping my involvement a secret is the best way to assure there's no tampering with, or pollution of, the evidence."

She blinked a few times. "You think that Suzette would blab? I'd trust her with my life, she would never endanger—"

"You'd be surprised how often these situations are perpetuated by those we trust most. Even if you're right, Suzette wouldn't have to intentionally discuss it to harm you. This way is best."

"You're the professional," she said, inhaling and holding her breath for a few seconds. "I ask my patients to trust me every day. It's odd to be on the other side of the advice."

"Once I find this guy, and I start to tail him then we'll know what we're up against. After that we can revisit letting Suzette in, depending on what turns up."

She nodded and left the couch, without releasing his hand. "I have to go back to work, and I guess you do too."

"You're always safe here, even if I'm not around. Blaser has good security and would never let anything happen to any of his girls."

"I'm not really Blaser's girl, am I? You introduced me to this place."

Hmm, his head tilted. "You saying you're my girl?"

"Maybe," she said. Her lips curled and her eyes lit. Their still joined fingers wrapped tighter. She moved in closer, her leg brushing against his. "For a minute there, babe, it sort of sounded like you cared." She bent over, giving him an up-close unhindered view of her cleavage. It was distracting until her lips touched his earlobe, then his head went in a totally different direction. "I won't tell anyone."

She winked.

Damn, she was a whole lot of trouble. "Get back to work, Cherrypop," he said, giving her ass a smack to send her on her way.

He remained on his perch for a few minutes after she left. Recovering from Lyssa Cutler always required some bonus time.

But he couldn't stay there thinking about her forever, so went to his desk to hit speakerphone and dialed his youngest brother.

"Yo, bro!" Ruger answered. "What's up?"

"Where are you?"

"Mom's."

Colt sank into his desk chair. "You're in town?"

"Just got back," he said. "It's late. What's bugging you or did you just roll out of a chick's bed? Not like you to love 'em and leave 'em."

Grabbing a pen, Colt tapped the end on the desk. "Have you ever…?" He closed his eyes and sucked it up. "Have you ever been attracted to a client?" Nothing but silence answered him. "Ruge?"

"Hold on, I'm getting out of the kitchen."

Their mother was always in the kitchen; the woman lived in that room. If she wasn't in the kitchen, she was on her way to the kitchen.

A door closed and Ruger exhaled. "What's her

name?" he asked.

"She's a doctor. Been stalked for months by an as yet unknown perp. I just caught the case from Mig."

"What kind of doctor?"

"Therapist," Colt said.

As anticipated, Ruger laughed. "Sounds perfect for you. Brunette?"

Covering his eyes, he propped an elbow on his desk. "How did you guess?"

"What's the problem? If you're hot for her, go for it."

"That's the kind of advice I'd expect from Blase, you're supposed to keep me in check."

"This is an ethical problem and you're the one with the strongest moral compass," Ruger said on another laugh. "I'd tell Blase to back off and leave her alone because he would probably hurt her. He can be casual about women, but you can't."

"I've had one-night stands."

"Not since before you were married. By the time you're telling me you like a woman, you're already invested. What's her name?"

"That's confidential."

"Protecting a client from me? You know I can keep a secret… which means there is more to this than simple client confidentiality."

He wouldn't confess Lyssa's work at Risqué thus revealing her study. "Could be," Colt said.

"She's pretty?"

"Oh, yeah," he said, the corner of his mouth edged upward.

"Sexy?"

"As hell."

"Can you talk to her? Do you trust her?"

"She trusts me," Colt said. "She's savvy and audacious. She's confident and bold, but humble too. She's curious and smart, and enticing—"

"Colt, man, you've got to marry this girl."

Ruger was known for telling it like it was and was remarkably perceptive. Colt had to laugh. His brother's finesse sent him slouching in his chair, flooded with relief or maybe it was reassurance.

"She makes me think about sex," Colt said. "Hardly a basis for marriage."

"So screw her."

"She's a client…"

"Solve the case, then ask her out," Ruger said. "Stop struggling with it, bro. Go with it. Give yourself a break… it's about time."

"You think this is about Emma? That I'm worried about getting my feet wet—"

"I think you need to dive in headfirst, Colt. Trust your instincts, remember those?"

"Always so sure about everything, aren't you?" Colt said.

"Ever known me to be wrong?" His brother strutted a little, as he'd expect. "Don't think so. If you don't trust yourself, trust me. Go with it. Let it happen… trust this gal because if she caught your eye, she's worth it."

"Okay, kid, let mom feed you then get her to bed. You know she gets cranky when she's up past midnight."

"Take it easy," Ruger said and hung up.

Colt was used to confiding in Ruger, or rather having Ruger confide in him. Certainly, his baby brother was right about one thing: he was never wrong. Acting on an attraction to a client was something he'd never had to worry about acting on. That was until Lyssa Cutler.

Ruger could be right, maybe he should cut himself some slack, but he wasn't in the habit of doing that. Lyssa might have come into his life at the right time, if not socially then professionally, because right then, it felt like sitting with a shrink was long overdue. But a shrink with a body like hers led a man to think with an organ not located in his skull.

For the moment, his role was to solve her stalker problem. In that area, he had plenty of practice. So, for now, that's where his focus would stay.

TEN

MED SCHOOL REQUIRED CRAZY shifts and long hours. It was like the law. Her fellowship hadn't required as many nights. During that time, she got out of the habit of going without sleep.

As Colt pointed out, with everything that was going on, she struggled to sleep through the night. Completing her first full shift at Risqué was exhausting. Maybe she'd sleep better because of it.

Locking her front door, pepper spray in hand, she went through the routine of checking each room. Nothing sinister awaited her in the lower hall, office, or waiting room.

Flicking on the back porch light from inside, the illumination flooded the glass in the rear door. Or it should have. Something was in the glass on the other side of the door. A flared shadow of… what was that? The shape…? It looked like… an inverted bouquet.

In the past, flowers were left on the external stairs. This time they'd been hung up.

Lyssa's heart hammered. She didn't want to open the door. What if he was still out there? The worst he ever did was watch… She had never been approached or attacked. He'd never attempted to cause any harm, physical or otherwise.

The cops wouldn't do anything. There wasn't anyone who could move them for her. With a shaking hand, she selected the back door key from the ring still looped on her thumb. Keys could be a great weapon and the pepper spray rose, ready to be used as she unlocked and opened the door.

Snatching the bouquet, she brought it in and slammed the door, locking it as fast as she could. It took a minute to slow her breathing and soothe her thumping heart.

Once she'd come back down, Lyssa removed the card and dropped the stems.

"Where were you when I needed you?"

The typed words on a rectangle of white card made her shiver. On autopilot, she checked that the door was definitely locked then ran up the stairs, flicking on every light switch on the route. Grabbing the phone from the wall, she speed-dialed Suzette.

It rang and rang. "Come on," she murmured. "Pick up, honey… please, pick up."

A click. The ringing stopped.

"Lys?" came Suzette's sleepy response.

Turned out her pulse was still high. "He left flowers."

The ruffle of bedcovers carried down the line.

"What?" Suzette asked in a yawn. "What time is it?"

"Early," Lyssa said, pushing a hand into her hair. "Or late… I don't know. I'm sorry, but… he left flowers."

"At this time of night?" Suzette asked, more alert. "Did you see him?"

"No. I… I was checking the house and they were hanging in the window of the back door. He wanted me to find them tonight."

"Oh my God, do you want me to come over?"

"No, I…"

"I can come over if you don't want to be alone. If I wake Pete, I can—"

"No," Lyssa exhaled and sank into one of the kitchen chairs. "There's no point. He's obviously gone, it's not like he ever comes inside. I just had to tell someone."

"You know that you can call me anytime. Maybe I should come and stay with you for a while to keep you company."

"There's no need for that," Lyssa said, feeling pathetic.

The idea of company was a good one. At these times, living alone was a burden. Leaning on someone was what she needed to do, except there was no one.

"This has gone on long enough, Lys. We have to end it. We have that fitting tomorrow." Bridesmaids' dresses. Right. "My sisters will be there. We can't talk about this with them around. Do you want me to cancel so we can go to the cops? Maybe if we talk to Chavez—"

"What can he do? What can any of them do?"

"I hate to hear you like this."

"Maybe I should move, change my name, and go into hiding."

"Others might believe you're joking," Suzette said. "I can tell from your tone that you've considered it."

She sighed. "At this point, I've considered everything."

The card slipped from her fingers. She'd take the flowers to the dumpster in the morning. Going out into the night held no appeal.

"You could go stay with your parents. They're only an hour away."

"I'd have to come back to the office every day and get every message he left. It's not worth it."

"Okay, I'm going to keep thinking about this. Let's do dinner tomorrow night, we'll put our heads together."

Suzette had said the same thing many times. Why did her best friend put up with the mess? They made plans to have an early meal and after some more reassurances, hung up.

A brief notion to call Colt flitted through her, but he'd told her not to. She didn't actually have a number for him and doubted that he'd be listed. Calling the club and leaving a message was an option, but he wouldn't like a physical trail connecting them.

He wouldn't appreciate her whining to him anyway. They weren't friends or romantically involved, she had to adhere to rule number three. Flowers weren't dangerous in and of themselves. The bouquet wasn't even wrapped in plastic. The flowers were tied with standard twine; no evidence could be gathered from them.

Sleep would elude her, but she had to take a shot at it. Resolving to tell Colt when she saw him at the club tomorrow night, she went to her bedroom thinking she'd love to shower off the day. Given how jumpy she was, it would do more harm than good, so she passed.

There was a shower in the locker room at Risqué. From then on, she'd shower and change after every shift. That way she wouldn't have to do it at home.

Planning her life around the actions of an unhinged individual in need of help frustrated her. Until Colt came up with the goods, that was her deal.

ELEVEN

RISQUÉ WAS UNEVENTFUL that Sunday night. The women were warming up to her, which presented the opportunity to ask leading questions and take mental notes. The Risqué groove was fun and fascinating.

Time was ticking on. Her feet were aching. She'd held off from taking her break, waiting for Colt to come in. The clock above the bar revealed it was one thirty and there was still no sign of him.

Zipping around behind the bar, Lyssa put her tray away and grabbed her water bottle from a lower shelf. "Heard anything from your brother tonight?" she asked Blaser.

He continued wiping down the bar. "Which one?"

Blaser tossed his cloth aside to take an order from Destiny, the waitress leaning over the bar.

"Either of them," Lyssa said.

Blaser smirked, he had to know that she meant Colt. He was her friend, according to him. Though, she couldn't deny being curious about the youngest Warner brother.

"Ruge called, but I was too busy to talk much. He just got back into town."

"That's nice. Where has he been?"

He shrugged. "Beats me," he said, filling the order.

"Colt's a better bet if you want to know that. Chances are he won't know either."

"Ruger is secretive?"

"He's always on the move. Always up to something. You kind of lose track."

Tracing a fingernail around the edge of the beer tap, she asked what she really wanted to know. "Is Colt coming in tonight?"

"Haven't heard," Blaser said.

Damnit. She wouldn't push the issue. If he didn't show, he wouldn't know about the flowers or the note. Maybe he'd got a better offer. One case at a time was his rule. Could be that he was done with hers and had found something more interesting to do.

Some rowdy patrons on the edge of her zone with almost empty glasses gave her a goal. Encouraging them to buy more liquor was part of her job. Drunk was in full swing with them, they sang and flirted. One touched the back of her thigh.

She kept her smile in place but shook a finger at the fondler. "You know that's not allowed," Lyssa said, ladling on the Cherry charm.

"Oh, you love it," the fondler said.

The others cheered.

A hand came from nowhere and touched her waist. Someone else squeezed her ass. She tried to back away when the men on either side of her rose.

"Dance with me, darling," the fondler said.

He reached for her hip but was intercepted by a hand that appeared from behind her. Tugged backwards, disorientation swirled. Her protector yanked on the fondler's arm, twisting it around to his back, thrusting it upward, earning a pained yelp.

"These guys have had enough," the protector snarled. Colt.

Security men, dressed in black Risqué emblazoned shirts, rushed in. They took the fondler from Colt to cart him and his protesting buddies out of the club. Colt turned to watch the exit over the top of her head. She was more interested in the scowl he had trained to the harassers.

"You know how to make an entrance, babe," she said, threading her fingers through his, drawing his eyes down to hers. With patients it was hands off, with friends, she leaned into the tactile, and often forgot that others were not so touchy feely. "I hoped to see you tonight. I need to fill you in and I'm due a break."

Colt glanced at the bar and tightened his hold on her hand. "Let's get out of here."

Keeping her close behind him, Colt led her backstage and up the stairs into his office.

"Are you okay?" he asked, flicking on the light, nudging her toward the couch. "Maybe you'll reconsider working in a place like this now?"

"Oh, I'm not worried about men like that," she said, unfastening the buckles on her shoes and tucking her feet up under her. "But thanks for jumping in, that was hot."

"Hot?" he asked, pausing on his way to the fridge in the corner.

"Sure. A big macho man coming to my rescue, that's sexy. You can protect me. My primitive brain values that… though so much for you not being security."

"Like I said, I am when Blaser needs me."

Security wasn't stretched. What he did hadn't been for Blaser, did he know that? She'd give him a break… for a while.

"Do you want a drink?" he asked, retrieving a soda from the fridge.

"Water would be good."

He took a bottle to her and opened his can, then dropped onto the couch beside her, glugging down half of his drink.

"What did you want to tell me?" he asked, setting his can on the coffee table in front of them.

"He left flowers."

Slowly, he turned to her. "What?" he asked. "When?"

"I don't know exactly when. They were hanging on my back door when I got home last night."

"Last night?"

She nodded. "I have a ritual I go through every time I get home in the dark."

"Yeah, I've seen all the lights go on and off. Do you carry a weapon while you check the place out?"

"Keys and pepper spray," she said. "I've never found evidence that he's violated my property. I'm paranoid, I guess."

"He left the flowers while you were here?" Colt asked. She nodded. "He's never followed you to Risqué, so he can't know you're working here. That's good."

"There was a note on the flowers," she said. His eyes narrowed. "He wanted to know where I was, it said he needed me."

"For what?"

She shrugged. "He didn't say."

"My guess would be he went to your place looking for you last night. Probably waited around and got mad or anxious when you didn't come back."

"It's creepy to think of him watching my house when I'm not there."

"Would you rather have been there?"

The rhetorical question hung in the air.

Intense thought hardened his expression. Scooting closer, the length of her thigh met his. Just being close to him increased her intrigue. What was in that mind of his?

She propped an elbow on his shoulder to rub the pad of her thumb down his forehead. "Do you try to get into their minds?"

Their eyes met but his frown remained. "Hmm?"

"I'm curious about how you do what you do."

"You're curious about every damn thing. How you doing with the research?"

"For my book?" she asked, lighting up with the chance to talk about the secret.

Without her best friend to share with, Lyssa was left pondering her work alone.

"Yeah. Tell me what it's about."

"Sexual objectification," she said. "It's a very relevant topic in today's world. A fascinating subject."

"Just to be straight, are you in favor or against?"

Facing him, she interlinked her fingers and draped them across his shoulder to prop her chin on them. "It's not as straight forward as that. I'm exploring how pressures on each gender influence the sex lives and sexual behaviors of individuals and sections of society. In relation to the angle and weight of sexual objectification."

"I see why Risqué was a good bet."

"The women here are great. Their attitudes and behaviors differ greatly between back and front stage. They know how to objectify themselves; they're critical of their appearance and ability. Yet, out on the floor, they have all this confidence. And the men watching them raise so many more questions."

"You love what you do, don't you?"

That was an understatement. "There are so many facets to human nature. Sexuality is surrounded with deception and revelation, vulnerability, and arrogance. So many of these women dislike themselves and have low self-esteem, but they walk tall in public. They have power over these men who think they're the ones with the power because they have the money... And then there's you."

"Me?" he asked, blinking in surprise. "You're researching me?"

"Not professionally, but I'm a stickler for a conundrum like you."

"I'm a conundrum? How?"

"Downstairs, just now. You took a simple drunk customer overstepping his bounds and escalated it. Security is all over the place, nothing would have happened to me."

"I saw a problem and I fixed it," he said.

Many people weren't accustomed to her direct manner... the vast majority of people, truth be told. Telling it like it was, bring open and candid. "The puzzle is, why did it matter to you? You're handsome and smart. You try to play it aloof, but I can tell that things move you more than you let on. You're dedicated and not afraid of hard work, but what's your motivation, Colt? What makes you tick?"

He reflected her mood right back. "That's what it

comes down to for you, isn't it? You have to know what drives people."

"I have to know what drives you. Why do you do what you do?"

"I have my reasons, but I'm not on your shrink couch now, Cherrypop." His defenses weren't exactly up; they weren't down either. "This isn't one of your sessions and I am not one of your patients."

She almost laughed. "Oh, I'm very aware of that and thankful too."

"Why thankful?"

Tipping her cheek to the back of one hand, she let the other drift down his chest. "I can't be honest with patients or reveal any of myself, but I can do both with you. More than that, I want to be honest with you. You know about my work here and my book, and you're helping me find my stalker. Right now, you know more about me than my best friend does."

"Except we're not friends," he said, taking her hand from his abs and putting it on her bare knee.

"Why does he feel it necessary to put up these walls?" she asked herself, eager to figure him out.

"Why does she feel it necessary to unpick my agenda?"

"Oh," she said, straightening a little, ready to tease now that she had his attention. "Agenda. That's an interesting choice of language. Haven't you been taught to watch your word choice around us head doctors… What is your agenda, Mr. Warner?"

"To uncover the identity of your stalker, do my job, and get my money."

"Okay," she said, nodding, folding her hands in her lap. "Is money important to you?"

"It's what makes the world go round, right?"

"That and sex," she said. "You're getting cash from me. Who is giving you sex?"

"You think that sex is a necessity?"

"No. But you spend your time surrounded by attractive women. I doubt you're short of offers. If you're not taking advantage of what's available, there has to be a reason. Bad break up?"

"You always have to know the answers?"

"It's in my nature to want to help," she said, easing closer again. "By getting defensive you're setting me up to be your enemy. Do you see me as a threat?"

Snatching his soda can, he left the couch and crossed to prop himself on the front edge of his desk to drink. "I think I could take you in a fight."

"Do you think of all threats as combative?" she asked, peeking over the back of the couch.

"They are the most prominent ones and they're often the most difficult to protect ourselves from. You must understand that, given your current predicament."

"Have you ever had difficulty with sexual climax?"

"Man, you never switch off. There's nothing wrong with me. I don't need you to diagnose me."

Kneeling on the center cushion of the couch, she linked her fingers on the back, waiting. After a few seconds of silence, he came back to sit on the couch beside her.

"If he's leaving flowers then at least we know he's still around," Colt said, deflecting to a safer subject…

Did he have a problem with sex or just talking about it?

"Is that a good thing?" she asked.

"Yes, if he's around I can find him and start compiling the evidence you need to end this and get on with your life."

"Then your job will be done, and you can move onto the next one."

"Something like that," he said.

"Have you seen Ruger since he's been back in town?" she asked to which he frowned. "Blaser told me he was back."

"I spoke to him last night and today while you were at dinner. Who was the shirt with Suzette and Pete? Hot date?"

"Is that what's got your nose out of joint? He's Pete's best man, Keith."

"My nose isn't out of joint," he protested.

"So how come you never came in here to see me earlier tonight, huh?"

"I was outside looking for unfamiliar faces. If I'd known that something happened last night, or you had something to report, I'd have come in."

"You told me not to call you."

"Don't call me to soothe your female insecurities, but you should keep me privy to updates about the case."

"I'll note that for the future. But what would you have done?"

"Come over," he said.

"Why? To soothe my female insecurities? Are you the type of man to take advantage of a woman at a vulnerable moment? Because last night I probably would have let you."

While surprise crossed his face, his gaze darkened. "Would you?"

"A strong, attractive man like yourself," she said, leaning in to rest her bust on his bicep. "I've already told you how my primitive brain sized you up. You have a toned muscular physique; you could protect me. You protected me tonight." Even though she hadn't really needed saving. She walked her fingers from his belt to his chest. "You have the brains to outwit lowlife criminals, loyalty to family, and a sense of responsibility. Instinctively, my body is ready to mate with the prime specimen you offer. You would be a bold, but reliable, choice of sire for my offspring."

"Offspring?"

"Mm hmm," she pouted, draping one arm around him as the other slipped to his thigh. "That's what it's all about, babe, isn't it? Sex for the purpose of procreation."

"Teasing me isn't going to work, Cherrypop," he said, one side of his mouth slinking up. "I wasn't born yesterday. I know you're trying to goad me into revealing something of myself."

"Smart, but suspicious," she whispered, inching closer, swept up by the heady scent of man swirling around her. "But who's teasing?"

Skimming her hand upward, she closed her palm over the solid length of him behind his fly. "Is this where you ask me to submit to a physical?" he asked.

Smiling, she brushed the tip of her nose along his jaw. "Nothing so cliché," she said, overjoyed that he didn't flinch. Instead, he looked her straight in the eye. "You're erect."

"You're perceptive," he grumbled. "Professional curiosity? You wanted to see if I could get it up, so you thought you'd squeeze your tits in my face."

"I'm a woman before I'm a doctor, Colt. I've been physically attracted to you since I first saw you. There's an air about you that hypnotizes me."

"Are you always this honest?"

"I try to be," she said. "You can't ask for honesty if you're not willing to give it." Working her hand gently, she massaged him through the denim. "I was personally curious, I wanted to know if I had any effect on you."

Withdrawing her hand, she was ready to move away, but he snatched her wrist and pressed her against him, pushing his hips up in the process.

"No one told you to stop," he murmured.

When she started massaging again, his hand moved to her hip and up to the curve of her bare waist.

In the private room, the intimacy of skin-on-skin contact, and the strength in his certain caress was enough to make her tremble. He registered the effect he had on her and narrowed his eyes, stealing some of her gumption. That confidence morphed to something more vulnerable but equally as potent. It had been a long time since she'd been with a man, had the sensations always been so raw and arousing?

Their eyes stayed locked. Her hand slowed as his skated up and down, she sloped her body onto his, welcoming the caress. Helpless with need, she sagged against him, slanting her mouth to beckon his.

The moment their lips met, he clenched her waist and his hips rose, giving her every permission to consume his welcoming mouth. His tongue came to hers and their greeting slammed all hesitancy from each of them. Hormones and hearts rushed to provide facility for the union that their bodies craved. This wasn't about fornication, but it was intuitive.

Primal. Hands clambered to test flesh and lips screamed silently for more from the other.

Then before any conscious decision could be made about the destination of this kiss, he jerked away. "Bad idea," he said, turning his face down. "Very bad idea."

"For you or me?" she asked, not deterred.

Her body had become curled against his, so her knees were over his lap. She had one arm still along his shoulders. Bending her elbow, she finger-combed the hair on his crown, down the back of his head.

"You're a client," he said.

"I'm not a client right this minute. You don't have to worry about the ethics of this. I want to be intimate with you, Colt. I'm attracted to you."

"So we have sex while you're on my brother's dime?" he asked.

Though he was serious, she laughed. "I've paid you a retainer, does that make you a gigolo? We're a man and woman exploring a sexual connection. Sex doesn't have to be complicated, it's a biological drive."

"Are you trying to sweet talk me?"

"Charm you out of your underwear? No. If you're uncomfortable, I would never dream of pushing the issue. But I'm ready."

"Excuse me?"

Leaning over the edge of the couch, she felt around for her shoes and put them on. "In all sexual relationships, communication is key. At this stage, we can't possibly know the outcome of any intimacy that we share. Mixed signals complicate things. While I may tease at times, I want to be clear. I'm open to having a sexual relationship with you, I'm ready."

"You're a client."

With her shoes on, she clicked her heels on the floor and landed her smile on him. "If you're not interested, that's perfectly acceptable."

She got to her feet, but he caught her wrist before she could leave his side. "How many other guys have this offer at the moment?"

"You've seen my life, babe. There are no other men in it. You're the only one I've offered to share my body with."

"Not Keith?"

"Definitely not Keith," she said. "You can think it over and if you change your mind: act. I'll be receptive."

Something resembling shock made him slump back on the couch. He freed her and she went back to work. After taking an extended break, the least she could do was be there for kicking out and clearing up.

TWELVE

BY THREE A.M. most of the clean-up was done. The dancers were gone, and the waitresses were starting to say goodnight.

Since she'd sashayed out of his office after that kiss, Colt struggled to concentrate. His ears were still ringing. She wanted a sexual relationship. Just like that, she'd put it out there. Upfront worked for her... though not so much for him. Now all he could think about was getting naked with her.

In the background, a waitress brought over a stack of empty glasses. Colt still stared into his.

"You can take off," Blaser said to her.

"Will you be around for a while?" Lyssa's voice rattled his thoughts. "Or are you eager to get out of here?"

There she was, six feet away, talking to his brother. Damn, she was beautiful, even at three in the morning.

"I'll be around for a while," Blaser said. "What's up?"

"Can I shower here?" she asked.

"Sure thing. Need someone to soap your back?"

Lyssa glanced over, meeting his eye. "Make sure he keeps his ass behind that bar, will you, babe?"

His brother laughed. Agreeing with a nod, Colt twisted in his stool to watch that sweet ass of hers sashay backstage.

"Been a while since I've seen that look in you," Blaser said, carrying on with cleaning up the glasses. "You've always been strict about not messing with employees."

"I'm not messing with her," Colt said, turning back to finish his soda.

"She's worked here less than a week and she's already taken up residence in your office. What happened to our rule about upstairs being off-limits to employees?"

"Crystal's in your office all the time."

"She's worked here since we opened, and it took her forever to be allowed up there. You told Ruge about Cherry?"

"What does that matter?"

"That's a yes," Blaser said, pausing. "You told mom?"

"No," Colt said. "What's your interest in my sex life? Your own failing?"

"I'm off women," Blaser said, going back to his work. "They give me too much grief."

"Someone trying to tie you down?"

"More like ratting me out."

"Ratting you out to who?" Colt asked, reality slammed back into acute focus. "You know that Ruge and I gave you the cash for this place on the condition that you kept the club and yourself straight."

"And Colt jumps to the worst-case conclusion about me, what a surprise. How come you have all the patience in the world for everyone except me?"

"Maybe I've given you the benefit of the doubt one too many times, Blase."

"I'm not your great shame anymore. You're not the hotshot cop. You're a regular joe, just like the rest of us."

"'Cept you're about to tell me you got yourself in trouble again, right?"

"Yo! Where's the party gone?"

The twins were interrupted by their six-foot five little brother striding into the club.

"Hey! It's the baby!"

Blaser rounded the bar to bro-hug Ruger. After some back slapping, Ruger came to him for the same kind of greeting. Owning a club wasn't so bad in moments like that. Blaser was quick to open three cold beers, instantly turning the night to social.

"I sense tension," Ruger said, after slugging from his bottle.

"Blaser was about to tell me he's in the shit," Colt said.

"Oh, yeah? Of which variety?"

Maybe it wasn't fair but expecting the worst from his twin was justified given his history.

Still, even he wasn't expecting the next word that came from Blaser's mouth. "Bri."

His first love. High school sweetheart. Troublemaker.

Ruger hissed. "I thought you'd learned your lesson with that girl long ago."

"It was supposed to be casual," Blaser said. "Her idiot brother was never supposed to know."

"Gary can't stand you. He nearly killed you the last time you messed with his sister," Ruger said. "'Cause you were bad news."

"Back then maybe," Blaser said. "I'm legit now."

"Do you think that Gary's going to give you time to explain that?" Ruger asked. "He's the shoot first type."

"It doesn't matter, we're done."

The blank look in Blaser's eye as he drank his beer told Colt there was more to the story. Either that or losing Bri, again, meant more to him than he wanted them to know.

All of them drank in silence.

Typical that Ruger would be the one to break the tension. "I'm so glad I rushed home to the warm bosom of the family," he said. "Have you two been bitching at each other the whole time I've been gone? You're supposed to get along when I'm not here to bang your heads together."

"They've been getting along."

Lyssa's voice attracted all of their attentions. Skinny jeans and short cowboy boots under a boob tube and hooded top, more clothes didn't equal less hot. She swayed with the same confidence that mesmerized him on her departure.

"Hello, pretty lady," Ruger said. "You're new here."

"As are you," Lyssa said, pushing her damp hair over her shoulder while straightening the strap of her backpack.

"Ruger Warner," he said, offering his hand.

"The enigma," Lyssa said, shaking his hand then going to Colt's other side, putting him between her and Ruger. She snagged Colt's beer from him and took a swig. "Your reputation precedes you. I know who you are."

"Need a ride home?" Colt asked.

He might not be able to actually take her home, but he could tail her to ensure her safety.

"No, I'm good. Will I see you this week?" she asked in a lowered volume though they both knew his brothers were listening.

"Probably not," he said. "But I'll be around. Call the club if you need me."

She could also report developments to Chavez, the message would filter through to him, but he wouldn't complicate things by saying that in front of his brothers.

"Need you?" Lyssa asked with a smile. "And if you find yourself ready, you know how to find me." She sipped his beer again and let her eyes slink to his when she put it back in his palm, then turned to Blaser. "I'll see you Thursday, boss."

"Sure thing, Cherry."

"Nice to meet you, Mr. Warner," she said to Ruger.

"Call me, Ruger."

"I doubt we'll meet again. Word is that you're a bit of a drifter."

"An adventurer," Ruger grinned. "But we'll meet again, I have a feeling Colt will make sure of that."

"My favorite Warner," she said with innuendo that drove fire to his loins.

Turning to her, he read her mischief. "Behave yourself."

"I'm going home," she said, brushing her fingers across his ass as she moved past him. "Night, Warners."

Lyssa took her time leaving, but he was glad to see the smile on her face, she deserved to have a good time.

"Now I get it," Ruger grinned and slapped a hand on

the bar when he turned to Colt.

"Yeah, yeah," Colt said, prepared for the ribbing.

"What do you need to get ready for."

"Don't ask." Because that would set his mind on the preoccupation path again.

"She's a beaut," Ruger said. "Where did she come from?"

Colt drank his beer, having no intention of answering, which Ruger gleaned, so he turned to Blaser.

"She came in here the week before last looking for him," Blaser said. "They disappeared upstairs then she came back this week asking for a job."

"Really," Ruger said, switching focus back to Colt. "You've got no problem with her working here?"

"She's waiting tables," Colt said.

"And when she graduates to dancing?" Ruger asked. "You're going to be okay with that?"

"She won't be here that long," Colt said, trying to erase the mental image of Lyssa grinding and stripping for other men in this place.

"That right?" Blaser said. "Are you going to run off one of my waitresses?"

"She makes her own choices," Colt said. "I just get the impression that this is temporary for her."

"You know her better than I do. You two spent a while upstairs tonight."

"Talking," Colt said, omitting the truth about the kiss.

"Whatever," Blaser said. "But our staff turnaround isn't high here unlike other strip clubs because we treat our girls well. Maybe Cherry will like it here and want to go all the way."

He didn't appreciate his brother's attempt to rile him, but Ruger laughed which alleviated some of the tension.

"If Colt gets that girl, you know he'll protect her body with his life. He's a possessive sonofabitch."

"Like you've ever shared a woman you cared about," Colt said to Ruger.

"Oh, now he admits that he cares," Blaser said to Ruger's jeer.

"Foreign to you though, isn't it?" Colt said to Blaser. "You've never cared about another soul in your life."

"Whoa, hey," Ruger said. "Let's keep this friendly, Colt, if you want the girl, go get her. We'll support you. Blase, you should know better than to piss Colt off, he still has buddies down at the precinct. And you know I'll tell our future sister-in-law this story next Christmas."

Blaser laughed and Colt shoved Ruger off his stool. "You're not too old for me to kick the shit out of you, you know."

They began rough housing in good humor until Blaser came around the bar and gave them both a shove.

"If there's going to be bloodshed in my bar it'll be shed by me," Blaser said.

"Are you kidding? Mom wants us all around for dinner tomorrow night," Ruger said. "I don't want to explain all your bruises. She'll ground me or something."

"Your worst nightmare, staying in one place for more than twenty minutes, Colt said.

"And what about your bruises and broken bones?" Blaser said. "Colt's right, you know we can kick your ass. You're a little wimp."

"In your dreams," Ruger said, shoving Blaser.

"Grab the beer, let's go upstairs and play a few frames," Colt said. "We've got to catch up before Ruge disappears again."

"I missed you too, bro," he said, trying to yank his resistant brother into a headlock while Blaser went back for the beer.

"Knock it off you two and get moving. I'm in the mood to play for high stakes tonight."

"No problem," Ruger said, taking the case of beer from Blaser. "I could use the money."

The three laughing brothers headed up the stairs for a rare, but overdue, night of male bonding.

THIRTEEN

"I CAN TELL that this is important to you. It's a breakthrough and you should be proud," Lyssa said to Bobby, her last patient on that Wednesday night.

When he'd called to reschedule his Monday appointment, she'd worried that his reluctance to attend suggested a loss of faith in therapy. That was sometimes a problem with patients who felt like they weren't making progress fast enough.

"I am," Bobby said. "It's taken me so long to get to this point."

"Yes," Lyssa said. "But it's proof that everything we've done together is working."

"You've been so positive," Bobby said. "You're so understanding."

"We've been here for nearly an hour, and you haven't mentioned your date on Saturday night. How did it go?"

Bobby paled and pushed his palms into the couch by his thighs. "I called it off."

"No," Lyssa said. "You liked this girl, Deshana, and she sounded nice. Why did you cancel?"

"I just… couldn't I… if I went out with her, she would eventually want to go to bed and… I'm not ready for that."

"There's no pressure for you to do anything physical. I've explained that to you before."

"It starts with the goodnight kiss, that's when a girl knows how a guy feels."

"Have you kissed her?"

"Sort of," he said, though she wasn't too sure what that meant. "I didn't want her to get any ideas. So I kept it brief."

"Your anxiety about this is what causes the issue. You have to remember your exercises and how far you've come. We're going to get through this."

"You're the only woman who hasn't abandoned me," Bobby said. "When I go through the steps you taught me, I think about you."

"And that's fine," Lyssa said. "A calming influence can help before you try to initiate intimacy. Be patient with yourself and let it come naturally."

"Thinking about you helps me," he said.

She got the sense that he meant as more than a calming influence. "I am your doctor, Bobby. I'm here to help, but you can't rely too heavily on me. I won't be around forever. Eventually you'll progress enough for us to end our sessions." His eyes flared in panic. "But we're a way away from that. We're out of time this week, but I want you to think about calling Deshana and making another date, okay? Think about it."

They set their next appointment, then Lyssa went about bringing Bobby's file up to date. On a clock, she'd have to get upstairs and prepare for hosting a dinner party. Suzette insisted they do it. Initially, her best friend spoke of making plans later in the week or at the weekend. Risqué caused an availability issue that she couldn't share. To cover for her lack of availability, she jumped on the dinner party idea.

Not known for her cooking skills, Lyssa did her best to throw together something simple. Something that could cook while she showered and got changed. She had just finished tidying up when the front door opened.

Suzette's voice carried up the stairs. "It's us, Lys!"

She appreciated that her friend called out. Always best to have that confirmation the stalker hadn't just flounced in. Suzette had a key, the stalker did not… or he shouldn't. If he had to bust down the door to get in, that would be a big clue. But who knew what skills the perpetrator had?

Putting out placemats to set the table, Lyssa glanced up as Suzette walked in on the arm of her tall, charming fiancé Pete Harding. Ready to greet them, she faltered when Keith, Pete's best man, came in behind them.

"Keith," Lyssa said through her plastic smile. "I didn't realize that you would be joining us."

"The more the merrier, right?" Pete said, helping himself to a beer from the fridge and then giving one to Keith.

The men went to the living room, giving Lyssa the chance to glare at Suzette on her way to the flatware drawer.

"What harm can it do?" Suzette whispered, tiptoeing closer. "The guys can entertain each other, and we can talk."

"You could've left the guys at home."

"He likes you," Suzette said, earning another glare. "It's a good thing. Keith is a great guy, and he makes good money."

"And that's a reason to date him? I make my own money. I'm not interested."

"Why not? He's cute and having a man around wouldn't be so bad. Maybe it will scare off the obsessed madman."

Except Colt had already told her that the stalker wasn't on the street watching her constantly. "So I should sleep with him and keep him around just in case someone is watching? What if it pisses him off?"

"Keith?"

"No, the stalker," Lyssa said, contemplating how her stalker would react to the introduction of a man into her life. Dating hadn't been a priority for her of late. So far though, her admirer hadn't threatened physical harm. For all she knew, romance wasn't his ultimate goal. His motive was still unclear. The roses indicated perhaps amorous feelings but weren't conclusive on their own.

"That better not be the reason you've stopped

dating," Suzette said, straightening a fork.

"I didn't consciously stop," Lyssa said. "It's not a priority right now. Have you forgotten what the dating scene is like? You found Mr. Wonderful. Congratulations. It isn't as easy for everyone."

"You don't have to do the dating thing with randoms. I've brought you a Mr. Wonderful direct to your dinner table."

Through the arch to the living room, she took a long look at Keith's profile. He was about five eleven with short brown-blond hair and blue eyes. His appearance was fine... until she thought of Colt. As far as her libido was concerned, there was no comparison.

"He doesn't measure up," Lyssa said, finishing with the table.

She took a glass pitcher from the kitchen cabinet to fill it with ice water for the center of the table.

"To what?" Suzette asked, retrieving glasses for the table. "The idea of fairy-tale Prince Charming? You, of all people, should be more realistic. Sex and relationships are your specialty. You've been married too! In a real relationship. How—"

"I met someone." That revelation shut her friend up. The women stared at each other for a few seconds. Her friend's shock bred her smile, then a laugh. "Is that so unbelievable?"

"Yes!" Suzette said. "I didn't know you were looking. How long have you been keeping this from me?"

"I haven't been hiding it," Lyssa said.

Revealing her attraction to Colt was a compulsion. She was already lying to Suzette about too many things. Being dishonest with such a valued friend was just sickening. A line had to be drawn, and she was making the call.

"Who is he? Where did you meet?"

Lyssa put the water on the table and was about to put the salad beside it. Before she could get the bowl from the counter, Suzette pulled her around.

"We met in a bar."

"You went to a bar alone?" Suzette asked. "Why did you do that?"

She hadn't gone to Risqué alone. One truth led straight to a lie. "Sometimes being alone in this house sends me nutty. I needed to get out."

The shock in Suzette was subsiding… a little. As she relaxed, her smile began to emerge. "And you met Mr. Wonderful?"

"I wouldn't describe him as that. He's contrary and aloof, but he's got a great sense of humor… and he knows how to kiss."

Suzette gasped and lowered her volume. "Have you had sex with him?"

"Not yet," Lyssa said. "I left the ball in his court."

That perplexed her friend. "You're waiting around for him? Is there something wrong with him? Oh, is he a virgin?"

"He's divorced, so I doubt he's a virgin," she said. Suzette let her go to the salad. "There's nothing wrong with a person who is a virgin at any age, there are often extenuating circumstances."

"I just insulted one of your patients, didn't I?" Suzette said, springing up to sit on the kitchen counter. "Well, this gives us cause to celebrate… though, hmm… Keith will be disappointed."

"Can we keep this between us?" Lyssa asked. "Just for now, until I see how things go."

"If you want," Suzette said. "Tell me about him, when can I meet him?"

She moved on to pouring wine. "One step at a time. Let's not rush him."

"You do know how to make a guy last," Suzette said, smirking. "You're fully trained."

The women laughed as the men came in.

"What's so funny?" Keith asked.

"How long until dinner?" Pete asked.

"Everyone take a seat and I'll serve," Lyssa said, sharing a smile with Suzette.

Since they were all there, and the food was ready, it made sense to be social. The wedding required them to spend time together anyway. Lyssa had no objection to forging a friendship. With the union of Pete and Suzette, they'd be a part of each other's lives for a long time… hopefully. She'd be civil but make it clear there was no scope for intimacy between her and Keith.

THE NIGHT WAS DRAWING to a close. Conversation around the dinner table was pleasant but benign. The food had been edible, pleasant, nowhere close to spectacular. Night was all around them. She and Suzette had finished a bottle of wine. Pete was driving so had stopped drinking after his first beer. Keith, on the other hand, had moved onto the Scotch.

"Only a few short weeks," Suzette said, patting Pete's thigh.

Frequently, talk returned to the wedding. Made sense, it was something they had in common.

"Plenty of time to plan your escape," Keith said.

Pete laughed. "Not a chance, this is it for me," he said, putting an arm around Suzette who pressed a loud kiss to his cheek.

An echoing crash splintered the mood. Glass shattered; a thud followed. All of them shot to their feet.

"What was that?" Pete asked, looking left and right.

"A window broke," Keith said. "Sounded like it came from downstairs."

The men headed out to the hallway, Lyssa started to follow, but Suzette seized her. "Let them check it out."

Leaving it to the men wasn't right. That was her home. Her sanctuary. "I want to know what it was."

"If he's down there—"

"You think that the stalker crashed through the window?" Lyssa asked. "Why? He always keeps his distance. This is my problem. I have to see it."

Tugging her arm free, she ran after the men, Suzette beat a path behind her. In the waiting room, at the back of her property, beyond her office, Keith stood at the broken pane. Splintered glass was scattered over the grey fabric couch and the floor beyond. Pete was in the center of the room holding the heavy projectile, a rock… maybe a brick.

"This was no accident," Keith said, peering into the darkness of her yard. "Whoever did this couldn't have done it from the park. He had to be in your yard."

Pete stalked to Suzette shaking the concrete block, which was not much bigger than his fist. "This is what's going on? You're here when this kind of shit is going on?"

"He's never done this before," Suzette said.

"Who are you talking about?" Keith asked.

Suzette took her hand. "You have to call the cops," she said. "This is a violent act. It's vandalism."

Lyssa nodded. Suzette was right, though she didn't relish the idea of giving a statement. Half a bottle of wine didn't lead to a clear head. Tomorrow she'd have a Risqué shift after a day of patients. What she should really be doing is going to bed. But there was no excuse not to alert the authorities.

"We're going home," Pete said, dropping the block and grabbing Suzette's arm.

"No, we can't go." Suzette pulled back. "We have to stay and support Lyssa."

"The police will need our statements," Keith said.

Pete resolved himself with a sigh. "Fine," he said. "Where's the phone?"

"I'll do it," Lyssa said. "I'm used to it now."

FOURTEEN

BY THE TIME the police arrived, the adrenaline had worn off. Pictures and statements were taken, with the witnesses being interviewed in separate rooms. Eventually the cops left, and her heart began to slow to a sane speed.

She got a broom to sweep the glass from the hardwood floor. The rock had gouged the wood. Of course it had. The last thing she wanted to think about was having her floors refinished.

The outside breeze invading her home curled like unwelcome fingers around her vulnerable shoulders. She couldn't even bring herself to turn her back on the broken window. The ink of black sky and the gentle rustle of distant trees whispered like voices of intimidating warning. Turning off the light wasn't an option. But with the overhead light on she would be lit up to the outside world, framed in the shattered pane for anyone outside to admire or despise.

Voices upstairs grew louder, carrying down the stairs, giving her the excuse to leave the cleaning up until later.

In the living room, Keith was seated but Suzette and Pete were facing off.

"Get your things," Pete demanded of Suzette.

"I'm not running away, leaving my best friend alone."

"You're not staying here," Pete said. "I had no idea that the danger you were in."

"If it's dangerous, we should take Lyssa back to our place, now."

"No way," Pete said. "I don't want her bringing her mess to our home."

"He's right," Lyssa said, drawing the attention of everyone onto her. "You should go home, all of you."

"What if he's still hanging around out there watching, waiting for us to leave?" Suzette asked.

"You can come back to mine," Keith said. "Or I can spend the night."

The chirp of her cellphone saved her from responding to that either selfless or sordid offer. Pete and Suzette were arguing again by the time she got to her purse in the kitchen.

Given preceding events, she wasn't thinking straight. The fact that it was almost midnight didn't factor in her thoughts until after she answered.

"Hello?"

"You'll have to cover that window, Cherrypop."

Just hearing his voice loosened her body. She inhaled a long, cleansing breath. "Colt," she whispered.

"Staying there isn't smart, honey."

"I've already had an offer to stay elsewhere."

"Suzette?"

"No, Pete won't have me endangering her and he's right. This is my mess to deal with and no one else's."

"Except mine," he said. "You're paying me to deal with it."

"I guess," she said, drooping into a dinner chair.

"So Keith wants into your panties?"

"How do you know he's the one who made the offer?"

"There's no one else there," he said. "And twice in one week for dinner says he's interested in more than conversation."

"Suzette says he likes me, he knows I'm not interested."

"None of my business," he said with what sounded like distaste. "Just be careful about hooking up with unknown men while this bullshit is going on."

"No one else gets the offer you did, babe. I'll wait until you're ready."

"You're a client, Lys."

"You said that already. But my curiosity isn't satisfied. Kissing only fanned the flame." Teasing with him felt good. Better than she'd felt all night. "I want you."

"Do you think that now is the time to talk about this?"

"Okay, you be sensible and responsible," she said and exhaled, fingering the strap of her purse. "I'm glad you called. I feel safer just knowing that you know."

"Do you want me to tell Blase you'll be taking tomorrow night off?"

"Tell him? He's my boss. If I need the night off, I'll ask Blase if it's convenient for him. But I don't want the night off, I'll feel better out of the house… and I want to see you."

"What makes you think that I'll show face at the club?"

Her smile flared of its own volition. "You'll want to check that I'm okay."

"I'm doing that now. And you sound fine."

"Because by calling you've proved that you care about me."

"I care about staying in the loop," he said.

"You can probably get a copy of the report," she said, still sure that she was right. "Have you been outside for a while?"

"I was at the front of the property and didn't witness the act," he said, frustration straining his voice. "I did my perimeter check less than two minutes before. I just fucking missed him."

"We all missed him…" Taking a serious line, she confessed the truth of her tension. Until then, she'd hidden behind false indifference. "He's escalating."

"He is. He couldn't find you the other night and now he thinks that you're dating Keith."

"By dating and changing my routine he's gotten mad?"

"Maybe."

"I don't want him to hurt Keith. It would be unfair. The man has never laid a hand on me."

"Unlike me."

She relaxed into another smile. "You can take care of yourself, babe. Unless those sexy muscles are all for show."

"If he came after me," he said, "my job would get a whole lot easier."

"I don't want him coming after anyone."

The voices in the living room rose again, distracting her.

"What's that?" Colt asked. "The shouting?"

"Pete and Suzette are fighting. I better go and diffuse the situation. Tell me I'll see you tomorrow."

"You'll see me," he grumbled like he'd been busted. "Cover that window with plastic or cardboard and call a glazier first thing."

"I will."

"Do you want me to do it?"

Startled, it took a second to respond. "Come in and cover my window?"

"Arrange to have your window replaced," he said. "I'm not sure that the guy won't be back tonight."

"Thanks, I'll definitely sleep better knowing you think that, especially since you're the expert in this field."

"I'm round the back, I'll watch the back window all night," he said. "No one will sneak inside, I promise you, Cherrypop."

"If you're up all night watching my window then you won't have a chance to sleep. Why would you do that?"

"Because otherwise you won't settle, and you don't need the stress."

Did he know how much of himself he'd revealed in that conversation? It almost seemed like he'd been scared too. Or maybe his professional pride was wounded. Beyond that, their relationship was growing more personal… in her opinion. Did he feel the same?

"That's very kind of you to be so considerate."

"Ruger's sitting outside the front," he said. "Far enough away that he won't be noticed. You're safe, Lys."

Such an act of kindness spread warmth through her. "Send your brother home. Come inside and protect me from my bedroom."

"You're a client," he said in an almost sing-song voice.

"Is that all that's stopping you?" she asked. "If I was to put my hand in your jeans now, what would I find?"

"You'd find yourself in trouble, doc, because you shouldn't mess with patients."

"You're not a patient," she said and laughed. "That was a smokescreen appointment… but if you want me to stop pursuing you, I get it. I'll give you a reprieve… at least until tomorrow night."

"You're a saint," he said. She heard his blessed smile. "Cover the window and get rid of your guests. Ruge and I will watch your ass."

"I know how you enjoy doing that, babe."

"I do but watching is allowed."

"So is touching," she purred. "If I didn't think he might be watching, I'd be tempted to give you a show… Think about that while you're watching my bedroom. Goodnight."

Hanging up, she took some time to immerse herself in her hormonal response to Colt. The first man in a long time to stir her feminine desires… Mmm… then she got up and went to do exactly what Colt had told her to do.

***

BLASER DIDN'T GIVE ANY INDICATION that he knew about the previous night's incident when she arrived for her shift. Everything went on as normal. Life was so often like that. The world always kept on turning.

More than halfway through her shift, Ruger showed up. Colt was MIA. Although she'd have preferred her potential squeeze, she was curious about what the younger Warner knew of her predicament. Her cover could be blown any second if this was the first time that Ruger was seeing Blaser. Did he know that Blaser didn't know?

Moseying closer, she tried not to make her urgent impetus too obvious.

"I should thank you," Lyssa said.

Ruger didn't lift his head. "Cool. Gratuitous gratitude is gratefully received."

"For last night. I should say thank you," she said, keeping her volume as low as the music would allow. Thankfully, there were no speakers right at the bar, so conversation was still possible. "I don't know what you were doing when Colt called you to come over to mine, but I'd guess that a guy like you doesn't spend many nights alone."

Tipping his focus, he peered at her. "How's that?"

"You're fit, attractive… smooth. I can tell you have the gift of the gab. Ladies must find you difficult to resist."

"Are you hitting on me, doc?" His half smile could be hiding a laugh. " 'Cause my brother will be here before closing. If he thinks I'm cozying up to his girl, he'll kick my ass."

"I'm not Colt's girl, he's made that clear to me," she said, looping an arm through his, so that they leaned on the bar together. "You're a sweetheart, but it's not sex I want from you."

"What do you want?" he asked, swilling his beer.

"Information. You called me, doc, and you were at my place last night. Did Colt tell you everything?"

"No idea what you're talking about," he said, proving he was the most playful Warner.

"You're going to play dumb?"

"Most women want me for my beauty, not my brains."

Something in his tone was dull and distracted. Her psyche-senses tingled. "Do you have a problem, Littlest Warner?" she asked, aiming for non-threatening.

"No problem," Ruger said. "My life is easy sailing."

"Everyone has problems. You're preoccupied

tonight."

He sucked in a long breath. "If a girl's family hate a guy, but the girl keeps pursuing the guy, is it worth it?"

"This is kind of my area," she said, pulling up a stool. "How does the guy feel about her?"

"I don't know," Ruger said. "It's sort of about sex for him, it started that way, but… I think maybe he cares more than he lets on."

Trying not to smile, she watched him pick at the label on his bottle. "And how does she feel?"

"God knows," Ruger said. "I don't trust her."

"Then you come to the question of whether you can have love without trust. How much does the family hate you? How does that hate manifest itself?"

"We're not talking about me," he objected, showing his first smile of the night. "Everybody loves me, how could anyone not?"

Charm came naturally to him. "Okay," she said, unconvinced. "Who are we talking about?"

"That's confidential," he said.

Blaser came over. "Tables, Cherry. Get with it, girl," he said. "What are you two chatting about that's so important?"

"Your love life," Ruger said.

"Yeah, right," Blaser said, clearly not believing his little brother, because he laughed. "Tables."

She headed to a table in need of service and glanced back to see the brothers conversing. Ruger was being honest, though Blaser didn't believe it. She wouldn't correct him and could be discreet. When she got the chance, she'd get more of the story from Colt.

FIFTEEN

AROUND AN HOUR LATER, Colt came in. Although they made brief eye contact, he didn't come to her. He turned to nod at Ruger and the two of them disappeared backstage. To Colt's office? Did Ruger have an office too?

The speedy move was intriguing. Colt hadn't missed a step. The brothers exchanged something without words and then they were on the same page.

Rather than investigate, she concentrated on her job and went over to the three men who had just entered. After going through her usual spiel, she began to take their drinks order.

Blaser appeared at her side, interrupting. "What do you want, Gary?" he asked, angling his body in front of hers.

"Came in for a drink and to see the show, what's the problem?"

"Only reason you and Marshall hang out is to cause trouble. You forget that I used to run with your crew. And you brought Zeke to up your odds."

"Heard Ruge was back in town."

The menace in Gary's voice was backed up by the hostile expressions of the other two. If they wanted to cause trouble, Blaser could have security throw them out.

Mentioning Ruger made whatever was going on personal. These men could lie in wait for Blaser. She didn't want him to get hurt and didn't want Colt or Ruger hurt either.

"Yeah," Blaser said.

"He owes me a debt."

"No, he doesn't," Blaser said. "Your demands are bullshit."

"He gave me his word you wouldn't lay your filthy hands on my sister again… think he broke that promise."

Backing away, Lyssa tried to blend into the shadows. None of the seated men were interested in her. Blaser was intent on Gary who stared right back.

Without drawing attention to herself, she spun to make a beeline for the backstage door. Running up the stairs, she hurried into Colt's office without knocking. The brothers, on opposite sides of the desk, looked at her.

"Cherrypop, give—"

"There's a guy called Gary in with his friends," she said in a rush of breath. "I'm worried he and Blaser are about to tear strips from each other."

The brothers didn't hesitate; they were on their feet, stalking in her direction. Ruger almost bowled her over, but Colt paused.

"Wait up here," he said and actually ducked to kiss her before disappearing in the wake of his brother.

As much as she wanted to know that the trio would be okay, she trusted Colt's professional judgement, just as she asked her patients to do with her. Closing the door, she took a seat on the couch and waited.

The imprint of Colt's lips on hers kept her company. His subconscious act was a comfort and a curiosity. The familiarity of it drove her bubble of desire to something deeper. The intensity of it grew until it shimmered through every inch of her.

Colt had shown concern and prioritized her safety tonight. That wasn't his standard procedure. What made her different? She wanted to spend time with him, quality time.

Sex wasn't a dirty word. Just because she could discuss it openly didn't mean she gave it away freely. On the contrary, she understood its importance and the bond that could be forged through it. Colt was a good man. She wanted to explore every facet of him behind his strong exterior.

The office door burst open. The three brothers piled in, Colt and Ruger shoved Blaser along in front of them.

"Give us a minute," Ruger said to her.

Something must have transpired. None of the brothers appeared injured. Ignoring her instinct to ask questions, she got up and slunk out, making brief, reassuring eye contact with Colt.

Music pumped through from the main floor. As she descended, Crystal disappeared through the curtain to the stage indicating everything was okay front of house. Crystal had the skills to distract patrons from any drama they may have witnessed.

Unexpected developments were always the most intense, Lyssa made a stop in the locker room to use the restroom and check her makeup.

Washing her hands, scrutinizing her reflection, a yelp from the locker room startled her.

Crying came next, then the growl of a male voice. "Shut up! Get in there!"

"Get your hands off me!" a female snapped.

Was that Destiny? The youngest of the dancers.

"Beg all you want, baby," a second male voice. "Won't help you now."

"Someone will come in here," Destiny said, fire in her voice though it trembled, undermining her confidence.

"Hope they do," one of the males said on a laugh. "Got plenty of uses for more babes like you."

Lyssa grabbed the restroom door handle, yanking it open to stride out. Two men had Destiny trapped against the lockers. One fondled her breasts as the other held her throat.

Her intrusion didn't go unnoticed. When the men turned, she recognized Marshall and Zeke.

"What's going on?" Lyssa asked.

"Another one!" Marshall, with his greasy black hair, said.

The exit door was on the opposite wall. How could

she get over there?

"You shouldn't be back here," Lyssa said.

"And who's going to chase us out, baby?" Zeke asked, leaving Marshall with Destiny to slink toward her.

"Just do what they want, Cherry," Destiny said. "They rushed me out back."

Where the girls went to smoke in the alley.

"Cherry?" Marshall said. "She's Colt's girl. She got Lenny and his crew tossed out of here last week."

Either the community was small or the lowlifes in the neighborhood had a phone tree.

"You're not welcome here," Lyssa said. "Didn't the Warners make that clear?"

Zeke snatched her throat to plant her back on the restroom door that had clicked shut behind her.

"Hey!"

Panic never got the chance to take hold. Colt's shout gave instant relief, even though Zeke didn't let go. Within seconds, he wasn't given a choice. Colt came up behind him and jerked him away, throwing him toward the waiting Ruger.

"You boys weren't listening the first time," Ruger said. "You'll get the extra special escorted exit this time."

Blaser appeared with security to bundle the cursing men out. Destiny followed on cursing right back.

Colt turned, paralyzing her with his gaze. "What happened?"

"Nothing, no one got hurt," Lyssa said, taking his hand.

"We threw them out. The bastards must have got in the back. They'd never have got through the—"

"Don't worry about it. Why were you in here?"

"I came looking for you," he said. "I pulled some strings with Chavez. The cops are going to open a case. They'll do a full investigation. You're on their radar. Officially."

That was... astounding. "Really?" she said, almost unable to believe it.

The broken window debacle may have contributed to the decision. Or Colt had been fighting her corner, pulling strings.

"Officers will come out to talk to you tomorrow. They'll increase patrols and video surveillance in your area. We'll install an alarm and panic button for you."

"We…?" she said, tipping up her chin and closing in on him, touching his abs.

"I can install it for you."

"If the police are following up, I don't need to employ your services anymore."

He put his hands in his pockets. "I guess you don't. I wouldn't want to step on the cops' toes."

"No, so… you're fired," she murmured. "Which means…"

"You're no longer a client."

Before she could speak, he grabbed her hips and slammed her back against the wall. Yes, this was the Colt Warner she wanted to know.

"I guess this changes things for you," she said without containing her smile.

He remained intent, holding her tight, his grip digging into her flesh. "I guess it does," he said. His fingertips met her cheekbone and arced down to her jaw, thrusting her head back. He stooped to settle his lips on her neck beneath her chin. "Let's get one thing straight upfront, doc. You might have started the engine, but I'm the driver."

"Do you always make your intentions clear up front?" she asked, luxuriating in the sizzle of stimulation left in the wake of his travelling lips.

"I like to show my lady a good time and know how to make sure I have one too."

"Is that a failing of your trust in me?"

"Stop thinking and deconstructing, doc," he said, his mouth teasing her throat. "Consider all rules rescinded… except number two."

Rule number two: do as she was told. The simmer within her simmered to a boil, splashing desire throughout her senses. Her focus narrowed to the contact of his lips on her skin. The gentle contact continued across her neck up to her ear.

"I like that," she exhaled, sliding into bliss.

He touched her waist then lifted her arms up to guide them around his neck. "Yeah?"

"Yeah," she said. "Your mouth is warm. You're respectful, but you want me. There's urgency in your touch that says you want all of me."

"Oh, yeah."

"I want you too," she said.

Her eyes closed; she absorbed his seduction. The pulse of bass from the club came through the wall from the main floor. A mist of feminine perfume scented the air, mingled with the smell of stage make-up and other cosmetics.

The breadth and stability of Colt's wide shoulders was strength. Security. All the baser needs were met by the man tantalizing her hormones.

Capturing her body, he slid her up the wall, and wrapped her legs around him, bunching her skirt at her hips. "Untie—"

Anticipating him, she untied her halter top, peeling it down to expose her breasts. Grinding her hips on his, she pushed her shoulders back, giving him a full view.

"Nice," he muttered and levered her up to bring her chest in line with his face. He sucked one nipple then switched to the other, kissing circles around the tingling mound until he sampled the sensitive peak.

"Firm and sure," she said, each breathy whisper for her own benefit. "Makes me hot, oh I want more. Colt, keep going."

Her body slithered down his as he eased her lower to kiss her lips again. Crushing her center to his, she undulated, awakening her own core in preparation for the promise of completion.

"You're hard," she said. "So hard."

"You're soft," he said, nuzzling her neck. "I'm going all the way right now, honey. You've teased too long. Are you going to stop this or give it up to your man like a good girl should?"

"How quickly can you open your fly?"

"All the way?" he asked, kissing her quickly.

If he was surprised, she was just eager. "All the way,

babe. I've never been aroused like this. I'm slick and hot, my body craves a union with yours. I don't ignore my hormonal drives. Our bodies tell us what they need by flooding our brains with chemical endorphins—"

"All that lingo is hot talk for an orgasm, right? You want me to get you off? Is that what you want?"

"Well translated," she said and smiled.

Locking her mouth over his, she forced her tongue between his lips. His pleasure was as important as hers; she recalled what he'd said in her office. She wouldn't let him marginalize his own gratification in favor of hers.

Trusting him to keep her weight, she released him from his jeans and began to squeeze his length through her palms, one after the other, causing him to groan.

"If you want to get me off," she said, "you'll have to let me feel you deep. You're long and thick, so big that you'll fill me up. It might be a tight squeeze for you."

In work with patients, it wasn't her place to talk, or describe her sexual experiences. But in the fog of thrumming hormones, her sanity slipped. As this strong, capable man devoured her mouth, her hands moved faster and squeeze tighter. A sure finger slipped past her panties. His deft fingers found all the right corners, the gentle brush, the plunge of needs, and the quick, hard stimulating end.

Her cry of ecstasy stalled him.

"You're some picture, Miss. Lys. I think my dick is in bliss."

"Not yet," she panted, elevating her hips to bring the head of his penis to her opening.

His fingers slipped away giving room for him to progress with aching leisure. God, he was torturing her with ecstasy, one slow inch at a time.

"Faster," she pleaded, but he only smiled when her gaze met his.

"You're not driving this session. I'm in control."

That grumble sent a quiver through her. From the way he froze inside her, he'd experienced what his voice did to her.

"Then do with me what you will."

Pinning her hips to the wall, he thrust himself into her, surging forward until there was no more of him to give. "No going back," he said.

Struggling to remain still, she squirmed against this steel rod occupying her. "No, not a chance," she whimpered, whining when he began to move in and out.

The pace picked up until he was hammering into her. With each pound, she squeezed him tighter until like a vice she clamped around him in climax. Holding back a scream, her teeth grabbed her lip. The pulse going through her was satisfaction. Pure gratification. The mood of the club, the heat and arousal heightened in her gut, enlivened the crest cascading through her. Just as hers slipped from its apex, his hit and he slammed in hard, filling her with his seed.

Her chest tightened with every vibrating aftershock. Thought wasn't possible. Nothing was. Which was probably why it took him at least a minute to shift back enough to look at her.

He smoothed her damp hair from her temple. "I wasn't planning that," he panted and exhaled a smile.

"The best moments in life are often spontaneous," she said, kissing him once, then he kissed her longer and slower. Breaking that union was painful, but she had no choice. "I have a shift to finish."

He took another look at her body then put her on her feet. "I should check on my brothers."

Lyssa fixed her skirt and tied her top. "You should."

Colt came toward her. Another kiss would probably take them onto the floor. Maybe they'd lose their minds completely and split before the end of her shift.

At that moment, the locker room door opened. A naked Crystal came in chattering with a couple of other girls, paying.

Blithe adrenaline bubbled up in her, they had a secret. A hot, thrilling, carnal secret.

She pressed a hand to his arm. "Go and check on your brothers."

He nodded. A twitching smile came and went so repeatedly that she guessed he was experiencing the same high as her. This was a new bonding experience. Their connection was strengthening, and she wanted to explore it further.

"Okay," he said.

She wished he'd kiss her again. Instead, he followed her suggestion and left the locker room.

Taking herself into the restroom, she cleaned up, all the while smiling and giggling like an idiot. Whatever they were starting had the potential to be something real.

SIXTEEN

LYSSA DIDN'T FINISH HER SHIFT. After returning from the restroom, she served two tables, then Blaser told her to head home. And it wasn't as a favor to Colt. His own issues were distracting him, yes. But she read guilt in him too, obviously over what she and Destiny were subjected to by Marshall and Zeke. Not that there was much of a trauma.

Destiny had been due to go on stage. Blaser had given her a pass and another girl took her spot, leaving Destiny free to go home as well.

Protesting the invitation would've drawn attention to her. Who would elect to do cleaning rather than skip it? Others would jump at the chance to bunk off. Refusing to do the same might raise suspicions. After agreeing to leave, she went through the usual routine of showering and changing her clothes. She wasn't procrastinating… no, she was… in hope of seeing Colt.

He didn't appear and she wasn't going up to his office. It was never wise to add pressure to a man in the early stages of a courtship. Appearing too clingy could scare him off. Many women made the mistake of rushing to make a mark on a man. In contrast, her excitement was savoring the burgeoning stage of what could be a lasting relationship.

So she bid goodnight to Blaser and went home. If Colt wanted to follow her, he could, and she would gratefully receive him.

Except he didn't come to her that night.

The police came at midday on the Friday. She gave them a full statement and answered all their questions. Since starting work at Risqué, she'd switched her Friday schedule to allow her to sleep later in the morning. During the day, she worked on compiling her notes and writing her book.

Taking a late lunch, she went upstairs to call Suzette. With all that had happened at the club, and in her relationship with Colt, it hadn't occurred to her how much time had gone by. She and Suzette hadn't spoken since the night of the window incident.

The phone rang and rang, which was unusual. Suzette usually answered on the second or third ring. This time, it took seven rings for her friend to pick up.

"Hello?"

"Hey," Lyssa said, noting by tone that something wasn't right with her friend. "It's lunchtime, are you busy?"

"Actually, yeah, I am."

She could understand that. Suzette worked full time while maintaining a relationship and planning a wedding.

"Sorry..." Lyssa said, trying to remember if Suzette had ever been too busy to talk to her. For the chance of a chat, usually Suzette would put other tasks aside. "Should I call later?"

"No," Suzette said and sighed. "I'm sorry, I didn't mean to be a bitch. Pete and I had a fight."

"Another fight?"

"Several actually, we've been fighting since we left your place."

"About what happened?"

"He doesn't want me coming over to yours anymore," Suzette said. "He's not wild about us hanging out while a madman is watching you. Those were his words."

"Wow," Lyssa said, leaving the kitchen to go sit on the couch. "He doesn't want you to associate with someone who could put you in danger."

"Trust you to react with that damn, calm doctor voice. You should be pissed. I'm pissed. He has no right to tell me who I can spend time with."

"Not explicitly," Lyssa said. "But he has a right to voice concern, and you should listen to that concern and appreciate that he cares for you so deeply."

"Maybe he's just being a jerk and trying to exert dominance. If I let him get away with that now, what will it be like when we're married?"

"You have to show that you won't be bullied, but you also have to be open to compromise. You're merging your life with another person's. Both of you will have to make allowances."

"You're okay with this? You want to throw away our friendship because some guy's throwing his weight around?"

"We're not talking about throwing our friendship away. I've voiced my own concerns about your safety during this. Maybe Pete is right. We can talk on the phone whenever you want. This could be over soon; the police are taking things more seriously now."

"Will that last? What if they don't find him quickly?"

"Then we'll revisit," she said, mustering a smile. "You'll never guess who I missed a call from this morning."

"Who?" Suzette asked.

Her friend's need for gossip outweighed her melancholy. "Archie."

"No way," Suzette gasped. "Your ex-husband, Archie?"

"Yes. I was busy"—with the cops—"when I missed the call on my cell."

"Are you going to call him back?"

"No," Lyssa said. "I haven't heard from him in two years. If it's that important he'll call back."

"What do you think he wants?"

"With Archie, who knows? He'll be boasting about something. He'll be starting a new business, or marrying a new model, or something."

"He'd phone you for that? Does he think you'll be jealous? Maybe he's experiencing some issues and needs to employ your professional services."

Suzette had relaxed enough to laugh and because it was at the possible misfortune of Lyssa's ex-husband, she smiled at the solidarity.

Archie was seventeen years her senior, but he'd never had regular sexual dysfunction issues that she knew about. Treating him would broach on the unethical, though they hadn't had a personal relationship for years. Anyway, she wasn't sure she'd want to coach him through issues like that.

"If he does, he's on his own," Lyssa said. "He can afford the best in the business."

"And that's you," Suzette said.

"You're biased… But thank you for saying so."

"I wish we could make plans to get together. But I don't want to get into another fight with Pete. Thank you for being so understanding. Maybe you're right. Maybe if we lay low for a week or two, he'll start thinking about something else."

"I'm always here to talk, call if you need me."

Saying goodbye felt solemn, like it was final, though it wasn't. Things would get back to normal between them as soon as the stalking stopped. The sooner the better. There was so much she wanted to talk about: the study at Risqué, her work with her book so far, and Colt. She couldn't wait until that day when everything could be out in the open.

SEVENTEEN

"IT MAKES NO SENSE why I feel so anxious about this," Lyssa said to Ruger who'd been propped at the bar since her arrival an hour ago.

"Because your best friend's fiancé is trying to push you out."

"He isn't," Lyssa said. "It's reassuring that he cares so deeply for Suze. I wouldn't want her marrying someone who didn't."

"Just because something makes sense doesn't mean it's easy to take."

"That's logical."

"Not everything is rational," Ruger said. "You feel marginalized. Pushed aside."

"You're good at this," she said, impressed that he was both listening and offering sensible reassurance.

When someone touched her waist, she turned to Colt standing just behind her.

Before they could exchange a word, Blaser shouted from behind the bar. "Cherry," he called. "Stop moping and clear your tables."

"Moping?" Colt asked, concerned. "Why are you moping?"

"She got dumped," Ruger said, bringing his beer bottle to his mouth.

"Ha, ha," she sneered sarcastically and slipped past Colt to clean up the vacant tables in her section.

Each night, according to the schedule, she worked a different section. The ones closer to the stage tipped more. Were those men bolder? Drunker? Or just too mesmerized by the show to pay attention to their wallets?

"Put that down," Colt said, materializing beside her to take the empty glasses from her hands. He linked their fingers and led her out of the club and up to his office. "Sit down."

As soon as they got there, he took off his jacket and pitched it to the loveseat. With a few gentle nudges, he got them seated on the couch.

Intrigued, his actions suggested purpose. "Have you got something to say?"

"First off…" he said. "I didn't dump you."

Despite it probably being secondary, his reassurance improved her mood. "Ruger wasn't talking about you."

His contrite expression snapped to a frown. "How many other dudes are you seeing?"

She laughed. "He was talking about Suzette. Pete doesn't want her to come over to my place anymore."

"Suzette dumped you?"

"Yes," she said. Picking up his hands, she slithered in close to lie against his chest and wrapped his arms around her. "Talk is all Ruger can do to make me feel better. You can do this."

"I can get physical?" he asked, leaning forward to scoop her legs over his lap.

With one arm still around her, he removed her shoes and tossed them to the floor.

"Probably not a good idea to do that while I'm on shift," she said as he began to massage her toes. "I might ask you to massage other places too."

"Why did you run off last night?"

"Blaser said I could go home early."

"I would've come home with you… I thought we

started something in here last night."

"We did," she said, guiding his arm around her again. "I don't want to pressure you. I'm going to ease you into falling for me."

"I'm no good at casual sex," he admitted. "I had a fling after I was divorced, lasted about three months. I like to know I'm the only guy with access to the goods, if you get me."

"I get you and you're the only one with access to my goods," she said, tipping her chin up. "And this doesn't have to be casual. I don't want us to be casual."

"Then you better start letting me spend the night," he said, broadening his smile as he dipped lower to kiss her.

"Tonight?" He nodded. "You're not worried about being seen coming in and out of mine?"

Without further explanation, he acknowledged her concern. "He doesn't watch the house," Colt said. "I don't know how he does it. But I've seen no evidence that he monitors your doors."

"Or we could stay at yours…" she said, wriggling closer. "Where do you live?"

"A couple of streets away from here, in an apartment building my cousin owns. Blaser manages it."

Turned out her boss did go other places, other workplaces. "Blaser? Downstairs? Your brother?"

"Yeah, he owns a garage as well. He's a mechanic by trade and used to chop cars."

"He's a busy guy, isn't he? How did he manage to get himself in trouble with Gary?"

His mouth opened, allowing a deep breath to pass his lips. "That goes back to when they were teenagers, it's a long story."

"One I shouldn't ask you to tell me while I'm working," she said. "Maybe you'll tell me another time?"

"Sure. No running off tonight. I'll take you home… We're not hiding from this guy. I'm not working for you anymore; I don't need to hide my identity. If he wants to come after me, let him."

"Don't go looking for a fight," she said. "I was

worried about Suzette's safety when she spent time with me. I have to give you the same warning."

"Don't worry about me, Cherrypop. My brothers watch my back and I know what I'm doing."

"Okay. Your apartment is closer, and I'd love to see it."

Exaggerating the flutter of her eyelashes made him smile out a laugh.

"Whatever makes you happy, Miss. Lys."

Rising from his embrace, she sought out her shoes to slide them on again. "The quicker I get to work, the quicker time will go, and we can get home… to bed."

COLT STAYED AT THE BAR with Ruger throughout the rest of the night. His attention was never far from Lyssa as she buzzed around the room and back to the bar to fill orders. Occasionally they'd flirted, but it was the touches that drove him crazy.

She'd come over and loop her arm around his or rest her head on his shoulder. Or she would relax her body on his back and wind her arms around him. Lyssa wasn't afraid of publicizing their relationship, he was the only one to get the special treatment.

Blaser filled an order for her and put the last glass on her tray. As Lyssa slid it from the bar he squeezed her ass, earning himself a smile. He kissed the ball of her shoulder before she turned to go serve the drinks.

"We've got rules about touching the girls," Blaser said from his side of the bar. "You do it again and I'll have to call security."

"I didn't see her complaining," Ruger said, wearing a mocking grin, giving him an exaggerated nudge. "I think our brother has got himself a girlfriend."

Colt just laughed.

"You move fast," Blaser said. "She's a good girl. Shame she sucks as a waitress. It's a good thing that she's sexy, that ass could hypnotize a guy."

The sway of her hips was another distraction. Though

it was one he didn't mind, one he was proud of. Despite the environment being so alien, she exuded nothing but confidence. Her ambition was admirable; she'd go to any lengths to follow her dream. The book, her reason for being there, was something she'd wanted to do all her life.

Blaser filled another order for one of his servers then came back to him and Ruger. That coincided with Lyssa coming up behind him. At least he hoped it was her because the female lifted the end of his shirt and trailed her fingernails up and down his lower back.

Ruger leaned back, making an obvious show of watching her actions. Colt kept his elbows on the bar and slurped his beer.

"Are there rules about the girls touching customers?" Ruger asked Blaser.

Leaning toward Ruger, she kissed his cheek. "Are you feeling left out?"

"Hey," Colt said, while his brother grinned like an idiot. "No more of that."

"He's easily riled," Ruger said. "You'll have to be careful what you do with those lips from now on."

"Yeah, the only male they're allowed to touch is me," Colt said.

"So I can make out with women?" Lyssa asked.

Ruger swung around, leaving his weight on one elbow while he observed the rest of the room. "Plenty here to choose from, pick any one you want. Any girl is fine with me as long as we get to watch."

"We?" Colt said.

"You'd keep that show all to yourself?" Ruger asked. "My birthday is coming up."

"No, it's not."

"It could be. She didn't know any different, I could've got away with that," Ruger said and shrugged. "You're a spoil sport."

Blaser sauntered over. "You can head off early if you want."

Lyssa propped her cheek on his upper arm. "Why do I get to leave early... again?"

"You're doing management," Blaser said. "You can pretty much do anything you want."

Lyssa picked up his arm to hook it around her so that she could move in against the bar. "Your assumption is that I'm starting a relationship with your brother in order to get perks here at work?"

"I'd have thought that the perks came in the bedroom," Ruger muttered into his beer bottle.

Colt resisted the impulse to smack his brother because Lyssa was intent on Blaser and probably hadn't heard Ruger. The earnest, blinkered expression on her face was familiar. She hadn't been offended by Ruger's glibness, not that he'd ever seen her offended. In times like that, her training kicked in. He'd witnessed it many times, those moments when she believed the comments said more about the speaker than the person they were speaking with.

"What other reason would you have to date such a loser?" Blaser asked, not missing an opportunity to rib his twin.

"It couldn't be that I'm just immensely aroused by this knockout hunk of a man?"

Both Ruger and Blaser laughed. Her eyes narrowed, betraying she was about to launch into some deconstruction of their reaction, so he planted a hand over her mouth.

"Get your shit together and we'll bail," he said, resting a hand on her bare stomach.

"I have to have my shower." She glanced over her shoulder at him. "Will you wait fifteen minutes?"

"Shower at home," he said.

"I shower here because…" Her saucy smile grew as she relaxed to kiss him. "Okay."

After another kiss, she left him to retreat to the locker room backstage. Blaser went to fill an order for one of the waitresses.

"Why does she shower here?" Ruger asked.

"A creep is stalking her and might sneak into her house while she's vulnerable in the shower in the middle of the night."

"No danger of any stalker sneaking in while you're

there," Ruger said. "You'll be the one doing the sneaking."

"That's the idea," he said, finishing his beer. "I hope the bastard makes a move; I'd love to take him down."

"Don't borrow trouble. This guy could be crazy. He won't like the idea of her having a boyfriend."

"Lys has already said this to me."

"She's a smart cookie. A very smart cookie."

"She has a medical degree, that's not an easy get," Colt said. "Smart, sexy and sassy, I've hit the jackpot."

"Sassy is less important to me," Ruger said. "I like my women compliant."

"Do you enjoy wearing women's clothing?"

Both he and Ruger turned to see Lyssa standing behind them wearing her backpack and therapist face.

"Excuse me?" Ruger asked.

"Do you enjoy wearing women's clothes or shoes?" she asked. "Or make regular visits to the beauty salon?"

Ruger turned to Colt. "What is she talking about?"

"Men who feel the need to exert dominance over a submissive woman can have control issues. They may have been a victim of sexual assault or have a history of abuse in childhood. Sometimes the need to display overtly masculine traits can be a disguise for what may be deemed feminine fetishes, such as wearing lingerie, or make-up, or—"

His laughter cut her off. Ruger was so stunned that his expression hung in disbelief. He'd never seen his brother speechless.

"I think he's going to be stuck like that for a while," Colt said, still laughing.

"What's funny?" Blaser asked on his approach.

He rested a hand on Lyssa's hip. "Ask Ruger to show you his pink lace thong," he said, maintaining pressure on Lyssa's hip when she tried to pause to say more.

He got her out of the club. One of the bouncers went to get them a cab.

"I didn't say that to upset Ruger," Lyssa said, taking his arm to bring her body close to his, probably for heat.

"Maybe you got it right on the money. But I'd rather not know too much about my brother's fetishes."

They waited a few seconds. "Not all fetishes are unhealthy," she said. "We all have sexual preferences."

"We do?"

"If it elicits an erotic response or you have a fixation, which causes arousal, on any object, or non-genital part of the body, then it's classed as a fetish. Do you have a fetish?"

"Will you accommodate it?" he asked, putting his arms around her, enclosing her in his jacket while holding her.

Yeah, he could be a gentleman and give her the jacket, but any excuse to press her body against his…

"I might," Lyssa said. "I am quite open when it comes to sexual matters. Are any of your preferences illegal?"

"Aren't you professionally obliged to report it if I admit they are?"

"You're not a patient," she said.

The tolerance in her expression was so patient and non-judgmental. It was awe-inspiring just how good she was at her job.

"Are you going to let me read your book?"

She twisted around, remaining in the same space but putting her back to his front. "Eventually, when it's finished."

"Will I be in it?" he asked.

If he was going to be her sexual partner, he had a right to know if their antics would be shared.

"I keep my personal and professional lives separate. You're mine, all mine," she said, tilting around to kiss his jaw.

The cab pulled up, so she linked their fingers again and bounced forth to lead him into the vehicle.

EIGHTEEN

THEY COULD HAVE WALKED to his apartment from the club, it was only a couple of streets away. Though as she wasn't wearing a jacket and it was the middle of the night, the cab was appreciated.

The neighborhood was unfamiliar. They'd need to have a conversation about safety in the area. Yeah, okay, so she was no idiot, but she wasn't exactly street savvy either.

In the back of the cab, she'd unzipped his jeans while pressing her chest into his. The juxtaposition of her soft breasts squashed against his unyielding body heated her urgency. He'd been the one to join their mouths, something he probably regretted. In a millisecond, she'd gone from cool to searing. His hungry hands struggled to confine his animal urges. The sensation of his struggle, him at the edge of his control, spurred her on.

When they eventually stopped outside his building, he threw money at the snickering cab driver and hauled her out. Ignoring her exuberant laugh, he swept her off her feet and took the external stairs up to his second-floor apartment two at a time.

Sandwiched between him and his front door, her elbows clamped on each side of his neck as her hands grabbed the hair at his crown. Somehow the door gave from behind her, and with her legs gripped around his waist she could do nothing except let him catch her weight. She trusted him.

Inside, as she fought to free her arms from her backpack, his mouth met hers, swallowing her moan of impatience. The door slammed as they crossed the room, seconds before they started to fall. In reflex, her body braced around his, grasping the closest stable entity: him. Cherishing her, he guided her to the cradle of a couch. As they settled, instinct took her fingers to his belt. She didn't even think, she just acted. Within seconds of her freeing him from his pants, he pushed into her. Impatience was relieved for only a split second because he pulled back. In desperation not to lose their connection, her hips came up to meet his, wringing a growl from his throat.

Even in the darkness she could see the possession burning from his eyes. Still clothed, she wore everything except her shoes, but that didn't matter or lessen their need, not in this second. All that mattered was fulfilling their wish.

Her legs climbed his back, she needed him, all of him, now, more. His whispered promises didn't satisfy. Eager to have more, for skin on skin, she dug her heels into his waistband, shoving at his jeans, keen to gain access. Ensconced in their want, he nipped at her lower lip and sucked her tongue into his mouth. The distraction of his kiss didn't hide the clatter of him reaching out to flip the coffee table, throwing it out of the way.

When he rolled them off the couch she called out, but distress turned to desire when she found herself on top. He'd given her exactly what she wanted. All of him, so deep that if she wriggled, she'd come all over him.

The pulse of him trembled in her belly. This man knew what she wanted, before she did. She felt complete. Whole. Every second was vital. Essential. Like she'd never have another. Tearing her lips away, she sat up, relishing how deep he was embedded within her. The moment of sheer liquid pleasure felt private, and so profound that she couldn't share it with him. It belonged to her. He belonged to her.

Overwhelmed with primal sensations, her skin was

too tight, her clothes clung to her sticky body, stifling her. Barriers were out of place, unnecessary. As she stripped down, his hands explored new paths, grasping her breasts the moment they were exposed. While he massaged and enjoyed her, she grabbed the edges of his shirt, tearing buttons from thread when she yanked them apart, revealing his chest.

Shoving his hands from her breasts, she bowed, devoured by the need to taste him, to feel his flesh under her mouth, yielding to her. His groan of ecstasy tossed her into an abyss of her own pleasure. His commitment might be the greatest gift, but his body and hers belonged together, there was no denying it.

Shifting from her knees, she straightened her legs, resting her weight on him. He didn't seem to mind and caressed her calf, guiding her instep to his lips. Everything about him aroused her, even the tickle of his chest hair sent another barb of pleasure quaking through her.

Balancing her weight on her palms, she moved up and down a few times, but was stalled when his teeth grazed her ankle. The prelude to him sitting up, coiling her legs around his torso, his thick arm held her weight as though it was nothing.

His shirt was shirked, giving access to more skin, more truth. In the vulnerable position his groin crushed her clit between them. With just a few moves, the stimulation sent an orgasm ripping through her. Being with him reduced her to one raw nerve ending, sensitive to the pampering he showered on her.

Lit only by the outside light shining through the front window, her drowsy eyes sought his. In them, she read complete ownership and he wasn't the only one feeling possessive. His craving fed hers. How could she show him his value? How essential he was to her existence?

Shoving at him until he lay back down, she turned her back. He drew up his knees, the denim of his jeans rasped her nipples in contrast to his delicate caress of her back. Everything was right. Right there. Everything they needed in the world. Taking hold of him, she slithered down onto his cock. Just like that, all was right in the world.

His groan encouraged her, his hands steadied her hips, and they moved together. Slowing the motion when his fingers dug deeper into her, she wanted to keep him on the edge for as long as possible. The union may be the first of many, that didn't diminish its significance. Getting used to it might take time, but she wanted to blend with him, merge so completely that even outsiders wouldn't mistake their propriety.

In an oddly intimate move, while she glided up and down his phallus, she reached over his knees and unlaced his boots. Such a normal, everyday thing, yet in that moment, entitlement drove her. It became intimate, not because they were part of each other, but because it proved she had the freedom of him. Pulling his boots off clamped her inner muscles around him. He cursed her name, and sat up, kicking off the inconvenient boots. She squealed and arched her back against his chest. Sweeping her hair from her neck, he sucked hard and pinched her nipples.

One hand travelled south, if he touched her, she'd combust, but his destination wasn't flesh. His fingers curled into the band of her skirt, and with one motion, the flimsy fabric ripped. The tearing sound echoed throughout the apartment and her hormones. Climax came with a groaning scream; it was more than she'd ever experienced.

As the last quakes passed, he grabbed her knees, pulled them back, and sent her face almost to the floor. Thinking fast, she caught herself on her palms. On all fours, she pushed back against his body's invasion of hers as he pounded into her from behind, ready to complete his own cycle.

Fearing she wouldn't be able to hold out, she gasped his name, but tumbled over another peak. In the blast of his name on her lips, he followed, the roar in his throat paired with his fist grasping her hip.

Neither moved for what could have been a lifetime, savoring and reflecting on what transpired. When they couldn't delay anymore, she edged forward and turned over to lay on the hardwood, staring up at him, still high on his knees.

Again, they just existed together. They could have stayed there all night, except the floor was cold, and she was thirsty.

She got to her feet, seeking the kitchen in the open-plan space or more accurately, the fridge. Beer was the only chilled liquid there. Popping the cap, she gulped past the bubbles and quenched her thirst.

"There's a sight that'll have us starting all over again."

Lowering the bottle from her lips, the sight of him standing between the couch and toppled coffee table was humbling. The admiration of his adoring gaze was the answer. To what? Anything. Everything.

He sauntered over and she pushed the cold bottle to his chest. He flinched but took it to finish the liquid.

Hopping onto the counter, she slid her calves up and down his legs, to the back of his thighs urging him closer. He didn't put up any fight and scooped a hand under her hair to angle her head up for another kiss. Their mouths relished each other for a few seconds before his trekked to her neck.

"Maybe this time you could show me the bedroom," she whispered into his ear.

He scooped her up. "Doctor's orders?"

She laughed and nodded. He carried her toward the back of the apartment, past a bathroom into his spacious, night-soaked bedroom. There, she'd spend the rest of the weekend... naked.

NINETEEN

LYSSA WASN'T ACTUALLY NAKED the whole weekend. After a long lie, more sex, and a cooked breakfast, he'd shown her around the apartment complex. Just two stories, each front door led off an external terrace. Every property had a back door to a balcony that ran the full length of the building. All the apartments were one bedroom. Nothing flashy, but in that neighborhood, no one wanted flashy.

Blaser and Ruger had apartments there as did another of their cousins, Gus. Apparently, he did the lion's share of the management work. Gus's brother was the one who owned the building. The Warner family extended far. She'd had no idea that Colt was part of such a large clan.

Blaser spent most of his days in the garage which butted onto the back of the apartment perimeter. The public accessed the garage pitch from the parallel street, but a gate in the chain-link fence between the two plots allowed Blaser to move between them without setting foot in a street.

The other units in the block were mostly occupied by employees of Risqué or the garage. Every one of them was male. An apartment complex full of male residents raised all sorts of questions for her inquisitive mind.

"Are you hungry?" Colt asked, stroking her back.

She was quite enjoying lying face down in his bed, hugging the pillow, misting in and out of slumber. "What time is it?"

"Almost eight."

Sunday night, the last shift of her week at Risqué. Colt had taken her to work last night and stayed the whole time. Blaser let her leave an hour early again, probably at Colt's urging, explicit or otherwise.

"I have to get ready for work," she mumbled. "I should go home and find something to wear."

"You wore clothes from the club last night."

"I'm not a fan of wearing other women's clothes," she said, yawning, rolling onto her back. "Where was Ruger last night?"

"Talking about wearing other women's clothes makes you think of my brother?" he said, smirking. "He'll probably let you borrow from his closet, but I don't think any of his clothes will fit you. You have a much better figure."

"I hope I didn't upset him. You have to give me his phone number. I'll call and apologize."

"Ruger isn't easily upset," he said, stretching his arms above his head when he sat up, displaying the intricate, tough muscles in his back. "Anyway, you might have been right."

"Maybe," she said. "But he wouldn't have appreciated being outed in the middle of the club. That was inappropriate." Spreading her hand on the middle of his back, she sighed. "You have a beautiful body."

"Thanks," he said. Flopping onto his side, propping his head on a palm, his crooked elbow supported its weight. "You're pretty hot yourself."

"I do yoga."

"I know," he murmured.

She rolled her eyes at his semi-smile. "I forgot you stalked me."

"Only for a couple of weeks," he said. "Kind of wish I'd stuck at it for longer."

"Why? What do you think you'd have seen?"

"Who knows? You're sexy enough to watch day-in, day-out. You don't have to do anything."

He kissed her shoulder, continuing his exploration across her upper chest, descending toward her cleavage.

"Do you remember the last time you had sex with your wife?"

His lips stopped, his head came up, and he looked her in the eye for a few seconds colored by apparent confusion and surprise. "We're naked in bed together and you're thinking about Karri… I'd have lost money on that bet. What kind of fetish is that?"

"If you don't want to talk about it—"

"You *do* want to talk about it?"

"I'm just curious," she said. "How close to you moving out did you have sex with her?"

"In which direction? Before or after I moved out?"

She shifted away slightly to get a better look at him. "You had sex with her after you moved out of the marital home?"

He nodded. "Remember that three month fling I mentioned?"

"Your fling was with your wife?"

"Sex wasn't the problem for Karri and me. The problem was everything else."

"Before you moved out of the marital home, when was the last time you had sex with her?"

"The night before," he said. "We thought it was goodbye."

"Did she achieve climax?"

"I don't know," he said. "Probably not." Scrubbing his hands over his face, he sat up. "What is this about?"

"Did you cheat on her?"

"What?" he asked with a stab of offense and spun to glare at her. "I was always faithful to her."

"But you blame yourself for the demise of the relationship?"

"Don't psychoanalyze my marriage," he said, vaulting out of bed and wrenching on his jeans. "That's done with. You don't have to worry about Karri."

"I'm not worried about her," Lyssa said, sitting up. "You prioritize my pleasure over your own and I don't know if that's an inherent insecurity or if it comes from guilt over the break-up of your marriage."

"Maybe I'm just a good lover," he said, opening his arms.

Though he wasn't as pissed, the way he thrust his hands to his hips told her he wasn't completely calm.

"You are," Lyssa said. "But I want to satisfy you too, and if you have issues—"

"I'm not one of your patients, Lys," he said, coming around the bed to sit beside her. "Don't over think this."

And when he kissed her, it was easy to do just that… or not do that. Her intention wasn't to make him uncomfortable or pry. It was in her nature to ask questions, to establish people's motivations and how to help them.

Relationships hadn't been on her priority list. They hadn't been on any of her lists. She was out of practice, but if Colt kept kissing her, she'd quickly get back into the habit of going with the flow and switching off her critical brain.

Unfortunately, practice was interrupted. Her cellphone rang; both she and Colt groaned in unison. He snagged her backpack from the floor and handed it over so she could retrieve her phone. Reading Suzette's name was a surprise.

"Hey, is everything okay?" Lyssa asked.

"Disaster!" Suzette said. "There has been a disaster with the dresses."

"Your wedding dress?" Lyssa said. Her hand subconsciously went to Colt's shoulder for support, he kissed her gripping knuckles. "What's the problem?"

"All of them. The dressmaker called. She had some sort of problem in her workshop, something to do with her niece. She lost all of the alteration details from the time we were last in!"

"Oh my God, that's terrible. What are you going to do?"

"I've tracked down one of my sisters and she's corralling the other," Suzette said. "I hate to do this to you after our conversation on Friday. You probably hate me and Pete, and I know you have work tomorrow…"

"What do you need, Suze? I'll do whatever you need me to."

"Meet me at the dress store?"

"Sure," Lyssa said, noticing Colt's jeans were open, revealing his reaction to her naked proximity.

He took her hand from the bed to kiss her palm then coiled her fingers around his erection. Her smiling frown asked the question of what he was doing.

"Prioritizing my pleasure," he whispered.

She brushed her lips across his and took over the jerking. Leaning back, he propped his weight on locked arms.

"We need to do it tonight," Suzette said.

In just a few moments, Lyssa had almost forgotten the phone call. It took a few extra seconds to absorb her friend's words. When she did, her grip stilled and tightened. Colt cracked open one eye.

"Tonight?" she repeated, conveying her silent apology to Colt.

He sighed out his disappointment but took her hand from his dick and flattened it on his chest.

"Yes. I know it's short notice, but if you could meet me at the dress store in like half an hour? I'm heading over there now."

"Okay," Lyssa said, glancing at the clock next to Colt's bed. "But can we do my dress first. I have something on later."

"Later?" Suzette said. "On a Sunday night? Is this about that guy you mentioned?"

"Could be," Lyssa said. "I'll see you soon."

Hanging up the phone without further explanation, she tossed the device into her backpack.

"I'll tell Blase you won't be in," Colt said. "It won't be a problem."

"I have no intention of taking advantage of our physical relationship," she said. "I made a commitment to Blaser, and I won't let him down."

"What does she need you to do?"

"There was a problem. I have to go to the dress store for a fitting."

"I can drive you," he said as she climbed off the bed.

"You have a car?" she asked.

"My brother's a mechanic. There's a junkyard behind the garage, he fixes up cars and sells them in his spare time… not that he has much of it. We always have access to a bunch of vehicles."

"Legal ones?" she asked, pulling on the clothes she'd brought to change into after her Friday shift.

Thankfully she and Colt had their last tryst in the shower. That saved valuable time.

"Yes," he said, retrieving a tee-shirt from a drawer. "Would otherwise be a problem?"

"More for you than for me," she said. "You'll be the one driving… and you're an ex-cop."

"You're just dying to get the story behind that one, aren't you?"

Scrunching her face, she nodded. "How could you tell?"

"Ruger told me that you asked him. I'll tell you all about it, but not now."

They dressed and she stuffed her things into her backpack. "Will you pick me up too? I'd appreciate a ride to the club; I might be cutting it close."

"I'll wait," he said, opening the bedroom door. She took his hand and pulled him to the front door, which he held open for her. Somehow, he read her mind, and answered her concerns about him parking outside the dress store. "I'll stay far enough away that Suzette won't see me."

"I don't have time to answer her questions," she said. He locked the door, and they went down the stairs, their fingers intertwined. "It's not that I don't want her to know about us."

"You two have enough going on in your friendship right now," he said, pressing a button on a key fob causing the lights of a sedan to flash. "I don't mind skipping the new boyfriend parade." He opened her car door and closed it behind her then went around to get in the other side. "When is the wedding?"

"Five weeks from Saturday," she said.

Backing out of the space, they left the parking lot, following her directions. "You need a plus one?"

"Do you want to be my date?" she asked, grinning. "I'd be honored."

"I'm interested to meet the guy who told your best friend to stay away when you're most in need of support."

She sighed. "Pete is a good guy. He cares about her, that's all."

"But he doesn't care about you. An extension of caring about a woman is caring about people that she cares about. He should care about you because Suzette cares about you."

Interesting insight. "Is that why you're driving me to an impromptu dress fitting instead of coaxing me into having more sex?"

"I'm playing the long game," he said, flashing her a lazy smile. "By taking you to the fitting, you'll be so grateful that sex will follow in due time."

"Clever," she said, reaching over to stroke his arm. "Do you mind if we stay at my place tonight? I have an early patient."

"Sure," he said. "Tell me more about Pete Harding. He does something with computers, right?"

If he'd researched her and her friends, it stood to reason he'd know something about her best friend's fiancé.

"Yes. His department is next door to the hospital's admin department where Suzette works."

"Have they been together long?"

"About six months."

"He moves fast."

"Suzette is a romantic," Lyssa explained. "She's always wanted to be swept off her feet and I suppose that's what Pete has done for her. He proposed after six weeks. I was shocked, but who am I to judge? I was with Archie for years, knew him inside out, yet that didn't work out."

"Why not?"

"I wasn't the dutiful wife that he wanted me to be. He wasn't wild about my specialty and tried his best to talk me out of it. My book was a big bone of contention. Lots of arguments. I did some research in other undercover situations and he went nuts. I think he wanted me to be something I wasn't. When we met, he worked at the hospital, then he went into private practice and started to make a lot of money. I mean bags and bags full, he's a plastic surgeon."

"A lot of money in that."

"Right," she said, tossing her backpack into the backseat. "Our lifestyle changed. With that, he changed. I wasn't obedient and didn't defer to his opinion. I wasn't interested in the golf and country club parties that he wanted to frequent. Our lives diverged until we were basically living independently of each other."

"What about kids?"

"What about them?"

"You never wanted kids?" he asked.

"I wanted kids, but he didn't. You know he was older than me and had children from his first marriage? I guess he thought he was done with all of that, which I understood."

"That's a helluva sacrifice for you."

"I was too young to appreciate the gravity of it when I made it," she said. "My career was all I wanted then. My parents were so insistent on medical school. At first, I hated it. I mean I really hated it. I'm not big on blood and guts." He smiled. "But it was what they wanted, and they spent a fortune on it, so I persevered. Everything started to make sense when I did my psyche rotation. I realized that was where I was meant to be and what I was supposed to do."

"And the rest is, as they say, history," he said, pulling the car to a stop just around the corner from the dress store. "Give me your phone."

Reaching into the back she retrieved her pack and handed over the cell. She peeked to see what he was doing: adding contacts. When he finished, he rang his own phone, and then gave it back.

"You have three new numbers in there," he said. The three brothers. "If you ever have a problem or need anything, call them in order. What's the order?"

"You, Ruger, then Blaser."

"Good," he said, wearing a smile as he leaned over to

kiss her. "I'll be here when you're done."

"Thank you," she said, squeezing his thigh. "I'll show you how grateful I am on my break."

"That's what I was aiming for."

As she got out of the vehicle, he swatted her behind. In return, she pronounced the sway of her hips as she walked away, glancing back to check he was watching. With a wink, she rounded the corner to fulfil her latest maid of honor duty.

HAVING SUZETTE'S SISTERS around meant there wasn't much time for private conversation. More than once, Suzette glanced her way, and she did try to approach, but something, or rather someone, always got in the way.

One of the sister's had her dress done first. All through that fitting, Lyssa was preoccupied by the time on her phone. Eventually, when it was her turn, she got into the dress, measured, then out of it as quickly as possible. Hanging around wasn't an option, she still had to get to Risqué and changed. Bless Colt for waiting around the corner, he was probably going out of his mind with boredom. Or maybe he'd already gone, she wouldn't blame him, it had taken a while.

Coming out of the changing room, she hooked her shoe strap over her heel, and stumbled toward the door. "Great to see you all! I have to go!"

Heading straight for the door, she didn't see Suzette swoop in at her side until the door was open.

Suzette blocked her path. "You're pissed at me, aren't you?"

"Pissed? What? No. I'm not pissed."

"I feel terrible that this is happening, and I can't be there for you because of my idiot boyfriend. Should I dump him? Is that what I should do? You always help me make decisions and now I'm losing you…"

Maybe it was the hormones associated with the stress of planning the wedding, but Lyssa hadn't expected her friend to tear up.

Dropping the door, she took Suzette's hands. "I'm not pissed. It's strange not to have you around, but this is for the best. Pete isn't just your boyfriend; he's going to be your husband in a few short weeks. You know my stance on compromise. He's not trying to hurt you. He's trying to help you."

"It doesn't feel that way. He doesn't understand why I am so upset about this, or why you are so important to me. Guys just don't understand the relationship women have with their girlfriends. I feel like I should be doing something, taking action, isn't that what you always tell me to do? That I should take action to achieve the goal I want to succeed in."

"Leave this goal with me," Lyssa said, smiling and took Suzette into her arms. "I'll fix it, honey. I promise you. Just give me some more time."

"Do you really have to run off? Maybe we could go for a drink after this? Pete doesn't need to know."

"I really have to go," Lyssa said and opened the door again. "I'll call you later in the week. If you need me, call me."

Suzette nodded and Lyssa maintained her positivity, trying not to show the burden of scheduling. When she got out of there, she rushed down the street, but as soon as she turned the corner she stopped. Colt was still there, exactly where she'd left him, and he smiled when he laid eyes on her. This was a man she could rely on, no doubt about it, he'd proved himself that night and then some.

TWENTY

LYSSA TOOK AN EARLY BREAK and stole him away to his office. The unusual timing concerned him. Though his girlfriend working in a strip club worried him full stop. If any customer ever thought to put his hands on her… to corner her… Their relationship might be new, but it was potent. At sporadic moments, he got a flash, a mental image of her smile of bliss as he slid into her. He couldn't put a label on the satisfaction he got just from knowing they'd cut out the bullshit and claimed each other.

In his office, she'd wriggled out of the slightly too small halter top, barely managing to contain her breasts. He kept himself busy playing with those as she unzipped him and shoved him onto the loveseat. Right there, she showed him how that spectacular mouth of hers was proficient with more than just words.

Driving her to the thing with Suzette wasn't a big deal. To him. For some reason, it earned him beaucoup brownie points. He wasn't going to refuse her gratitude. Not when it came in that form.

As she swallowed his gratitude, he'd tried to take her onto his lap. His girl wouldn't have it and shooed him out of the office telling him to return the favor later. She'd never steered him wrong on their intimacy, so he agreed and travelled back towards the front of house.

Approaching the bar, Blaser stood behind it, while Ruger held up the other. Exactly where he'd expected them to be. His little brother was flanked by Crystal and Destiny… no surprise there either. They were all aimed towards something he couldn't see, something around the curve of the bar. He slowed and listened in to get a measure of what was going on.

"I want to see Trapper now," a female demanded. "You look like him, stand up!"

"Strip naked," Ruger said in return.

"What!"

"If you don't follow my orders, why should I follow yours?"

"I want to see Trapper. You must know him."

"Look, lady…" Blaser said. "Every single one of us has told you that Trapper has no appointments on the books tonight. That means you don't get to see anyone."

"I'll wait here all night. I don't care what any of you say. He'll have to show up eventually."

"No, he won't," Crystal said. "We can get security to throw you out."

"I'll come back tomorrow."

"And we'll throw you out again," Destiny said. "There are more of us than there are of you. Not like you're tough to spot in a room full of guys and half-naked women."

"You don't understand how important this is. I need to see him. Please, I'll pay anything, I'll do whatever it takes."

"You weren't interested when I hit on you," Ruger said. "And I could've got you in."

"I'm engaged," the indignant female said.

Her identity clicked.

Glancing over his shoulder, he saw no sign of Lyssa yet. Time wasn't on his side, he had to deal with this fast.

Going up behind Destiny, he showed himself over the dainty dancer.

"Miss. Blossom," Colt said, dropping his already deep voice an octave. "What are you doing here?"

"Ah," she screeched in relief. "I need your help!"

"My help?" Colt said. "I spoke to your friend about this, and we couldn't reach an agreement."

"You don't understand," Suzette said, clutching a velvet purse in both hands, leaning far over the bar. "Things have changed, and my friend is all alone now. I can't be there for her. I'm a terrible friend. A really terrible friend. We can't leave her out there alone. We have to catch this guy. We have to get him off the streets. If we do that, things can go back to normal."

So Suzette was feeling guilty about abandoning Lyssa at the urging of her fiancé. In theory, if they caught the person fixated on Lyssa, Pete would no longer have a problem and their friendship would not be in jeopardy. Coming to the club alone was a big risk that could have a huge cost for her.

"You shouldn't have come here alone," Colt said. His words to Lyssa in the car earlier echoed in his ears. "This could be a dangerous place. You don't know what you just walked into."

"The recommendation for your services came from a trustworthy guy and my friend walked out of here alive. When your security man got me a cab, nothing bad happened. I don't care about taking risks. Lyssa has shown me that sometimes risks are worth it. Sometimes we have to take a risk to achieve our goal. The struggle makes the destination more valued."

"Those are admirable words…" definitely quoted from Lyssa, "but they make no difference," Colt said. "I can't help you. You should leave."

"I won't," Suzette asserted, raising the purse to slam her knuckles on the bar. "I will stay here until you agree to help me. I don't care what it costs. If you want me to sleep with your friend, then I'll sleep with your friend."

"Wow," Ruger said, smacking his shoulder. "Thanks, friend."

"I thought you were engaged," Crystal said.

"She's desperate," Destiny said. "Maybe you should help her."

"Maybe you should butt out," Blaser said. "If he says no, he means it."

"And he doesn't have to give a good reason?" Crystal

asked. "He can't just send a desperate woman away without telling her why he's doing it."

"He doesn't have to give any damn reason," Blaser said, in a show of solidarity that epitomized their relationship.

His twin would fight with him tooth and nail, but he'd defend him just as vehemently to outsiders.

"Cherry is the reason," Ruger said. "We're defending her."

The girls, and Blaser, grew an inch. They didn't need to hear more. Those in the Risqué rabble closed ranks to defend their own.

"You have to leave," Crystal said.

"I'm sorry, but she's right," Destiny agreed. "We protect our own before anyone else, and you're not one of us, sister."

"Who is Cherry?" Suzette asked. "I don't even know Cherry. How can you be protecting—"

"How does everyone feel about cunnilingus?"

Damnit. That was Lyssa's voice. She hadn't reached him yet but would in a few seconds. He, Ruger, and the two women turned around to see her approach.

"I'm in favor," Destiny said.

"Is someone offering?" Crystal asked. "If it's the cute guy at table three tell him I'm ready, willing, and able."

"Abstract cunnilingus," Lyssa said, reaching for him before her arrival. Like it was automatic, she touched his abdomen, sliding her arms around him to curl her thumbs into his belt loops.

"I thought you went up there for fellatio," Ruger said. "Problems with your Latin, friend?"

"I was never good with foreign languages," Colt said.

If Suzette stayed on her side of the bar, behind the barrier of his group, they'd get away with sneaking Lyssa off… providing she didn't put up a fight.

"I don't know," Lyssa said. "You're pretty good at French."

Crystal and Destiny enjoyed that with an "ooh." Ruger laughed. Course he did. Lyssa pushed up as though to kiss him. He'd accept the kiss then shuffle her way. Would've worked if Suzette hadn't appeared in his peripheral vision… If he saw her, so did Lyssa.

She stopped and did a double take. "Suzie?" she asked, backing away from him. "What are you doing here?"

"Me?" Suzette said, wide-eyed. "What are you doing here? And why are you plastered all over that guy? Is he making you do this?" She gasped. "Is it some kind of sex for protection deal?"

"No! God no," Lyssa asserted. "It's nothing like that."

The pallor of her face didn't match the satisfaction he felt at her coming to his defense on impulse.

"We don't want drama in here," Blaser said.

"Why didn't you tell me about this?" Suzette asked, examining those in the impact zone of the catastrophe.

"I… I don't—"

"Because I told her not to," Colt said, stepping up to his responsibility. "I told her I wouldn't help if you knew about me, about us."

"Babe…" Lyssa said.

The truth was the truth; he wouldn't hide from it… though he didn't mind stretching it to cover his girl's ass.

Pushing Lyssa behind him, he approached Suzette. "Sex for protection isn't something a guy advertises," he said, dragging his focus over Suzette's figure, watching her shrink under the scrutiny. "She's safe here, safe doing what I tell her when I tell her… I see you trembling, are you feeling unsafe too, sweetheart? I can do something about that for you."

The thwack of her hand on his cheek was sort of expected. If Suzette's wrath was on him, not on Lyssa, he'd done his job. Suzette whipped around and marched off.

"What did you do that for?" Lyssa hissed as she passed him to chase her friend.

"Ouch," Crystal said, coming over to inspect his cheek with Destiny not too far behind, the smaller of the women had to cling onto him to haul herself up and poke at him.

"You know how to make an impression on a lady, don't you?" Ruger said.

"You want to stop bringing your shit to my club?" Blaser said. "Please. What the fuck was that?"

Incredulous, Colt wouldn't apologize. "You almost caused two brawls last week. My girl and Destiny were assaulted by the schmucks related to the woman you're shtupping."

Ruger propped an elbow on the bar. "Who'd have thought that I'd turn out to be the most respectable one in the family?"

"Aww," Destiny said, switching her fawning to Ruger. "Do you want me to corrupt you, big boy?"

"Maybe another time," Ruger said, patting Destiny's hip. "You're a sweetheart for offering."

"I'm going to get her," Colt said. He couldn't leave Lyssa on the street in her Risqué garb. If Suzette caused a scene, plenty of folks out there might take advantage of two distracted women.

"Is that a good idea?" Ruger said. "Maybe I should—"

A loud pop interrupted. Shrieking from outside carried into the club.

"Holy fuck," Blaser said, vaulting the bar.

"Gunshot," Ruger said.

Yeah, and his girl was out there.

TWENTY-ONE

PANDEMONIUM AT THE ENTRANCE delayed his exit, people were trying to get into the club and the security men were trying to keep them out. To his relief, two of the women seeking cover were Lyssa and Suzette.

Snatching Lyssa, he shoved aside the guy in his way, who whipped around, ready to fight. They made eye contact, identified each other, and that was the end. The bouncer went back to his job, leaving Colt to take Lyssa inside, Suzette too because his girl was holding her friend.

"What happened?" Ruger asked, meeting them at the internal club door.

"Someone… someone fired a gun," Suzette said.

Colt's only goal was making sure Lyssa was safe. He didn't stop for his brother and didn't care that Suzette was shook up. The customers in the club were scattered, some tried to leave, some were looking for a rear exit, and others hid under tables. Those who knew the area better remained in their seats, craning their necks, but otherwise unmoved by the events.

Dragging Lyssa through the club, he eventually got her to his office and sat her on the couch to crouch in front of her. Vaguely aware of a host of bodies crowding in behind him, he paid them no heed and instead focused on her.

"Are you hurt?" he asked, curving his hands around her hips.

"No," she said, stroking his forehead. "I'm fine. Are you hurt?"

"I wasn't outside."

"You're white as a sheet," she said. "Maybe you should sit down, you might be going into shock."

"I've been around gunshots."

"And I've seen blood before."

"Were you hit?" he asked, running his hands over her body to search for injuries.

"No one was hit," she said. "There was only one bullet, and it struck the concrete wall about six feet from us."

"Do you think they were aiming for you?" Ruger asked, seating himself on the coffee table next to where he was crouched.

"I don't know," Lyssa said. "I wouldn't think so."

"Where did the shot come from?"

"I was facing the street. I wasn't paying attention, but I'd say it was a dark sedan. The window wasn't even halfway down."

The road was a good twenty feet from the Risqué doorway. It would depend how close to the door they were, but at that distance she wouldn't have seen the shooter's features.

"Was he driving?" Colt asked. "Which direction was the car headed?"

"He was in the driver's seat, but I didn't see him."

"Did you?" Ruger asked.

Colt glanced around to see he was talking to Suzette; he'd forgotten anyone else was there. But there she stood, surrounded by Blaser, Destiny, and Crystal.

Suzette shook her head. "I just saw the wall explode."

Blaser seated Suzette, then retrieved water from the fridge for her. Ruger carried on questioning her, but Colt turned back to his priority.

"There have been shootings around here before," he said to Lyssa. "It's unlikely to be linked to your situation. But it's possible."

"Why would he do that now?"

"We still don't know his motivation, but I agree that it would be a massive escalation to go from flowers to murder."

"What's going on?" Crystal asked.

Too many people didn't know the full situation. He wasn't about to let them all in on it, so he stood up. "Would you all give us a minute?"

"I'm going to check the fallout," Blaser said, putting an arm around Destiny and Crystal to take them out.

"I'll cover your zone," Crystal said to Lyssa before she exited, Lyssa smiled in acceptance.

Crystal hadn't officially waitressed in years, the dancer was high up in the food chain. She'd likely serve a couple of tables then delegate the task to another of the girls.

He and his twin might sing from different hymn sheets most of the time, but Blaser must have recognized this was private business. He didn't try to involve himself, maybe he didn't care, more likely he understood how high the walls had grown between them.

It got to him then more than ever.

Ruger stayed, as did Suzette. After the door closed, Colt went to get soda from the fridge.

"Can I have water?" Lyssa asked when he handed her the cold can.

"No, you can drink what I give you," he said, hoping the sugar would calm her nerves… though she didn't look anxious or scared.

"She can drink whatever the hell she wants," Suzette said, trying to hand her water bottle to Lyssa.

Colt pushed it away. "The sugar will help."

"Lyssa is a rock in disaster situations," Suzette said. "She says it comes from her rotation in the ER, but the truth is, she's always been like this."

"I'm in the room," Lyssa said. "And I'm fine, so you can both stop worrying."

"I'm not worried about you at all," Ruger said, moving over to the couch to sit beside her. "You're made of steel; anyone can see that." He put his fist to her shoulder and pushed her a few inches.

Lyssa swayed back and socked his arm. "I could knock you out, Littlest Warner."

Ruger smiled. "Oh, you want to go?" he asked. "We can step outside. I'd take you down in a heartbeat."

"How up are you on your anatomy?" she asked. "Just the right amount of pressure—"

"What is going on here?" Suzette exclaimed. "I thought you were being forced into sex with him!"

"I am," Lyssa said. "But only by my overwhelming desire to copulate with him."

"Copulate," Ruger muttered, snickering. "That's a sexy word."

"It's the way she says it," Colt said, dropping onto the couch at Lyssa's other side, using his body weight to shift her down a few inches. "That sexy doctor tone… she doesn't get how hot it is."

"She uses it in bed?"

"All the time," Colt said.

"I do not talk like a doctor in bed," she said, threading her fingers through his and resting their joined hands on his lap, maybe a little closer to his groin than he was comfortable with in company.

"You talk me through what I'm doing while I'm doing it," he said. Ruger laughed. "You tell me how good it feels, what you like about it."

"I do?" she asked.

He nodded and leaned in to kiss her temple. "It's okay, it's hot. I never wonder if you're having a good time because you tell me, in detail."

"Sounds like you," Suzette said. "You never miss an excuse to talk about sex."

"Even while I'm doing it?" Lyssa asked.

"Apparently not," Ruger said. "What else does she say?"

"Are we going to talk about why someone is shooting at us?" Suzette asked.

"Might not have been shooting at you," Colt said.

"Could be they were aiming for one of the pimps on the corner. The police will show up eventually. Tell them what you saw… or didn't see."

"Which means I'll have to explain why I'm here," Suzette said. Her head fell into her hands. "Oh God, Pete is going to kill me."

"You can take off if you want," Ruger said. "No one has to know that you were here."

"I can't run away from the police," Suzette said.

"Why not? You didn't see anything."

"Pete doesn't have to know that you were here," Lyssa said. "You can talk to the police and get a cab home."

"I'm supposed to be home in twenty minutes! If I'm not back, he'll worry and call me."

Despite having no formal introduction to the guy, Colt didn't like Pete Harding already. If it wasn't bad enough that the guy was keeping Lyssa and Suzette apart, he didn't seem like the caring type. Lyssa excused his attitude towards the friendship as his need to protect Suzette. If that was true, he should be the first person Suzette called when shit like this went down.

"Anyone shoots around you again, you call me right away," he said to his girl. "Doesn't matter if you just think it sounds like a gunshot. Call me. Okay?

"Okay," Lyssa said, confused. "Why did you say that?"

"I don't care what you're doing. I don't even care if you're screwing another guy or we're in a fight, you call me."

"Why would I—"

"Because he wants to swoop in and save the day," Ruger said. "And he wants to protect you because he's so in lurve."

"Or you could call Ruger," Colt said. "Especially if it's at three in the morning and you know he has company, or a really early morning the next day."

"Are you telling me that I should call Pete?" Suzette asked.

"No, he's implying that your relationship is a crock because you can't," Ruger said.

Maybe he wouldn't have used those exact words, but his brother was right. Either Ruger had read his mind, or they once again were on the same page. They had the routine down pat. Weren't twins supposed to be symbiotic? That sure hadn't been his experience.

Suzette squealed, probably in offense.

Lyssa scooted to the edge of the couch. "He didn't mean it like that," she said, reaching for Suzette's hand. "We're here to support you; you don't have to call Pete. I understand that you don't want to worry him. He cares for you so much. Hearing you were in danger like this might upset him."

He appreciated the view of Lyssa's snug ass. If he wasn't distracted, he might've laughed. His distraction didn't explain why Ruger didn't laugh… no, the little punk was admiring the same view. Glaring, he reached behind Lyssa to smack his brother's chest with the back of his hand, Ruger only smiled and shrugged.

"You could tell Pete that you went for a drink with one of your sisters," Lyssa said. "They would cover for you, wouldn't they?"

Suzette griped. "You're the one always harping on about the importance of honesty in relationships."

That reminder would be a kick in the teeth for Lys having just been caught lying about him. "Sometimes we have to lie to the people we care about when we want to protect them."

"I suppose so."

"Just tonight I lied to Colt," Lyssa said. His ears piqued. "I told him that I didn't want him to eat me out after I blew him when actually I did."

His nose wrinkled in a cringe because that wasn't exactly the same thing. A cough of laughter came from Ruger, his hand jumped to his mouth to cover the hilarity that clearly wanted to follow. But Lyssa remained between them, reaching over to hold Suzette's hand.

Ruger's laughter stopped as horror seized him. "You didn't do that here, did you? I'm not sitting where you…?"

Colt shook his head and nodded toward the loveseat;

Suzette didn't seem to be paying attention.

"If you want him here, if you want to call Pete to tell him where you are and what happened, all of us will support you," Lyssa said.

"No," Suzette said, drawing in a breath. "You're right. I'll just tell him that I was with my sister. He wouldn't understand why I came here."

"Why did you come here?" Ruger asked.

"I wanted to help Lyssa. I thought I could persuade your friend to do his thing and trap the stalker so that everything could go back to normal. Pete wanted me to stay away from Lyssa, but he didn't say anything about helping without seeing her… I didn't know she would be here."

"Colt has handed everything over to the police," Lyssa said. "He had to so that he could have sex with me."

"What does that mean?" Ruger asked.

Colt shook his head; it wasn't worth explaining now.

"Colt," Suzette said. "Is that him?"

"You haven't been introduced, but yes, his name is Colt Warner."

"And he's the guy?" Suzette asked.

Lyssa nodded.

"Uh, what guy?"

Lyssa sat back to address him. "She wanted to set me up with Keith, but I told her I was interested in someone else."

"I told you he wanted to screw you," Colt muttered.

"Does it matter?" Suzette asked. "It seems that you got the girl."

"The girl who could be getting shot at," Ruger said. "Are we going to talk about that?"

"I don't think he was shooting at me," Lyssa said. "This is just a coincidence. Like you said, there have been shootings around here before. Maybe he was aiming for Blaser."

"Blaser wasn't outside," Colt said. "I doubt you were the target. It's not impossible but would be a helluva coincidence that your stalker was driving by at the exact moment you and Suzette went outside."

"Precisely," Lyssa said. "Are we all agreed that we

don't need to discuss my stalker situation with the police? It will just complicate things."

"Yeah," Ruger said. "If they're that interested, your information is at the precinct, right? It's up to them to do their jobs and put the relevant pieces together."

Suzette hadn't said much and sat staring at her legs.

"Are you alright?" Lyssa edged closer to her friend. "Are you sure you don't want us to call Pete?"

"You lied to me," Suzette said. "All of this has been going on, and you lied to me."

"It wasn't a lie—" Colt said.

Lyssa's hand on his knee stalled him. "I'm sorry," she said. "I know you're hurt. It was always my intention to tell you when everything had blown over. The case was handed over to the police and before I got a chance to clue you in, Pete said he didn't want us seeing each other and I… I didn't want to put more on your plate."

"That woman said she'd cover your zone, and how you're dressed… you're working here, aren't you?"

"Just as a waitress," Lyssa said. "You encouraged me to get back to my research."

"Come on, bro, we'll go help Blaser," Ruger said, standing up. "These two can stay up here and talk. If they're lucky, we might send one of the girls up with coffee."

"There's a coffee machine in the building?" Lyssa asked.

Ruger faltered. "Beer?"

"There's beer in the fridge," Lyssa said, smiling. "But we'd appreciate the privacy."

They'd just been excused. He wasn't thrilled about the idea of leaving her alone yet. Ruger stepped past Lyssa and grabbed his shoulder to haul him up.

"I'll take care of you, brother. We'll come get you if the police want to talk to witnesses," Ruger said to Lyssa while bundling him out the room.

"We didn't have to leave them," Colt said.

Ruger shoved him down the stairs. "You'd only have sat there jumping in to defend Lys every chance you got. They need to work this out themselves, and you don't want her best friend hating you. You need the best friend on-side if you want this relationship to work out. You want it to work out, right?"

He did. Being with Lyssa was more than he could've anticipated. His respect for her, his admiration, amplified his feelings. Ruger was right, as he so frustratingly always was. If he kept taking the flack and diverting it from Lyssa, Suzette would hate him. She'd blame him for trying to drive a wedge between the friends. Which was ironic given that's what her fiancé, Pete, was attempting to do, whether intentional or not.

At the same time, Colt did have some responsibility for the deception. He had told Lyssa to lie to Suzette. Granted, that was before they got personally involved, but his instruction led to Lyssa misdirecting her friend.

Thinking about their meeting spurred a reminder to call his cousin. He had to keep on top of what the cops were doing and their progress. So long as Lyssa's admirer was around, they would jump at every snap in the street. As they'd deduced, the shooting tonight was a coincidence, but he didn't want any hint of a possibility that Lyssa's life was in danger.

He'd get an update from Chavez, then he'd play nice with the cops who showed up for statements on the shooting. After that he was taking Lyssa home to her place. Immediately. Right now, it was important to send a message to anyone who might be watching her house. Lyssa wasn't alone anymore; he was watching her back. Anyone trying to get near the doc would have a hard time while he was standing in the way.

TWENTY-TWO

TALKING TO THE POLICE was becoming a habit, though not one she relished. As soon as the cops left, Colt took her home. Her objections didn't last long in the face of his determination; the shooting shook him up.

At home, he took her upstairs, into her own bed. Maybe for his own piece of mind, he'd left her there to complete the ritual of checking out the house himself. For her, his kisses were an easy, welcome distraction. With him in the house, vulnerability wasn't an issue.

On the new day, as she worked, the occasional footfalls echoing from the ceiling reminded her he was still there, watching over her. Hadn't she once suggested he come inside to protect her? Maybe now he was getting her point.

The end of her workday approached. Just a few more minutes and she could go upstairs. Would they spend the night together inside or go out? Which would she enjoy more?

"You should see this as a triumph," she said to her final patient. "It's natural to be nervous before a date, Bobby."

"It's a Monday," he grumped. "Who has sex on a Monday?"

Lyssa tried not to think about what she and Colt had done that morning… and on her lunch break. "Is that what you want from your date tonight?"

"I'm a guy, right?"

"Yes, you are." His insecurity about that fact flared in anger on occasion. "But developing this relationship is important to you too."

"I feel like I have to do it. I have to get this done. Maybe after I won't be so stressed about it, you know?"

"Don't be impulsive," Lyssa said, repeating advice she often gave. "Do you care about Deshana?"

"Yes, I think so… maybe."

"Breathe out," she said, sensing his rising panic. "Tell me what you're thinking. You can say anything here. This isn't a place of judgement."

"All I can think about is her breasts," he admitted, shaking his anxious legs, his attention fixed on the carpet. The tent that grew in his slacks made him mutter and grab one of her cushions onto his lap. "I'm sorry, this is mortifying."

"You have nothing to be embarrassed about. I'm a doctor. It's good that you have a positive reaction to your memory of Deshana. She must be very beautiful."

"She is."

"Bear in mind, Deshana will be nervous too. I'm sure she wants things to work out between you both. It's possible she's not ready to be physically intimate with you."

His leg stopped shaking and his eyes shot to hers. "You think she's not attracted to me?"

"She wouldn't have agreed to go out with you at all, let alone agreed to go out with you again, if she wasn't attracted to you."

He began to shake his head. "I can't do this. I'm not ready for this. I don't know what I'm doing."

"You do," she soothed. "We've spent many sessions talking about what you should expect from physical intimacy and how to react to the sensations you'll experience. You just have to remember the techniques we discussed. This date, your relationship with Deshana is the last hurdle, Bobby. Look how far you've come. You should be so proud."

"Okay." He nodded. "Okay. Yeah, okay."

"It's natural to be anxious, but once you've done this,

once it's over with, you'll wonder what all the fuss was about. Being with someone, relationships, are positive things that can be very fulfilling."

"If I don't do it now then I never will," he said.

She checked the time. "Next week, you can tell me how it goes. Baby steps still show progress, it's all forward motion. Remember that and don't put too much pressure on yourself. This is a marathon."

"Not a sprint," he agreed, somewhat bolstered.

They scheduled the next appointment, and she maintained her smile until the front door closed. She slid her pen and pad onto the desk. After updating Bobby's notes, she'd be free to spend the rest of the night with Colt.

"Did you ever think about converting the attic?"

There he was, sauntering into the room, tall, broad, sexy, and already raising her temperature with his presence.

"I did actually," she said. "But I thought I would wait until I decided it was time to have children."

"Whoa, forward," he said, holding up his hands then dropping to the middle of her patient couch. "You're on the pill, right?"

"You never asked and that's quite an assumption, Mr. Warner." She picked up her notebook again. "Do you think you made the subconscious decision that you were ready for children?"

"I'm thirty-five, I've thought about kids. But my lifestyle isn't conducive to it."

"Nothing to do with the lack of a stable female in your life or a fear of choosing the wrong woman to mother your offspring?"

"Honestly? I think, as a guy, you assume you have all the time in the world."

Switching into doctor mode was natural for her. He didn't moan or point it out, he just went with it and answered her questions.

"What are you hiding?" she asked.

"Hiding?"

"You never shy from a question. I have patients who won't be so honest with me even after a year of treatment."

"I had a lot of secrets from Karri," he said. "I figure that's part of the reason it didn't work. She didn't know what was going on in my head, and my life… I don't want to make that mistake again… Besides, I have doctor-patient confidentiality, right?"

Slipping her pad and pen onto the side table, she pulled the clip and pins from her hair to shake it out, letting it fall around her chest. Popping open two shirt buttons, she rose, gathering her skirt up her thighs in her fists, revealing the stockings she'd donned that morning.

"Nice," he drawled, enjoying them for the second time that day.

Sliding one knee the length of his thigh, she sank down to straddle him.

"I'm feeling frisky."

"Isn't this against the rules, doc?" he asked, flicking her hair out of the way with his head to suck her neck.

"You need a more hands on approach, Mr. Warner. You know how I value my patient's satisfaction."

"Satisfaction is still a way off."

The swelling in his groin, protruding between them, begged to differ. She wriggled forward, getting closer. "We have lift off," she whispered, taking his hands around to splay them on her ass while squashing her breasts against him. "Is it my butt or my boobs?"

"I'll consider that while you're laying those sugar lips on me."

"Take your time," she said, meeting his mouth on its descent to hers.

Something about his chest drew her hands, she yanked up his tee-shirt, spreading her fingers on his pecs, purring as she widened her legs to grind down on him.

"Nice," he growled on her lips and ripped open her shirt.

Arching into the exposure, she was shocked to see a gaping Bobby standing just behind the couch.

"Bobby," she stuttered, snatching the edges of her shirt to hold it closed.

Colt frowned, obviously not appreciating that she'd

said another man's name.

"Doctor Cutler, I… I didn't realize your services extended this far."

Colt twisted and hooked an arm over the couch to sneer at Bobby. "Boyfriend, not patient, get lost."

"Don't talk to him like that," she muttered and clambered off Colt, holding her shirt closed with one hand while yanking down the hem of her skirt with the other. "Why did you come back, Bobby? Is there a problem?"

"I forgot my scarf," he said, pointing in the direction of the hat stand, though his fixation was her chest. Yep, he'd seen a lot more of her than usual… which explained the new tent in his pants. Unfortunately, she wasn't the only one to have noticed it.

Colt flew up off the couch, stalking toward Bobby. "Get the fuck out of here!"

"Colt!" she said, scurrying after him but Bobby spun and ran out, slamming the front door on his frantic exit.

"Little prick!" Colt said, whipping around, except his glare couldn't match her fury.

"What did you do?" she hollered. "Why did you scare him like that? He's my patient!"

"The jerk had a boner! He was checking out your tits. I'd have knocked his teeth out if—"

"Bobby is not a threat to me. Do you think I've never seen an erection before? Dicks are my bread and butter, you idiot! I've seen more than you, I guarantee it. I spent years specializing in sexual issues. There were days I had twenty different dicks in my hands."

"Those guys didn't see you half-naked, making out with a guy."

"That doesn't matter. This is a non-judgmental space. Now you've scared him, he might not come back."

"So what? He's a little pervert—"

"No!" she said, eliminating the space between them. "We do not use that word in here. We heal here. I have to be accepting."

"Of that? You accept men getting hard in your company? Does that happen when you're alone with him?

Does it happen with other guys?"

"Just because a man gets an erection doesn't mean he'll use it. And not all erections are sexual in nature. Men can't necessarily control a physiological reaction."

"Are you kidding me? You think that doctor shit will work with me?"

Now toe-to-toe, Lyssa's rage became feverish. Her anger management and serenity training abandoned her. All she wanted to do was shout and beat him about the head.

"Please leave," she said.

Faltering, his brow hardened. "You're kicking me out? We have one fight, and you break up with me? Where are all those conflict resolution skills you must have studied?"

"This is them in action. Get out!"

"Nice, Miss. Lys," he snapped and stormed out of the office. "Very nice!"

When the front door slammed, she jumped. A well of moisture rushed to her tear ducts, but she wouldn't let it out. She distracted herself by buttoning her shirt as best she could, though most of them were missing. Marching to the desk, her impulse was to pick up the phone to Suzette, except that may not be allowed.

Colt had paid for Suzette's cab home after the police excused them the previous night. She didn't know what happened with Pete when Suzette got home. If he suspected that his fiancée lied, Lyssa's name had come up, or the truth had come out, Pete wouldn't appreciate her calling.

She was too riled to update Bobby's notes and couldn't sit still upstairs. So after changing her shirt, she grabbed her purse, shoved the strap up her arm and slammed out of the house. Everyone else had done it, now it was her turn.

When her and Archie argued it had never been like that. Her blood scalded her veins; anger bled from her primal core. The blast of wind pushing back on her as she strode down the sidewalk offered a welcome cleansing to the built-up adrenaline. To clean it all out, she'd have to walk for miles.

There was no destination, just moving and breathing. Her friendship with Suzette was on the rocks. Her new lover had declared them over when all she'd wanted was a timeout. Suzie and Colt were her priorities, but she worried about Bobby too. About her admirer. Oh, and her research at Risqué.

More drama didn't help. This was her timeout; things would be better after… wouldn't they?

TWENTY-THREE

BY THE TIME SHE GOT HOME, night had fallen. Despite being tired, she went through her ritual of searching every room before checking for messages. Zero messages.

Stripping down, she climbed into bed, inhaling the scent of Colt where she'd left him sleeping just that morning. Tears didn't take long to sneak out again.

Life went on, despite her own personal drama. She had no excuse to see or speak to Colt until her next Risqué shift on Thursday night.

Not being a woman to play games in matters of the heart, she decided to give him until the end of her working day. If she hadn't heard from him by then, she would call him, and they would talk things out. Her decision helped her fall asleep with a greater sense of optimism.

The optimism didn't last. Just before her penultimate patient arrived, two unknown men walked into her office.

Her panic was short-lived, they identified themselves as detectives and then used the word "homicide."

"Why are homicide detectives talking to me?" she asked, descending into her doctor chair while they sat on the patient couch. "Is this about the shooting?"

"You've flashed on the police radar quite regularly of

late, Doctor Cutler," Detective Hoburn said.

"I suppose so," she said. "Will you tell me why you're here?"

"There was a homicide last night. We have reason to believe you have information about the victim, and that you may be one of the last people to see him alive."

"The last one to see him alive?" she asked. Sickness swamped her. Colt. He was the last person she'd seen yesterday. "Who…? Who are you talking about?"

"A Mr. Robert Julius."

"Bobby," she said, exhaling a rush of relief that instantly made her feel guilty. Reorienting herself, she absorbed the new information. All positive feelings vanished. "He's dead? How?"

"At this time, we're trying to establish his final movements," Detective Hoburn said.

His colleague remained stoically silent, observing her, and scrutinizing the details of the room.

"His final movements?"

"He had an appointment with you yesterday evening, is that correct?"

"Yes, he had an appointment at five o'clock," she said.

Her fingertips went numb, ice continued up to her knuckles. She couldn't quite bring herself to look at the police, too many possibilities preoccupied her.

"It was in his calendar," Hoburn said, producing a small notebook from his pocket to take notes. "Can you tell us the nature of your work with him?"

"I won't discuss the specifics of his condition or treatment, but I can certainly answer any specific questions that you have relating to your enquiries."

"Did he tell you what his plans were after he left his appointment with you?"

"He had a date," she said. "The woman's first name was Deshana; I don't know her last name."

"We have her details and are trying to track her down now. They met through work?"

"Yes," Lyssa said, meeting his eye. As the shock

subsided, she mentally crept back into her doctor's cloak. "He's a data entry clerk."

"Do you have any reason to believe that relationship was acrimonious?"

"They had only been out a couple of times. He did stand her up on their last date, but he called to apologize and reschedule. As far as I know, everything was fine between them."

"Did he have any enemies?"

"No," she said. "Not that he mentioned to me. He had a very difficult childhood but was an only child. His mother died several years ago. He has no other family." Talking of him in the present tense was incorrect. Reminding herself of that brought back the numbness. "As far as I know he got along with everyone. He wasn't very social because he had been isolated as a child. He lacked the social skills that many of us take for granted."

"It's possible he pissed someone off?" Hoburn asked. "That he was rude or disrespected someone?"

"I don't believe so," she said. "He tended to withdraw if he felt threatened. The only anger he exhibited was towards himself. If someone tried to start an altercation with him, I would surmise that Bobby would choose retreat rather than attack."

"Did he discuss neighbors with you or friends?"

"He didn't really have friends," she said. "I'm sorry, but can you tell me what actually happened?"

"We're not releasing any details at this stage," Hoburn said and flipped his notebook shut. "Thank you, doctor, you've been helpful." He handed her a card as he and his partner stood up. She fumbled the card and mirrored their action. "If you think of anything specific, anything at all that may be helpful, please be in touch."

"Of course," she said.

The detective filtered out and held the door for her next patient to enter.

The patient perked up after scrutinizing them, then paused to frown at her. "Were they cops?"

"I'm sorry, Lee," she said. "I have to reschedule;

something has come up."

"Is everything okay?"

"I lost a patient."

"That can't be common in your line of work," he said. "What was wrong with him?"

"It was unrelated to his treatment here, don't worry about that. Do you mind if we reschedule?"

"No," he said and shrugged.

Letting down a patient was the last thing she wanted to do, but there was no way she'd be able to concentrate. Not paying attention to a client wouldn't help him. When the appointment was rescheduled, she canceled the following one and those in the morning too. A drink… or a few, would be needed to process the tragedy.

Calling Suzette still wasn't an option. Her and Colt were in a fight. She wasn't sure he'd want to hear from her… except she'd made a promise to herself to call him after work. At least she had news, a reason to call, terrible as it was.

His cellphone went to voicemail. Ruger's too. Blaser didn't even know the truth of her profession, so she couldn't call him. Instead, she went upstairs to change her clothes and then grabbed a cab to Colt's. Showing up might be heavy handed. Scaring him off now would spell the end of their relationship. At least she'd know. And she needed a mission to distract her anyway. Tracking him down was it.

Except he wasn't at home either. No one answered his door, or Ruger's, the next one along. Blaser's place was directly underneath Colt's. She knocked there too and got no reply.

Damnit.

Blaser could be at the garage or the club. Before her hunt went any further, a man poked his head out of the door next to Blaser's.

"Can I help you?" he asked.

"No," she said, wondering why he was interfering. "You can't help, Random Creepy Man Who I Don't Know."

"That's my name, how'd you guess?"

He came outside and she backed up a step. Blaser's door was under the external stairs, she was cornered.

"I know Colt," she said, hoping if she made him aware of the association, he'd be less likely to do anything sinister.

He didn't look like a particularly scary guy. His hair was too long, his body stretched and lean, but his sense of propriety unsettled her.

"That's not Colt's door."

"No, it's not," she said. "But no one answered upstairs."

"I heard you knocking on Ruger's door as well," he said, coming so close that he propped a shoulder on Blaser's doorjamb.

She shuffled back against Blaser's kitchen window. "Is that a crime?"

"No, but none of them are here."

Yes, unanswered doors usually meant no one was home. "I guessed that."

"Maybe they're avoiding you."

"Why would they do that?"

"I don't know. I'm guessing that you tried their phones and got no answer either. You're in a pickle."

Now he was playing with her, and she didn't appreciate it, or have the time for games. "Look, Strange Man, either you know where they are, or you don't. If you don't, then I have to be moving along."

Striding forward, she intended to pass except he spoke again, stalling her. "Their mom hates cellphones, especially at the dinner table."

"Their mother?" He nodded. "They're at their mother's?"

Where was the Warner family home?

"You wouldn't be Cherry by any chance, would you?"

That startled her. "How do you know my name?"

Her fake name anyway.

"Sexy girl knows the brothers but hasn't been in their lives for long… Plus, Colt talks about you, and Ruger likes to rib him about it. I haven't heard Colt talk about a woman in a long time. Karri screwing around with his partner really fucked his head."

His wife cheated on him with his partner? Was that the reason he gave up his professional law enforcement career? More pieces of the puzzle. They really needed to have less sex and do more talking.

"I don't suppose you know where their mother lives," she said, aware he may not divulge the address even if he knew it.

"Auntie Pru lives in the same house she has for all their lives."

"Auntie," she said, brightening up. "You're Gus Warner, their cousin. Your brother owns this building."

"He does," Gus said. "Never done a day's work in his life though."

If he owned a building, he must have done something to earn it, but she wasn't going to question him. "Can you give me her address, please?"

The nonchalant expression on his face morphed to a smile. "You're going to show up at their mother's house?"

She wasn't sure she got the joke or appreciated the sentiment of it. "I have something to tell Colt."

"Oh, please tell me you're pregnant."

Still, the joke was lost on her. "What business is that of yours?"

"Damn, Aunt Pru asked me over for dinner. I wish I'd said yes now. Hang on, I'll get a pen and write it down for you."

Gus went back into his apartment. She stayed outside, waiting for him to return. Showing up at Colt's mother's house probably wasn't a good idea, and it felt like Gus had goaded her into it somewhat. She couldn't change her mind or he might think she was scared. Certainly, no one could accuse her of being chicken.

TWENTY-FOUR

"I HAVE TO GO," Blaser said for maybe the fifth time since their mother had filled his coffee cup, but the Warner mother was no pushover.

"Dinner isn't finished," she said, seating herself at her husband's side.

Colt wanted to leave too. The sooner he got out of there, the sooner he could get to Lyssa's. He needed to apologize. Would she be understanding? It was Lyssa, she had to be... right? Maybe she wouldn't. But he wouldn't walk away from their relationship because of one stupid fight. They'd barely had a chance together. Their relationship deserved a fair hearing. Lyssa was beyond worth it.

"He has to go to work," Ruger said, but happily took another slice of cake from the center of the table.

Prudence Warner wouldn't let anyone leave the dinner table until everyone had eaten their fill. So as long as someone was eating, Blaser was stuck at the table, and Ruger knew it.

"He works too much," Pru said. "He'll never find a woman who will put up with that."

A groan went around the table. "Jesus, mom, don't start," Blaser said.

Taking her hand from her cup, she held it up in surrender, but shook her head. "I just don't see why three strapping, handsome men, in their thirties, are all single. You should be married."

"Some of us have been," Blaser said.

Colt didn't look back when his twin locked him in his sights.

"Karri wasn't a keeper," Ruger said. "But it's funny you should bring up women because Colt is actually seeing one, a pretty fine one too."

Pru perked up. "Oh?"

Colt slammed daggers from his eyes into Ruger. His younger brother was the only one at the table who knew what had happened between him and Lys last night. Yet, he was bringing Lyssa up, a woman with whom he may not have any future at all.

"I don't think now is the time to talk about it," Colt said.

"I think now is probably the best time," Ruger responded.

"Oh, yeah, why's that?" Colt asked. "Want a laugh at my expense?"

"No, because she's walking across the front yard right now."

Everyone at the table stood up to peer out the front window at the long front yard and the street beyond. Their collective movement must have been visible from outside because Lyssa stopped, like a rabbit pinned by headlights, then lifted her open hand in a tentative wave.

"She's beautiful," Pru said, brimming with excitement. "I'll make her coffee and we'll—"

"No," Colt said, already shoving past his brothers. "I'm going to talk to her. You all stay here."

How did she find him? The fact that she had was worrying. Showing up at his mother's was bold; she'd shown no bunny boiler tendencies so far. Something had to be wrong.

The moment he got out his parents' front door, Lyssa started toward him. He picked up the pace until they met.

"Something happened," she panted as though out of breath.

"What? The stalker?"

She was already shaking her head. "No, not that, no… I… I lost a patient."

"Suicide?"

"Murder," she croaked.

He took hold of her shoulders, fearing she could pass out. This news had knocked her sideways.

"Murder?" he said. "What happened?"

"The police wouldn't tell me. They showed up at my office tonight asking questions."

"Which patient was it?"

"Bobby," she said. "Bobby, who we saw last night… I didn't tell them about what happened. I didn't think and… they didn't ask and…"

It seemed like she was trying to get out a mishmash of random unprocessed thoughts. "You're shaken up."

"We saw him last night; he was my patient. You shouted at him; you scared him."

"I didn't scare him to death," he said, taking his hands off her. "Is that why you came here? To ask if I did this? If I hurt him?"

A spasm in his gut took his body further from hers.

"No! What? No, that hadn't even occurred to me… I came here because… because I didn't know what to do. I was distressed and I thought I might feel better if… you would hold me."

That was the truth. She didn't come to question him; she came for support. She chose him above all others and took a risk in pursuing him at this personal location, especially after their fight.

His anxiety evaporated. He pulled her into his arms, against his chest, holding her tight. She sagged against him, releasing a long exhale.

"All night long," he whispered into her hair.

"I know we were fighting and—"

"That doesn't matter," he said. "I'm sorry for being a jerk."

"You were a jerk, but I shouldn't have reacted in anger."

"Lys," Ruger hollered. "Mom wants to know how you take your coffee. Said I'd get you coffee, didn't I?"

While holding her, Colt turned so they could see his younger brother hanging out of the front door.

"I shouldn't come in," Lyssa said. "There are too many questions."

"Are you kidding? There will be more the next time you're here if you don't come in now. I'll field the questions; you've got enough on your plate. But if you're up for it then you should come in and say hello. It's just Blaser and Ruger."

"And your mom and dad," she said.

"Yeah, but my dad won't say much. My mom takes care of the talking in their relationship."

"Smart woman."

Hooking her under his arm, he took her across the yard into his parents' house. He'd have to call Chavez and his contacts in homicide to get the details on what happened. This development was suspicious. Too many coincidences were piling up. Usually that meant they weren't coincidences at all.

"A DOCTOR? YOU'RE A DOCTOR," Blaser said when they were in the car travelling away from his parents' house an hour later.

The questions hadn't been so bad. Colt had done as promised and dealt with most of them. After a brief, whispered conversation with Ruger—in which she imagined Colt filled him in about the murder—Ruger did his part in diverting his mother's attention when he could.

No one could prevent one thing: Blaser finding out the truth, or at least part of it. And although he hadn't questioned them in front of his parents', it seemed he'd chosen that moment to say his piece.

"Yes," Lyssa said.

Ruger was driving. Blaser was in the passenger seat, giving her and Colt the backseat to themselves.

Blaser hung over the shoulder of his chair, glaring at

them. "All this time you've been what? Studying us?"

"Not you specifically," she said. "But the customers and your employees? Yes, I suppose you could say that. I think of it as research, you're not like lab rats."

"Forgive me for struggling to see your side. You came in and gave me a sob story," Blaser said, then trapped Colt in his gaze. "And you knew about this?"

"Me too," Ruger said. "You were the only one out of the loop."

"You're not helping his anxiety," Lyssa said. "Don't you think that maybe this is why there is animosity in your relationship? Maybe if you all trusted each other—"

"You don't know the history," Blaser said, flopping into his seat to stare forward. "You're fired by the way."

"I figured," she said.

"You can't fire her for having qualifications," Ruger said. "She's a good worker."

"Actually, she's not. She kept her job because she's sleeping with my brother. Her mind is never on the job, she has ducked out of more shifts than she's seen through to the end, and she never keeps on top of her tables."

He had a point. "You've been very kind to me, Blaser. I appreciate the opportunity that you gave me."

"You got shot at outside of his club, one of your patients was murdered, and you're being gracious to him?" Ruger asked.

"One of your patients was murdered?" Blaser asked, twisting around again. "How?"

"I don't know, the cops wouldn't tell me."

"Shot," Colt said. "He was shot."

"How do you know that?" she asked, bringing their joined hands to her abdomen.

"He still has contacts in the department," Ruger said. "Who has the case?"

"Hoburn."

"He hates you," Ruger said.

Lyssa couldn't imagine why anyone would hate Colt.

"The feeling is mutual," Colt said.

"I need to check my messages," she said and sighed.

"You can do that from my place, you're staying with me tonight."

No question, just a command. "What if the police need to talk to me again?"

"Then they'll track you down," he said. "They're the cops. If a detective can't locate a woman at her boyfriend's apartment, he's not worthy of carrying the badge."

When he put it like that, it made sense. "Okay. I cancelled my morning patients, so we could go out for breakfast."

"Or have a long lie," Ruger said.

"I have an early meeting," Colt said. "But you can stay in bed."

"An early meeting with who?" she asked though it was none of her business.

"You got one of your spooky hunches, brother?" Ruger asked him, glancing in the rearview mirror.

"Something isn't sitting right with me about this. I want to check out a few things."

"He wants to solve the mystery," Ruger said. "You can rest easy, Lys, you and this Bobby dude. Once Colt has something in his teeth, he won't let it go."

"I don't want you getting involved," Lyssa said, twisting to look at him. She lowered her voice. "You were fighting with Bobby last night. If the cops find that out—"

"We're not going to hide anything from them," Colt said. "Just because I was fighting with the guy doesn't mean that I killed him."

"You were fighting with him?" Blaser asked. "How come?"

"He got a hard-on staring at Lyssa's tits." Jabbing an elbow into Colt's ribs, she frowned at him. "What? That's why I was fighting with him."

"Sounds like a reason to take a guy out to me," Blaser said. "Where were you last night?"

"Your girlfriend's apartment," Colt sneered, then leaned down to her. "I'm kidding, he doesn't even have a girlfriend."

Yeah, she got that.

"Colt and I got drunk last night," Ruger chimed in. "Solid alibi, must be a couple of dozen people who saw him."

"No one suspects Colt of anything," Lyssa said.

"Only because you haven't told them the truth yet," Blaser said. "You didn't tell them about Colt's tête-à-tête with the dead man, did you?"

"No," she said. "I didn't think about it. I just answered their questions."

Lyssa hoped that by omitting the details of Bobby's return to her office, and the ensuing outburst, she hadn't made things more difficult.

"Don't worry about it," Colt said. "We'll clear it up."

"I can't believe that he's dead."

"Yeah, you lose your second job and a patient," Blaser said. "You'll have to tighten your belt."

"Hey." Colt dived forward to shove his brother. "You want to be a jerk? Aim your shit at me."

"Great, now you've had a go at me," Blaser said, facing the windshield. "Wonder if I'll turn up dead tomorrow."

Bobby was dead and as far as she knew he hadn't achieved his goal. She wanted to know if he'd gone on the date with Deshana, and if there had been any success between them physically. After the therapy they'd worked through together, she really hoped he'd found happiness before he lost his life. To die without accomplishing it would make his demise all the more tragic.

When she and Colt were alone, she would ask him if the cops had a time of death and a location. Those facts might answer her questions. But answering the material questions didn't answer the biggest questions of all: who would want Bobby dead, and why?

SPENDING THE NIGHT with Colt was the perfect medicine. He made dinner, and then they put on a movie. Neither spoke about their argument. Thank God. She didn't want to think about more drama, she just wanted to relax and feel. Colt obliged and then some. A gentle, soothing massage in front of the movie quickly became something more. The heat of his certain hands surrounded her with security. With Colt, she was safe, she was treasured.

Turning toward him, she sought his mouth, wishing she could do more, everything, all at once. Kissing him, touching him, she wanted to taste his body as much as she wanted to feel him move inside her.

Just like always, he anticipated her and took control, freeing her from those thoughts. He carried her from the couch to the bedroom and tossed her onto the mattress. As he stripped off his own clothes, he stared down at her, his eyes glowing with the pressure of his need. With ideas of hurrying the formalities, she began to take off her own shirt.

He grabbed her hands and pounced down on top of her, holding her immobile. "I'm going to do that myself," he said and bit into her lip, then her earlobe.

The sting of his teeth made her wince, but he didn't apologize. He elevated his weight enough to grab the neck of her shirt and ripped it apart. That sound did something to her, something he must have noted in the past. A satisfied pant cascaded over her chest when he yanked away her bra to take one of her nipples into his teeth.

"Pain," he said, tugging the nipple tight until she squealed. He released her and lapped the peak. "It's only temporary." When he blew the dampness, a spear of pleasure made her arch. "We cause it in those we care about without intending to."

"You were defending my honor last night," she whispered, stroking his shoulders. "I am thankful that you feel so deeply for me. I'm just very protective of patients."

"I understand that," he said. "But you have to understand that I don't want to share this body."

"You don't have to, you'll never have to," she said. "But what I do requires me to talk about intimate things with other men. I don't discuss my own intimacies; I only discuss theirs. This, our time, is entirely private. And you are the only one who gets to share this side of me."

"I'll come to terms with that. Give me time. Don't expect me to always be understanding of other men getting erections while they're alone with you."

"It's not sexual."

"Maybe not for you, but it might be for them."

"Colt, this is what I do. You will have to get used to that. Just as I will have to get used to what you do. I'll have to make accommodations for it."

"Enough talking," he said, kissing her, pushing his tongue against hers, filling her mouth and mind with ideas of having him inside her soon.

For now, he only played with her breasts, fondling and stroking, then kissing every inch of them in circles of increasing circumference. His fingers skimmed down the center of her abdomen, she anticipated them in her center. Instead, he spent time circling her belly button, pushing into it, massaging the disc, which transferred a spiral of arousal down to her core.

The bulge of his cock rubbed against the cotton of her skirt. She tried to wriggle to bring the hem up, but he kept her wrists in his hand, above her head, keeping them out of commission. Her whimpers grew impatient prompting his fingers to continue their route south. The button and zip of her skirt were loosened. She held her breath, waiting for his intimate caress. For an inordinate amount of time, he massaged her outer thigh, sliding between them without actually touching her pussy.

"Colt," she breathed and tried to force herself upward, but he pressed down until she struggled to catch her breath.

"I like to see you writhe and whimper," he admitted. "It turns me on to know that you're desperate for me to satisfy you. I want your mind clear, thinking about nothing except me inside of you."

"I'm thinking," she said. "I'm definitely thinking about that. Please."

"Not yet," he said, moving his hips to rub his dick on her thigh. "Are you thinking about that?"

"Mm hmm. Yes."

"Open your eyes and look at me."

When she did, the darkness in his eyes and the twist

of pleasure on his mouth amped her arousal. He was enjoying the teasing, kneading the length of his shaft against the flesh of her quaking thigh. Her attempt to move it aside drove him to stop and thrust hard against her, shunting the air from her lungs. He kissed her throat, using his head to force her chin up and licked the column he'd kissed before rubbing his face on her damp skin.

"You're a lucky girl, you know that?" he said, taking hold of her breast again. "I'm going to make sure you spend the rest of your life craving the ecstasy that only I can give you. Your pleasure will be delivered by me, in every way imaginable. Sex will be part of your everyday diet; I guarantee that I'll deliver each and every time."

"In your own time," she murmured, groaning at the flood of unsated desire that was livid within her.

"Do you feel that desperation now? Feel what it is to be desperate for me?"

Keeping still was a distant memory. Her eyes closed again as he let a fingertip touch her opening. Was this how some of her patients felt? To be aroused yet unable to accomplish release must frustrate them beyond belief.

"Pleasure me, Colt, please."

Gently, his finger slid in, the rest of him remained pressed against her, clamping her hips down, making it impossible for her to respond with anything other than a moan. Another finger joined the first; they pushed in deep and curled, tickling that cushion inside her.

Panting was the only way to get oxygen as he moved his fingertips back and forth, bringing her closer and closer to the brink of ecstasy. Just on the cusp, his fingers slid free, and bam, in less than a heartbeat his dick filled her up and she was screaming in climax.

Colt knew what he was doing with a woman, with her. As he pumped into her, and she lifted to meet his thrusts, orgasm wasn't the only cliff her hormones fell over.

Opening her eyes, she saw the intention in his eyes, every bit as enamored as the intensity of emotion in her. How it had happened so quickly she didn't know, but Lyssa was sure she loved this man. If they got through this, she'd prove her dedication.

TWENTY-FIVE

COLT DID GO OUT IN THE MORNING, after waking her for pleasure. When he returned, she'd asked questions, but he hadn't answered them. Instead, he went to Ruger's. She'd thought the point was to retrieve his brother and return. Evidently not.

Twenty minutes later, she took matters into her own hands and went to Ruger's. Taking the chance that the door was unlocked, she opened it to find both men sitting at the kitchen table. They were drinking coffee, all serious like, apparently righting the wrongs of the world.

"You ditched me?" she said to Colt.

"I'm updating Ruger," Colt said.

"Without updating me? This is my life, my patient, when were you planning on updating me?"

"I don't want you to be upset and you don't need to know the details. It might be best if you don't."

"Why?" she asked, coming into the apartment, closing the door behind her. "What did you find out?"

The men exchanged a look.

Ruger shrugged. "She's tough and smart, I'm sure she can handle it."

"I don't think that it was a coincidence," Colt said.

"What?" she asked, heading toward the enticing scent of java, helping herself to a cup of it. "What wasn't a coincidence?"

"Bobby was shot," Colt said. "After his date, on his way back to his apartment. His body was found in an alleyway, but it looks like the shot came from the street, possibly from a car. It could be a drive-by, just like at Risqué when you and Suzette were outside."

"Do you think he was aiming for me outside the club?"

"No. I think he was showing you what he intended to do."

"Why would he want to kill Bobby? Why would anyone want to kill such a harmless person?"

"I don't know," Colt said. "I could be wrong, which is why I didn't want to say anything to you. I just don't think it's a coincidence that all these things happen to one person in such close succession. His obsession has intensified."

"But why? Why now? He's been doing this for months, why would he choose now to—"

"How many men have you screwed since this guy started leaving the flowers?" Ruger asked.

Resting back on the kitchen counter, she held her coffee mug in both hands. "Colt is the only man that I've… you think my admirer has taken offense to us being an us?"

Colt shrugged. "Possibly."

"But that… that means you could be in danger too."

"It's possible. Chavez says their investigation keeps hitting dead ends. So Ruger and I are going to take the case privately."

"Wait, you're back on the case?" she asked.

"Don't worry," Ruger said. "I'm sure he's okay with screwing a client now… especially since you won't be paying us."

"I never received a final bill," she said.

"Consider it paid," Colt said. "I never cashed that check you gave me."

"I thought you didn't take barter," she said and received a scowl in return. "What about the rules?"

"This guy could be hunting you," Colt snapped. "Do you expect me to stand aside and let that happen? Ruger and I know what we're doing. Forget the bullshit from before, this is serious."

"It's always been serious," she argued. "I don't want you getting involved."

"You don't trust me to solve this?" he asked.

"I don't trust you not to get hurt. If this guy has seen us together, has seen you... If that's what has set off this frenzy, then he can identify you. I want you in hiding not seeking him out."

"Maybe you shouldn't have told her," Ruger said.

Colt left his seat, ignoring his brother to approach and take the mug from her hands. "I'm not going into hiding. If you have a problem with what I'm doing, walk away from us. But you can't stop me from pursuing this guy."

"Walk away?" she said, startled. "If I leave you, will you promise me not to look for him?"

"I'm going to look for him no matter what you do. If he has a target on my back as well as yours, I deserve a chance to defend myself."

Yeah, right. Lyssa didn't believe it for a second. "So that's what this is? You're looking out for you?"

"Look at it however you want. You can't stop me from doing this," Colt said, walking away from her to snatch his jacket from the back of his chair. "Ruger and I have to talk to someone, do you want me to take you back to your place, or should I leave you with Blaser?"

"I don't need a ride and I don't need to be babysat," she said. "Let me grab my stuff from yours and I'll make my own way home."

"You don't have to go back there if you don't want to. I can—"

"Where are you going?" she asked, walking over to him.

All the while Ruger remained at the table, sipping coffee, and enjoying the show.

"Out," Colt said. "And I'm giving you a ride home."

"I don't want to go home. I want to go with you."

He laughed. "Not a chance."

"Why not?" she asked. "If you're looking out for me, I should look out for you."

"Why do you think I'm taking Ruger? He'll watch my back. You sit at home. I'll come over later."

"Sit at home and wait for you to come over to my house for sex? Will you tell me what happened at this secret meeting?"

"Probably."

"I don't think I believe you," she said. "I want to come."

"No."

"You can't tell me that I can't prevent you from doing this and then you prevent me, that's unfair."

"Life is unfair," Colt said, his tension visibly rising.

"Let her come," Ruger said. "What harm can it do?"

"She's the primary target. If he's following her—"

"Oh, so I'm a liability?" Lyssa said. "You'd rather leave me somewhere alone like a sitting duck where the loon can take me out without any hindrance?"

"You've got your pepper spray, don't you? I'll check out your house. I'll clear it, then you lock all the doors and windows and don't open the door to anyone until I get back."

"What if something happens to you and you don't get back?"

"I'll send Blaser over."

"This is fun," Ruger said, laughing. "You two could keep going at it all day, both of you have an answer for everything. Look, either she comes, and you get laid tonight, or she doesn't, and she gripes your ass about it for the rest of the month. She's right. If she comes, we can keep an eye on her."

"She has clients this afternoon," Colt said.

"Which means she would have to answer the door," Ruger said, leaving the table to rinse out the coffee mugs. "Bring her this time, but Lys, we're making an exception. If you get in the way, we'll hole you up in an empty apartment and leave you there until this is over."

"Leave me there?" Lyssa said. "What's to stop me

from leaving when I'm alone?"

"The chain we'll attach to your ankle," Ruger said.

When his eyes met hers, they were blank, nothing of the usual laidback, fun-loving Ruger existed in that stare.

"Okay," she said and nodded. "I would appreciate being a part of this as much as possible. I'll cancel this afternoon's clients and come with you. I want to be a part of this. I want to help myself too, and the people I care about."

"This better not be more of your damn research," Colt muttered when she headed for the door.

"Research on you," she said, stopping at his side. "You have to learn to trust me."

Without giving him a chance to respond, she left the apartment to retrieve her things from Colt's. She didn't want to slow the men down or get in their way, so was quick to make her cancellation calls.

Colt's speculation awoke her anxiety. She wasn't scared of being hurt; Colt would never let that happen. But what if he was right… what if Bobby had been killed because of her?

"THIS WASN'T WHAT I EXPECTED," Lyssa said when they pulled into a wide alleyway lined with service doors for the retail unit storefronts on the other side of the building.

"What did you expect?" Ruger asked. "Guns and ammo?"

"We have guns and ammo," Colt said.

"We grew up with guns and ammo scattered on the kitchen table."

"Okay, I get it, you're both macho men. What are we doing here?"

"You wanted to come," Colt said. "Are you having second thoughts? Do you want to stay in the car?"

"It took us almost an hour to get here. I'm not missing this chance to see what it is you do."

The men exchanged a look, then Colt turned to her in the backseat. "You think that what we do is in there?"

She shrugged. "Seeing you in action might be

arousing."

"Ha," Ruger burst out. "If you get turned on in there, honey, there is something seriously wrong with you."

"Why would you say that?" she asked.

"Because he gets turned on in there," Colt said, unclicking his seatbelt and leaving the car.

Now she was too intrigued not to follow. They'd parked at the side of the alley, so she shimmied across the backseat to get out. She was at Colt's side before Ruger was around the car.

Taking Colt's hand stopped him. Tilting his head, he examined the point of contact as though he didn't understand it.

"I'm not allowed to hold your hand?" she asked, without releasing him, curious about why it was such an alien thing when they held hands all the time.

What was going on in his mind?

"You can hold my hand," Ruger said, offering it.

Colt spoke, "I'm just not used to doing business with a… partner."

"You do business with Ruger," she said.

"He doesn't hold my hand," Colt replied.

"As far as I'm aware, he doesn't suck your dick either," she said with a triumphant smile. "Maybe when he does one, he can do the other."

Ruger leaned into his brother's ear from behind. "You'll be waiting a long time for that, buddy boy. A long, long time. You can hold your own damn hand as far as I'm concerned."

Slapping his brother's back, Ruger left the couple to head for one of the doorways on the other side of the alley.

"If it's about professionalism," she said, extracting her hand from his only to have him snatch it back.

"No," he said. "You wanted us to be in this together."

"Come on," Ruger shouted, holding open the door. "You can do lovey later."

Crossing the alleyway, hand-in-hand, Ruger let them enter first, then came in at their back. Metal shelving units, jam-packed with all sorts of electronic equipment, lined up vertically in front of them towering all the way to the ceiling.

"Pinch!" Ruger called from his place at the rear of their trio.

"Come on down!" someone replied.

They began to move through the columns of shelving.

Computer monitors and hard drives sat interspersed with laptops and webcams. Strange electronic boxes in all configurations lay between them. Miles and miles of cabling in all widths and colors coiled around like snakes protecting the treasure.

A tall guy, about the same height as Ruger, got up from a long, steel workbench. Monitors lined the wall in front of where he'd been working. They showed what had to be the front of the store from various angles. Half a dozen more didn't look like any retail space, except she had no time to figure out what they were.

The guy Ruger had referred to as Pinch, passed them. She, Colt and Ruger followed him to a shelf containing two long, rectangular black sports bags.

"Everything you need," Pinch said, pulling the bags from the shelf and handing one each over to Ruger and Colt.

Colt gave the guy an envelope.

"You always deliver," Ruger said.

"And you always pay," Pinch said, giving her a quick once over then leaving them to go back to his workbench.

They departed to the alley and the bags were stowed in the trunk. After faltering for a second, she clambered into the backseat and Ruger cranked the engine.

"That's it?" she asked. "That's the big, scary secret meeting that you were afraid to take me to?"

"No one said it was big and scary," Colt said.

Ruger drove out of the alley, she guessed, to head for home.

"Why didn't you want to take me if all you were doing was picking that stuff up?" she asked.

"You don't know what we picked up," Ruger said. "Maybe we're going to build a bomb, maybe you were just party to a crime."

The presented scenario didn't concern her. "If that's the case, how do you know I won't snitch to the police?"

"If you did, we'd know," Ruger said and nodded at his brother. "He knows every corrupt cop there is. We have a great alibi too. We could off you and then claim the crazy stalker did it. I feel pretty confident that you'll keep quiet."

"No one is offing anyone," Colt said.

Though he was irritated at his brother, his words were meant to soothe her, but Lyssa was fascinated.

Taking hold of the two front seats, she pulled herself as far forward as possible to peer at Ruger. "You're a whole lot more than a pretty face, aren't you, Littlest Warner," she said. "I don't suppose I could tempt you onto my couch?"

"He's going nowhere near your couch," Colt said.

"Everything would be completely confidential," she said to Ruger, paying Colt no heed. "You have seriously hidden depths."

"Much as that's a great offer," Ruger said. "If we're going to be sitting down to Thanksgiving dinner together, I'd just as soon not have you know all of my innermost secrets."

"I'll know Colt's," she said.

"Yeah," Ruger said. "But you've already pointed out a great difference between your relationship with him and mine. So unless you're willing to take our relationship to the next level and offer me the same perks—"

"Sex is a defense mechanism for you," she muttered, then turned to Colt. "Who was the last serious woman in his life?"

"They broke up at the beginning of last year, a woman named Eva."

"Hey!" Ruger chastised him.

Colt just shrugged. "What? She sucks my dick."

Judging by his expression, he got a weird pleasure out of reminding his brother of that. Like there wasn't a thing Ruger could do to prevent his honesty because she had special access to him.

"Sex makes you more open, babe," she said to him.

Colt's satisfaction dwindled. "Don't talk about our sex life."

"Why not? You just did."

"You started it," he said. "You brought up the sucking thing outside."

"I think he knows that I do that for you."

"You said that professional and personal were separate."

"Yes," she said. "But if I can't get Ruger onto my couch then all he and I have is personal."

"Fine, you can talk to him," Colt said.

"No way," Ruger chimed in. "I don't need a shrink picking my head apart."

"Is that what you think I'd do?" she asked. "Do you think that talking to a professional somehow diminishes your masculinity?"

"I haven't forgiven you for the women's clothing dig yet," Ruger said. "You're already on thin ice, you sure you want to keep going?"

"You're getting frustrated," she said.

"Which is unusual for him," Colt said. "He's usually cool and collected. Maybe you've hit a nerve."

"It's not his masculinity that's threatened," she said, edging closer to examine her rear-angle view of Ruger's profile. "He fears being exposed because he thinks that it will make him vulnerable. That's why he's always making jokes."

"Alright, alright," Ruger said. "You're never cancelling patients again. You obviously need your daily hit of deconstructing some poor schmuck. Leave me out of that mumbo-jumbo."

"Are you mocking what I do?" she asked. "Do you not believe in psychiatry?"

"I believe in proctology; doesn't mean I'm rushing to make an appointment. You do what you do, and I'll do what I do."

"You're using your skills to help me. Why shouldn't I do the same in return? There would be no charge."

"Yeah," Colt said. "Consider this one on me. I'll pay her for you."

Colt wasn't taking it seriously and that only riled Ruger more. But she had been serious. Every once in a while,

Ruger revealed a hint of what lay beneath his surface, and she wondered if he needed more help than he'd ever let on. He wasn't the type of man to reveal weakness.

Sliding back in her seat, she didn't push the issue because she didn't want it to become a joke. But she did vow to talk to Ruger again, when they were alone. Perhaps then he'd take her seriously.

TWENTY-SIX

"IF IT'S SOMETHING DANGEROUS or volatile then I don't want it in my house," Lyssa said, running up her front stoop, keys in hand, as the men followed with the bags from Pinch's.

"He's volatile," Ruger said, nodding at his brother. "And you let him into your bed."

"He doesn't have the potential to explode and kill me," she said, putting the key in the lock.

Ruger snorted. "No? Sure about that?"

"You, can it," Colt said. Coming up behind her, he kissed her shoulder. "It's nothing dangerous."

"Thank you," she said, appreciating his honesty, alleviating her concerns, as opposed to Ruger who was contrary for the sake of it. Obviously, her suggestion that he might need a bout on her couch had upset him. "You two wait here."

"Why?" Ruger said.

Colt crowded in behind her, ignoring her request. "You don't have to worry or go through your ritual when I'm here. Walk behind me."

"So if someone starts shooting, you get the bullet? No," she said, digging her shoulder into him to try overtaking.

They struggled for first position until they were in the hall at the bottom of the stairs and their jockeying became hilarious.

Ruger stopped just inside the front door and dropped his bag. "What's that?" he asked.

Following his line of vision to a thick white envelope on the floor, her curiosity piqued. It must have been pushed out of the way by the front door when she opened it.

"I don't know," she said, going towards it.

"Don't touch it," Colt said. "We might get prints from it."

Ruger turned it over with his boot. There was nothing written on the front, it was completely blank.

"It's from him," Ruger said like he just knew it.

The pressure building in her chest knew it too. Without need of her professional training, she could tell that her blood pressure was rising. "What do you think it is?"

Ruger retrieved a pair of latex gloves from his pocket, which he handed to her. "Take a look."

"Why would you be carrying around latex gloves?" she asked, taking them from him. "I have gloves upstairs but I'm a doctor. What's your excuse?"

"I'm a germaphobe," he said without an ounce of conviction. "Are you going to look or not?"

She snapped the gloves on and retrieved the envelope, which she took into her waiting room behind the office, because the office was locked. Sitting on the couch, she peeled open the self-adhesive envelope.

"No DNA on the flap," Colt muttered. "But there could be fibers."

Continuing, she reached in to grasp the documents only to discover on withdrawing them that they weren't documents at all, they were photographs… of her. All of them were black and white, the implications of them didn't fully sink in until she moved the top one aside and saw that the next one was of her, alone in her bedroom, getting changed.

She gasped and dropped the pictures, sending them cascading across the floor. The waterfall of violation went from her lap to a well in the middle of the hardwood floor where their momentum ran out.

"Jesus," Ruger muttered.

Colt bent over, scraping them together, using his jacket sleeves as protection. She saw flashes of the pictures. Her outside with Suzette. Her on her back step holding flowers. Her in her house. There were pictures of her living room, her bedroom, of her cooking, and putting on make-up, mundane things as well as the more intimate ones.

Her hands went to her chest. She sought out Colt, but he was spreading the pictures he hadn't gathered with his toe. The brothers were intent.

"Fuck," Colt said, his attention flying to his brother. "Do you see this?"

Ruger nodded and Colt dropped the pictures. Not in shock, he was on a mission. Both men turned and ran out of the room. She didn't see what they saw but sank onto her knees to fumble through the pictures, seeking it out. Flattening her hands on them, sweeping them out in an arch, she saw it. Pictures of her in bed, with Colt, taken from inside the property.

Pouncing to her feet, she went after the men clattering around in her bedroom. More cursing from Colt didn't bode well.

"No!" Ruger said.

Lyssa arrived in the bedroom just in time to see Ruger shove Colt against the wall and grab something from his hand, something small and round.

"What is that?" she asked. The brothers turned, but she already knew the answer. "He's been watching us, hasn't he?"

"The pervert has been watching from inside," Colt said, jostling Ruger out of the way to approach her.

"Watching us," she said. "Together. He's been watching us having sex?"

Her voice cracked. Clearing her throat, she needed to maintain the façade of strength and get through this. Colt took hold of her shoulders and pulled her against him. His strength bled into her; she'd never been more grateful.

"This is something else," Ruger said. "He's been

inside. Who has been inside your home?"

"Anyone can get in," Colt said, without releasing her from the hug. "You want to know who? Answer the when."

"When?" she asked, leaning back to look at him.

"Yes," he said. "We need to know if he broke in or if he just walked in when you were in session. Did he do it when you were here? How long has he been watching?"

"What difference does that make?" she asked. "He's been watching us… you and me… having sex."

"Filming it more likely," Ruger said, examining the device in his hand. "It's a webcam, wireless, motion activated by the look of it. I think it has a remote charging device too, which is state-of-the-art. I can take this back to Pinch, see what he thinks. Maybe he can tell us where it came from or where it's transmitting to."

"Get on it," Colt said. Ruger vanished from the room and, she presumed, the house. Colt stroked her face. "We have to look at the pictures and put them in order."

"In order?"

"A timeline. We have to establish when the first one was taken and where he's been."

"But if he's had a camera in here then he didn't need to be here."

"One of the pictures was taken outside Risqué," he said. "Did you see it?" She shook her head. "It's of you and Suzette talking. He was there. The night of the shooting, he was there."

She exhaled. "We have to tell the police."

"We'll call them, but they'll want to know which is the first picture and which is the last."

"But…" she said. A bitter taste moistened her throat. "They'll see us together."

"Yeah."

He couldn't be wild about the cops, his former colleagues, seeing them in bed together. Sharing something like that of himself and of her, wouldn't make him happy. But they couldn't pick and choose. If this guy was killing people, they had to cooperate fully. Modesty should be the last concern.

This man, the stalker, had been at Risqué on the night of the shooting. Knowing that made it even more likely that he had been involved in Bobby's demise. That meant, in an inadvertent way, the poor man, her patient, had died because of her, for her. Putting the situation in that perspective—fighting for Bobby rather than herself—made it much easier.

She squared her shoulders. "Come on then," she said. "We better get to work."

THEY'D SPENT TIME PUTTING the pictures in order but had taken a brief break to bring the bags up to the kitchen table. She just hadn't been able to stomach the physical proof of the stalker's intrusion anymore.

Colt must have sensed her growing unease. "I can do the rest on my own."

"No, you can't," she said. "You don't know where I was at all times. I'm struggling to identify the times and places of some of the shots myself."

"The angles are strange and not what you'd expect from someone sitting in a car or standing on a street corner," he said as though it had been perplexing him.

"What does that suggest to you?"

"I don't know," he muttered. "It's something, but I can't put my finger on it."

"Chavez said he and Ronson would be over later?"

"Yeah, I told them that we were going to work on putting them in order and that we were careful about disturbing prints."

"Do you think that we'll get any?"

He shook his head. "I could give you platitudes," he said, pouring her a glass of water. "But he's been careful in every other way. I doubt he'd be so stupid as to leave such obvious evidence now."

"He might not be on the system. If he's not on the system, then being careful doesn't matter."

"True. But why take the risk? We have no idea how long he'll keep doing this or what his plans are. He doesn't want to link himself to anything. Keeping his identity a secret is paramount to him, which is unusual. Most stalkers want to contact their victims eventually though, we have to hope he'll reveal himself soon."

"Before anyone else dies," she said. "We're waiting for him, taking the chance that a madman will make a mistake?"

"I know it's not comforting, but it's the way that most murderers are caught, by accident, like a routine traffic stop, or because they make a mistake."

"Not a great endorsement for your old department?"

His smile was tight, but it was there. "I didn't work homicide."

Glancing at the bags, she wondered what was in them. Should she ask? Sometimes not knowing was better. That was the moral of the day.

Ruger hadn't been in touch, but she had faith that in time, or if he had anything useful, he would call.

Before she had a chance to ask Colt about opening the bags there was a knock at the front door. It was the middle of the afternoon, sun was streaming in through her tall front windows, but the two of them tensed and looked at each other.

"I'll go," Colt said.

"No, this is my house," Lyssa said, heading for the hall and the stairway down.

Figuring a patient hadn't got her message, or maybe decided to come anyway, she was surprised to see Hoburn and his partner on her doorstep.

"Doctor Cutler."

"Detective," she said. "Is there something else that you need?"

"We need to talk again," Hoburn said.

"About what?"

Colt's voice came from behind her, he stood halfway between her and the stairs. She opened the door a little further so the men could see each other.

"Warner," Hoburn said. "I heard you were involved in this."

"And yet I never got your call."

"I think it would be clear that you're the last man I'd call for help with an investigation."

"I'm wounded," Colt said without intonation.

"What is it that we need to talk about?" Lyssa asked. "Did you find out something about Bobby?"

Her intention was to clue him in about the pictures.

Hoburn spoke before she could. "We need to talk privately."

"I trust Colt," she said. "We can talk in front of him."

"No, we can't," Hoburn said.

She didn't like the tone of accusation but granted them entry and unlocked her office to gesture them in.

Colt came to her side. "What do you think is going on?" she whispered.

"I don't know," Colt murmured, watching Hoburn and his partner sit on her patient couch. "Hoburn hates me, but he's good at his job. He knows what he's doing."

"You're telling me I should trust him?"

"I'm telling you we've got a good chance of finding out who Bobby's killer is with Hoburn on the case. That's about all I can say."

"Okay," she said.

"I'll do my best with the pictures that are left," he said. "I'll be right next door in the waiting room."

He kissed her and glared into the office again. Hoburn and his partner had their backs to the door, so they missed Colt's dirty look, but he bestowed it anyway.

Once Colt disappeared into the waiting room, Lyssa cleared her throat and entered the office. "Can I get you men something to drink?" she asked, hoping they would decline and tell her why they were there.

Pleasantries meant delays.

"No," Hoburn said. "We have some important questions, and we'd like to get on with it."

"Okay," she said, taking her regular seat. "Carry on."

As he had the last time, Hoburn took out his notebook. "How many of your patients are you having sex with?"

The shock of the question struck her dumb. She had

hoped that their specific questions might give her clues as to their line of enquiry. "It's a fundamental misunderstanding of sexual therapy that the therapists are intimate with their patients," she managed to say while maintaining her professional exterior, for which she was very proud of herself.

"I'm not talking about others in your line of work, I'm talking about you."

"Me? Why would you have reason to believe that I would be so inappropriate? I'd lose my license."

"We have more than a reason to believe it, we have witness testimony," he said. "Being honest with us now is your best course of action."

"I have never had sex with a patient," she asserted. "I would never do that. Your witness is lying."

"The eyewitness is dead."

"What?" The gravity of those words muddled their implication. "You're saying that Bobby… I never had sex with Bobby."

"No, but he caught you in the act, on the day he died… Why didn't you tell us that when we were here the first time?"

"Bobby… No—"

"He told Deshana what he saw, and she stated that your patient was angry at Bobby for interrupting the deed."

At least she didn't have to worry about anyone spreading lies. She relaxed and a smile began to form. Hoburn's eyes flared. "I wasn't having sex with a patient. I was making out with my boyfriend. We hadn't got to the actual act yet. Yes, Bobby walked in on it, but it was the end of the day, and we thought we were alone. I was off duty."

"Your boyfriend?"

"He's in the next room if you want to talk to him."

"Warner?" She nodded. "The stories of you and him are true?"

"That we're in an intimate relationship? Yes."

Hoburn closed his notebook and whispered something to his colleague who got up and left the room.

Hmm, ominous.

Hoburn met her eye. "You should be careful with

him."

"Who?" she asked.

"Warner. He's not the good guy he makes himself out to be."

"You came here to accuse me of breaking ethical rules, and now you're warning me off the man I'm seeing?"

"I don't know what he's told you about why he left the department."

"He hasn't told me anything."

"And that doesn't raise any red flags for you?"

Now that he pointed it out, it did. He'd been honest about his family and his ex-wife. He'd even invited her into his parent's home. But he'd never spoken about his work in the police, other than to mention he'd done it, and that his work interfered in his marriage.

"He'll tell me in his own time."

"He killed a woman," Hoburn said. "A woman under his protection."

She tried not to react to that news. Part of her training was to remain neutral despite the confessions of her patients, and she pulled on that training then more than ever.

"If that was true, he'd be in prison."

"He didn't pull the trigger, but he set her up for it," Hoburn said. "He set her up to die. He put her right where they wanted her to be and turned his back on her. It was jump or be pushed, that was why he left the PD."

Lyssa wanted to leap to Colt's defense. She couldn't believe that he'd ever do something so unbelievably callous. Except she had no other source of information to reference.

Hoburn tucked his pad away and left the couch. "Take care of yourself, Doctor Cutler, that's all I'm saying. You're an intelligent woman with a lot to lose. Don't sacrifice it for a man who hasn't been honest with you."

He left the office, and she remained in her seat. Hoburn didn't go out left to the front door, he turned right… in the direction of the waiting room. Colt was in there. She had questions of her own for him, but they would wait, they would have to.

TWENTY-SEVEN

COLT STAYED TO HAVE DINNER but didn't tell her what Hoburn said to him. Lyssa hadn't yet plucked up the courage to ask why he left the police, or if anything Hoburn said had any grain of truth.

In contrast, Colt wasted no time in plying her with questions. She spent more time talking to Colt about what Hoburn said than she'd spent talking to Hoburn himself.

They'd turned the pictures over to Chavez and Ronson when they arrived before dinner. The cops asked a million questions of their own. Her head was spinning.

As she cooked dinner, Colt went through the whole house, looking for any hint of further surveillance equipment. Although he didn't find anything, he did lecture her about safety throughout the meal.

He did also ask her to stay at his apartment. She was grateful that he'd asked, as opposed to ordering her, but had known he'd push the issue until he got his way. A command might have been quicker. While this was going on, she wouldn't fight living with him. Knowing that this person was watching gave her the creeps. Hard, irrefutable evidence had been dropped through her door. The man was everywhere, she just couldn't figure out how.

Packing a bag with her essentials, she was surprised when Blaser appeared in her house. Colt had apparently filled him in, and the twins went about packing more of her possessions. They seemed determined to take anything and everything that might be remotely important or necessary. As though she'd never come back to the house at all.

When they found this guy, she'd be back. It was her home, a few days at Colt's place wouldn't change that.

Work wasn't such an easy fix. Until the hospital could provide her with a workspace, seeing clients wouldn't be possible. The hospital had a floor of office space they rented to private practitioners. It shouldn't be too hard to get space there because she already had privileges.

So she bundled up patient notes and the basics needed for work, then climbed into Blaser's car. While she unpacked into Colt's closet, the brothers talked in the kitchen. Then Colt came through and told her that they were going out.

Not her and him, him and Blaser.

He'd gone through the safety spiel again, made sure she had her pepper spray, and told her that Gus was home if she needed reassurance or protection. Without giving her a chance to respond, he thoroughly kissed her on promise of following through when he came home.

Midnight came and went, so she'd gone to bed. Despite her worry, she didn't want to call and pester him. Still, sleep didn't want to come; she tossed and turned for a while.

Eventually, she drifted off.

A loud bang woke her sometime later, forcing her to sit bolt upright. The shuffle of feet and mumbling got her out of bed. From the ruckus of people coming from the living room, something had happened, and the bang was most likely from the front door being thrown open.

"Lys!" Colt shouted. She grabbed a pair of panties to put on. "Lys!"

The urgent tone of his voice set a fire under her.

"I'm coming!" she replied, donning a tee-shirt before rushing out to see the emergency.

Hope remained that she was jumping to conclusions.

That was dashed when she got to the living room.

Colt and Ruger maneuvered a pale Blaser to the couch to lay him down. She hurried over, evaluating the patient. A reddened rag was being pushed against his shoulder by Colt.

Tying her hair back with the band on her wrist she went to Blaser's side and fell to her knees to peel back the rag slightly to assess the injury. "He was shot," Ruger said.

"I see that," she said, checking for an exit wound. Damnit, no exit. "Ruger, I need towels and water. Get him a blanket and some water to drink. Colt, my medical bag is under the bed." The brothers ran off to complete their tasks. "Blaser, honey, you're okay. We're going to look after you. Can you wiggle your fingers for me?"

When Colt came back with the bag, the first thing she did was retrieve her scissors to cut off Blaser's shirt.

"If you wanted me naked, all you had to do was say," Blaser croaked as she went through her process of checking his vitals, nerves, and joints.

"I like my men vulnerable," she said, pulling supplies from the bag. "That way they can't run off."

"I'm going nowhere," Blaser said, his eyes closed.

"Stay awake," she said, patting his cheek. "Colt, keep talking to him. Ruger! Blanket!"

"I'm not going to pass out," Blaser said. "It just hurts like a sonofabitch."

"And it will," Lyssa said, cleaning out the wound, happy to see that most of the bleeding had stopped.

The next half hour was tense. The brothers did their best to keep Blaser talking and distracted while she removed the bullet, cleaned out the wound and sewed it up. While dressing it, she avoided looking at Colt at the head of the couch. She had a feeling he knew it too.

A doctor treated the patient in front of them. Blaser was hurt, she had to deal with the injury. Asking why they didn't take him to an emergency room wouldn't change the fact they hadn't. There was no time for talking while there was a chance of someone bleeding out. When she had the time to pause and think, she was proud of herself and her training for kicking in. She hadn't dealt with a trauma since her residency.

"Take him through to the bedroom," Lyssa said when she was finished. "He should sleep for a while."

"I can go downstairs to my own bed," Blaser said, groaning as he sat up. "I don't need to stay here."

Some color had returned to his cheeks, though she'd be worried about shock for the rest of the night. "I want to check on you," Lyssa said. "So if you're going downstairs, I'm coming with you." She packed up her supplies, then retrieved her prescription pad to begin writing. "Ruger, you can help me downstairs with Blaser. Colt, you need to find a pharmacy and get these things."

Tearing off the slip, she handed it over.

"An all-night pharmacy," Colt said.

Ruger was quick to offer. "I can do that."

"No." Lyssa got between the brothers under the guise of supporting Blaser. "I want Colt to do it. He'll get it right."

She continued with Blaser, who wasn't paying any attention to what else was going on. They were at the top of the stairs before Ruger caught up to them. He got Blaser downstairs without further injury and unlocked his brother's door to help him inside.

Together, she and Ruger took Blaser to his bedroom. She returned to the living room, leaving them alone so Ruger could help his brother get comfortable.

Vehicle lights came on and an engine started. Through the living room blinds she watched the light retreat until the sound of the engine faded to nothing.

"It wasn't his fault," Ruger said. She spun around to see him only a couple of feet away. "*I* said we should bring Blaser to you, he didn't want to."

"I don't know what you're talking about," she said, going into the kitchen to find something to drink.

"You're pissed that we brought a gunshot victim to you in the middle of the night and you're wondering what happened."

"No, I'm not," she said, slamming the fridge door. "I'm pissed that I thought I was falling in love with a man I clearly know nothing about."

"You know him. You two have been inseparable."

"No," she said, shaking her head. "It's been all about me because of this stupid stalker situation and my work at Risqué. I don't know anything about him, that's been made abundantly clear to me tonight."

"Colt didn't shoot anyone if that's what you think. We weren't doing anything illegal."

"So why not take Blaser to a hospital?"

"Because we were where we shouldn't have been," Ruger said, collecting a couple of beers from the fridge. "And we're not in the habit of getting others arrested."

Though he gave her one of the bottles, she ignored it. "Were you doing something illegal?"

He took a long drink, then lowered the beer. "No," he said.

"Is this the stalker? Was Blaser shot because—"

"No, this isn't that."

"So what is it?"

"I'll let Colt explain when he gets back," Ruger said, passing her to go sit on the couch.

"Hoburn told me that Colt killed someone and that's why he left the police."

"Did he now?" Ruger said. "My brother will be thrilled to hear that his former colleagues are interfering in his life."

Putting the beer on the kitchen counter, without drinking a drop, she hurried across to sit next to him on the couch. "Tell me if it's true, Ruger. Please."

"It depends on who you ask," Ruger said, examining the drink in his hand. "If you ask Colt then he'll tell you yes, which is the only reason I'm telling you anything. He'll crucify himself, but it wasn't like that. He didn't kill Emma; he was watching out for her. She was under his protection. She was convinced that her ex-pimp was watching her, that he was obsessed with her. Turns out, she was right. Colt was the only one to believe her. The department gave up on his crazy theories and all but pulled out of the case. Colt was the only cop left on it and his lieutenant only allowed that to shut him up."

"But she died?"

"Yeah," Ruger said. "Colt got a lead on the ex-pimp's location. He went to check it out, maybe talk to him if he was there, scare him a little bit."

"But?"

"Emma followed him," Ruger said. "Can you believe it? The stalkee becomes the stalker. I'm not convinced that the girl didn't have a thing for Colt, or the ex-pimp, or someone. She wasn't all put together if you ask me. But she followed Colt, he didn't know it, and she ended up dead."

"And that's why he quit?"

Ruger was drinking again, he kicked off his boots and put his feet up on Blaser's coffee table. "He didn't leave because she died, I mean yeah, it fucked him up, there's no doubt about that. But that wasn't the reason."

"What was the reason?"

"The PD had the resources to protect her. With backup or others on the case, they could've covered Emma or gone to that meeting for him… He got fed up playing by the rules because, as far as he was concerned, the rules and regulations got people killed. He's not wrong."

"He was bogged down by the rules and so wanted to do things his own way?"

"I guess that you could say that."

"And there was no one in the department he could rely on?" she asked, wondering if it was connected to what she'd heard about his partner.

"He was kind of working on his own then, he had trust issues, and didn't have a partner."

"Because his partner was sleeping with Karri?"

"You're a good detective," Ruger said, slurping from the bottle.

"So he went into business on his own." Contemplating this, she rested back on the couch. "He left because he thought he could do better on his own. But I don't get it. Why would Hoburn hate him now?"

"There was animosity before Emma's death, all connected to that case. Some thought Colt abandoned his post, or that it wouldn't have happened if he'd just given up on Emma like everyone else. Colt pulled in favors and tried to convince others of the danger that Emma was in. No one cared, at least they didn't listen. Then when she died, Colt made no bones about it, they'd let Emma down. Her blood was on the hands of everyone who refused to hear her out, just because of who she was."

"Who was she?"

"An ex-hooker," he said. "Well, I guess she was a current hooker, but she was freelance, trying to build herself up a nest egg to get to college and better herself."

"They don't like to look in the mirror, I guess," Lyssa said. "They thought less of her because of her position in society. But a death, any death, is still tough to come to terms with, especially if you have any feeling of responsibility yourself."

"Colt has gotten over it. In a way, his work since then has made up for previous shortcomings. He's mended some relationships in the department and still has favors that he can call in. He feels more useful now that he's not constrained by chain of command."

"But Emma is still dead."

"Yes, she is," Ruger said. "Colt won't let that happen again. He's more careful now, and more aware of what can go wrong. You're lucky, not just because he's on your case, but because he cares about you. Colt won't let anything happen to you."

"Tonight, when he left me, I didn't think he was going to do anything dangerous. What happens if, the next time, he's shot?"

"Then we'll bring him to you," Ruger said, smiling in an attempt to encourage hers. "Trust me, this doesn't happen a lot and it's great that you're a part of the team now. Seriously, Lys, thanks for helping Blaser. When he comes round, tomorrow, he'll be grateful too."

"I just did my job."

Colt was probably cursing himself for getting her involved, and she'd dismissed him like he had fault.

The details of what had happened to Blaser, and why it had happened, were still a blank. She wanted to know if Colt planned to put himself in more danger for his brother, or anyone else. They needed to have a conversation. When he got back. Questions would be asked, and she had to confess what Hoburn told her.

After speaking to Ruger, she wished she'd just been upfront with Colt as soon as Hoburn left.

They had to be open with each other. Their relationship would never work otherwise. Her current situation shouldn't prevent him from telling her the truth about his past, about where he came from. Everyone had skeletons in their closet, and she'd embrace him despite those skeletons.

Until she knew all of him, she couldn't trust their connection, or their feelings for each other. She had to make him understand that it was okay to be vulnerable, and that she would never judge him. If they couldn't build real trust, they may as well call it quits. How sincere could their love be without honesty?

RUGER SLEPT ON THE FLOOR, which gave her the couch. At some point, Colt must have come back, because she found him sleeping on the floor the following morning. Blaser's vitals were strong, and his wound would heal, although it would take time. He grumped when she woke him to check it was possible, so she let him go back to sleep.

Her clothes were upstairs, but she grabbed a quick shower and wrapped herself in a towel. As soon as she started to brew coffee, the men sleeping on the floor began to stir. She poured everyone a mug and laid out breakfast on the table.

"Ah, she's an angel," Ruger said, climbing to his feet and coming over to gulp down the scorching brew.

"I have to go upstairs and get changed," she said to Colt when he too picked up his coffee. "I've checked on Blaser and he's okay. You could take his coffee to him and give him some of the antibiotics and painkillers you brought in last night."

"Okay," he said, putting the cup down and starting

toward the back bedroom.

"You could kiss me good morning first," she said.

The big talk would have to wait, as they had an audience, and there were more pressing matters. But she wanted him to know there was no residual anger, only questions. His head tilted and a smile flirted on his lips when he came back to her. Ruger turned his back with a theatrical groan as she was swept into Colt's arms.

"Good morning," he said, and said hello in the best way there was: without words. "Do you want me to get your clothes?"

She shook her head. "No one will be around at this time, and they won't care."

"You obviously haven't met many of the neighbors," Ruger said.

"I'll be fine," she said and left the men to go upstairs and change.

When she got back downstairs dressed and with clothes for her guy, Ruger was nowhere in sight and Colt was coming out of the shower.

Dumping his clothes on the back of the couch, she inhaled. "Was this because of me?" she asked, wanting a definitive answer.

She wasn't convinced Ruger was forthcoming about the shooting.

"No," he said, tucking in his towel. "Wrong place, wrong time."

"I'm trusting you, Colt," she said. "I know about Emma."

His expression became gradually more serious. "Hoburn?"

"Yes, and Ruger gave me the details this morning. Why didn't you tell me?"

"We'd have gotten there eventually," he said. "But cracking your case, getting this guy off your tail, that's what we need to focus on."

"What about us? Aren't we important? Are we building a relationship or am I just a quick fumble? A distraction while you're dealing with other things?"

Coming over, he wrapped his arms around her. "That case still haunts me, Lys. It changed my life and… telling you what happened, trying to explain it when I can't come to terms with it myself… I didn't want it to change things between us."

"Things *are* going to change between us. You have to realize that, but we should grow closer with the more we learn about each other, not use our histories to wedge ourselves apart."

"It's easy for you to predict these things," he said. "You have an education that guides you in the appropriate way to act. I don't have that. It's been a long time since I've trusted a woman as much as I trust you."

"I'm grateful for that, but relationships take work. There's no great power looking down on us ensuring that we don't make mistakes. Those mistakes are what make our relationship unique. We make them because of who we are and the experiences we've had."

The weight of his expression cleared. Something struck him and he silently mouthed her words. "What an idiot."

"Excuse me?"

"Not you," he said, kissing her with full tongue force. "You're a fucking genius, Miss Lys. I'm the idiot."

He tossed his towel aside to yank on the clothes she'd brought him. "There's no need to dress so quickly," she said, sad to see his toned, naked physique disappear from her view so abruptly.

"I need to go out," he said. "I have to check something. Will you be okay with Blaser until Ruger gets back from his place?"

"Yes," she said, watching him gather his things. "What's going on?"

"I might have cracked it," he said, going towards the door then coming back to kiss her. "Actually, you might have cracked it."

She caught his wrist. "Clue me in."

"When I get back. I don't want to say anything until I've checked it out," he said, kissing her again. "You're a fucking genius."

He muttered the words again and managed to get out of the door this time without coming back. Lyssa was left clueless, but he'd had an epiphany. Who was she to stand in the way of that?

TWENTY-EIGHT

BLASER WAS A TERRIBLE PATIENT. He didn't listen, wouldn't follow instructions, and believed he knew better. Pigheaded, that's what he was.

To Ruger's credit, he backed Lyssa in every way, but it didn't matter. Blaser kept on insisting he was going to the club. On the condition that she and Ruger go too, they compromised. With the antibiotics and painkillers, she hoped he'd tire quickly. At the first sign of lethargy, they could steal him back to his apartment for more rest… but she wouldn't hold her breath.

Leaving a message for Colt—who hadn't appeared or been in touch all day—the trio went to the club. Blaser was immediately set upon by the girls who fawned over him and his arm, which Lyssa had put in a sling with hopes it would reduce movement. Although she had closed the wound, it could tear if he overexerted himself. For some reason, Blaser wasn't as worried about that or further injury. His lack of concern made her wonder if this was all in a day's work for him. Maybe it was a regular deal.

Ruger took over the role of chief bartender, frustrating the hell out of his brother. The Littlest Warner was more interested in showing off with the cocktail shaker than just getting on with the job. Watching them spar was fun, though having Colt in the mix would've been better, for her own peace of mind.

Without pressures of waitressing, she observed the comings and goings, and began to take notes. After telling Crystal the whole truth, things got more interesting. By the end of the night, all the girls were crowded around sharing anecdotes of their own experiences on the exotic dancing circuit. Each of the stories, and the women, were fascinating. She promised to keep returning until she'd taken note of all the tales.

Wondering if Colt would let her use his office to compile her notes, and maybe interview some of the girls, her mind turned to concern. Where was he? What was he doing? He'd been gone all day.

"He'll be fine," Blaser said, taking a seat on a stool beside her.

With the night winding down, he'd let Ruger have free rein and given up trying to control his younger brother.

"What are you talking about?" she asked. "Ruger has done really well tonight."

"Ruger's not who you're thinking about."

"No… he's not," she admitted, unable to lie. "He's been gone all day."

"He knows what he's doing."

"If this goes wrong, if something happens to me, like it did with Emma… he'll never forgive himself."

"He told you about that?"

"Under duress," she said. "I heard it elsewhere and Ruger filled in the blanks, but Colt knows that I know. I don't want him to carry guilt if anything happens to me, except… look at the way he's thrown himself into this, he's giving it everything and… it might not be enough."

"If Colt had gotten to do things his way with Emma, she would still be alive. Now that he does things his own way, his odds have gone up, which is great news for you."

"I trust him," she said, turning to look Blaser square in the eye. "But if something happens…"

Blaser slid a hand under hers. "We'll look after him,

Lys. He's a pain in the ass, Mr. High and Fucking Mighty, but he's family… just like you."

"Colt just called," Ruger said, coming over. "He wants you to stay at his place tonight, he said he'll come and see you at work tomorrow."

She shouldn't be surprised that while talking about her concern he got in touch, but she was. "How does he do it?"

Ruger shrugged. "He's freaky that way."

Blaser laughed, then winced. "No woman can ever claim he doesn't pay attention to them," he said, clenching his teeth in an attempt to hide his discomfort.

"Come on," she said, still with a hold of his hand. "I'm taking you home. Ruger can close up here."

"I'm being ditched?" Ruger called after them as they began to leave.

"Come to Blaser's when you're done," she called back. "I'll be on his couch tonight."

"You got it, sis."

Ruger wanted a reaction. It was nice to be a part of his ribbing, because it did make her a part of the family. He made fun of his brothers all the time. Being included brought her closer to the men important to her lover.

During the day at Blaser's, she'd called the hospital and arranged for workspace. She'd missed enough patient time, so suspended her adopted rule of not seeing patients on the last day of the working week. She'd called up the canceled patients, in the order that she'd missed them, and offered appointments in her new office at the hospital.

Many of her patients had questions. Being circumspect in her answers wasn't easy. Finding out that your therapist had lost a patient to murder was bad enough. Finding out the patient had been murdered because of his connection to her would be worse.

Were her patients safe from her stalker or was she putting them in danger?

THE DAY GOT OFF TO A FLYING START. Her new

workspace was perfect. Well, as would be expected, it wasn't as comfortable as her home office. Although there was nothing fancy, it had everything she needed, and had the added bonus of being in a busy building. People mixing together hopefully made it harder for her stalker to pick out her patients if he was indeed watching.

A desk and chair were provided for her, with a couch and an armchair for patient sessions. Her present client, Lee Zucker, hadn't spent much time on the couch during their session. Given the revelations he'd experienced in his own life over the last forty-eight hours, that was understandable.

"She let me think that I had a problem," he declared, pacing up and down in front of the window. "She let me think that I was out of line!"

"Calm down, Lee. I know this is a shock."

"I thought I was being too demanding, that my libido was somehow shot! I actually thought I might be sick!"

"Now we can't discount that your situation remains as it always was. It may just be that your wife—"

"She's having an affair!" He stopped pacing then came around to flop onto the couch. "She's having an affair. She's fucking around with another dude, no wonder she never wanted it from me!"

"I know," Lyssa said, wishing she could offer some comfort other than platitudes. "What she has done is terrible. It will take time to process it. You have to decide where you want to go from here. Is she still seeing her lover?"

He groaned. "Do you have to use that word?"

"I'm sorry. We need to establish whether you want to move forward and if she wants the same thing. I could offer you a session together if you think that would help."

"Do you think it would?" he asked. "You're really great but you can't... you know..."

"Erase the past? No, there are limits to even my powers. Did you tell Harriet why you come here? There was a time she believed you were here due to stress at work."

"I haven't told her everything, but... maybe I could talk to her and ask if she'd come along."

"That could be beneficial for you both. It would be

interesting to find out why she sought gratification elsewhere. Perhaps there are issues we could work on together. We may find a solution suitable for both of you.”

“You must have a perfect life,” he said. “Your relationships must be totally smooth sailing.”

“Just perfect,” she said, trying not to think about the state of her life. Movement in the small glass panel in the office door drew her eye. To her horror, the face filling the space was that of her ex-husband. “Oh my God.”

She hadn’t meant to speak aloud but the words tumbled out.

Following her shock, Lee turned to look over his shoulder at the window. “Who is that?”

“My ex-husband, believe it or not,” she said, with a frozen faux smile.

“Ex?” he asked, arching a brow.

“Maybe not as perfect as you’d think,” she said.

“And he gets to just walk in on sessions and kick out your patients?”

“I’m sorry for the intrusion,” she said. “But we are at the end of our time anyway. Let’s schedule your next session.”

Timing had always been an issue for Archie. Despite being at the end of her session, she left her ex in the hallway and took her time bidding Lee farewell. When Lee opened the door, Archie almost bowled him over when he ran in and closed the door.

“How long does it take to get rid of a patient?” Archie demanded.

“Good afternoon to you too, dearest,” Lyssa said, sinking into her desk chair to unlock her computer. “Some people may think it rude to randomly show up without an appointment. Do you need a consult?”

“This isn’t medical, Lyssa. I’m in trouble! Serious trouble!”

“Trouble?” she said, dropping the repartee. “What kind of trouble?”

“She kicked me out,” he said, sitting on her couch without invitation.

Archie was such a handsome guy. His salt and pepper

hair, and defined features gave him that sophisticated, desirable air, in the older man sort of way. Seeing him in distress didn't make her feel good. There had been a time when they'd been happy. Just because they wanted different lives didn't mean she wished bad things for him.

"What happened?" she asked. Abandoning her computer, she came around to settle in the armchair again.

At first, he said nothing, and various possibilities ran through her mind. When his gaze shifted, she could tell he was about to say something he was ashamed of, or at least ashamed to admit.

"Tax evasion."

"Oh, Archie," she said like a parent disappointed in a child and lifted her hands to drop them on the arms of her chair. "How could you be so stupid?"

"It snowballed," he said, making excuses. "The accountant said he could get me into this scheme, and I'd pay less tax."

"I don't want to know the details," she said, folding her arms, making no secret of her disapproval. "I don't want to be subpoenaed."

"Don't say that. Oh, God, Lys, what am I going to do?"

She was no tax accountant or lawyer, so answering from either of those perspectives was outside her skillset.

Instead, she went to her comfort zone. "This is… the receptionist you were living with who kicked you out?"

"She's a nursing administrator."

Lyssa wasn't even sure what that was. "Okay, and she's unhappy? She didn't know about the scheme?" He shook his head. "It's understandable that she's upset."

"Maybe, but she kicked me out of my own damn house!"

"You would rather she left?"

"No. She should stand by me; she should support me."

"Did you tell her you felt that way?"

"All she did was shout," Archie said. "Shout and shout… it's not my fault the assets have been frozen."

Her disapproval grew. "Everything?"

"Yeah," he grumbled. "So don't expect any alimony checks for a while."

She laughed. "That's not my primary concern."

"How can you laugh? That's very unprofessional!"

The office door opened.

Colt strolled in, only to stop short when he registered there was someone on the couch. "I heard you had an opening," he said, frowning at her "*patient.*"

That look in his eye… Colt recognized exactly who was on her couch.

"I did," Lyssa said. "But it was unceremoniously filled."

"The standard of your professionalism has slipped significantly," Archie said.

"Are you one to judge me?" she asked. Colt turned as if to go, but she stood up. "No, don't go. Close the door."

Colt did as told.

"We were talking," Archie said to her.

"Colt Warner, this is Archie Cutler."

"I know," Colt said, coming to her side.

She smiled. "I know that you know."

"Do you introduce all of your patients to random people?" Archie asked.

Being identified as a random person must have riled Colt because he sat in her armchair and yanked her down into his lap.

"Colt isn't a random person."

"Apparently not," Archie said. "You're fraternizing with patients?"

"Colt is my partner, he's my boyfriend."

"Really?" Archie said, examining her lover. "Your type has changed considerably."

"My previous type didn't work out in my favor," she said. "I reassessed my needs."

"Still, I didn't presume you to be the type to prioritize beauty over brains."

"Luckily, Colt has both," she said, arranging herself around Colt to leave no illusion as to their intimacy.

"He's sort of… brawny for you, is he not?" Archie said, as though Colt wasn't even there.

"Are you afraid he'll beat you up?" Lyssa asked. "He's actually very gentle."

"Providing you don't step out of line," Colt said.

"And what would be out of line?" Archie asked.

"Appearing at my girlfriend's place of employment without an appointment."

"Keeps a tight leash on you, does he?" her ex asked.

"Archie's having a problem," Lyssa said to Colt. "He came here to seek advice."

"Don't tell him my private affairs," Archie stated. "We have confidentiality."

She shook her head. "We don't. You're not a patient, I can't treat you and you don't get spousal confidentiality anymore either."

"I came here because I trust you," Archie said.

"You need something from me. I haven't heard from you in two years. I doubt you came to me for advice on your relationship issue with the receptionist."

"He's seeing a receptionist?" Colt asked. "Beauty over brains?"

"Youth and bust size over intelligent conversation," Lyssa explained. "Archie doesn't need a woman showing him up, so he likes them to be lacking in smarts."

"That why you got rid of him?" Colt asked her, then zeroed in on Archie. "It's hot as hell when she disagrees with me. I guess you've just got to know how to put her in her place."

"You do not put me in my place."

"Want me to prove it?" Colt murmured.

"When Archie's gone," she stage whispered. "I wouldn't want you to embarrass him."

"Do you have no compassion?" Archie asked. "This is not a time to be glib. I am in serious need."

"In a precarious position that you put yourself in," she said. "I have no compassion for those who do wrong and then expect to be pitied. You have, or at least had, more money than you knew what to do with, there is no excuse for your actions."

"You never used to be this judgmental," Archie grumped.

"Colt has friends in law enforcement. Maybe if you explained your predicament to him, he could see what he could find out about the state of the investigation."

"I think not!"

"Are you sure? His contacts go pretty high up," she said, without a clue as to how far his contacts extended.

"I have a team of attorneys on my case. They are working to disprove these ridiculous claims as we speak."

"What are we talking about?" Colt muttered to her. "Domestic abuse? Tax fraud? Kiddie fiddling?"

"I beg your pardon!" Archie spat.

"Tax evasion," she replied.

"Lyssa!"

The office door opened again, and Suzette rushed in. She came up short after identifying the occupants in the room.

"I feel like I should take a picture," Suzette said, her attention darting back and forth between the men. "The past meets the present. Seeing them side by side like this is… unnerving."

"How do you think she feels?" Colt asked. "What do you want?"

Lyssa was surprised that he asked the question before she had a chance to speak. "Are you okay, Suze?"

"I heard that you were on the complex and I wanted to… I thought that we could talk."

"She's busy," Colt said.

"What is wrong with you?" Lyssa whispered at him.

"There's a long line of people who want your attention right now, Miss. Lys," he said.

"Do you have something that you need to tell me?" she asked.

He'd been MIA for more than twenty-four hours. She was eager to find out where he'd been and what was going on. If there were any important, or urgent, updates, she figured he'd have been in touch in real time. Maybe her assumption was wrong.

"No," he said, still focusing on Archie who was staring at Suzette.

He'd just lied to her. Somehow, she knew it, but knowing him, trusting him, he'd have a good reason for the deception.

"How have you been Suzette?" Archie asked. "I heard that you are betrothed."

"Where did you hear that?" Suzette asked. "Have you signed up to the hospital gossip circuit? I thought you left that when you went uptown to your fancy building."

"I still hear things," Archie said. "He's a security technician or something."

"No, he's an IT manager," she said. "Not that it's any of your business."

"And I thought my invitation to the wedding just got lost in the mail."

"Unlikely," Suzette said.

Suzette's dislike of Archie had started early on in Lyssa's relationship with him. Colt didn't get along with her particularly well either. Should she take that as a bad omen? If Suzette's judgement of a man's character was accurate, perhaps that didn't bode well for the long-term prospects of her and Colt's relationship.

"I'm sorry," Lyssa said. "Archie is upsetting everyone today. I've already had a client upset that my ex interrupted a session. In my professional opinion, it's a case of misdirected anger."

"I think it's just his personality," Suzette said. "He has the kind of face that people take a dislike to."

"What time do you finish tonight?" Lyssa asked Suzette.

"Eight."

"Can you come over here around six?" Lyssa asked.

She would offer to go to Suzette, except Pete's office was on the same floor. Being caught together could cause her friend problems. Suzette nodded and glared at the men, then exited.

"What's going on with her?" Archie asked Lyssa, but she had no intention of answering the question.

"I can't help you, Archie," she said, extricating herself from Colt's lap. "I'm sorry about your troubles, I don't care about alimony, but thank you for coming to tell me."

"I didn't come here to tell you that," he said, leaping from the couch. "I need a place to stay."

"You came here because you need a bed? What's wrong with a hotel?"

"The bank accounts have been frozen," he said through his teeth, pained to admit such a humiliating truth in front of Colt, who didn't help matters by snickering.

"You can stay at my place," Lyssa said.

"What?" the men said in unison.

"As it happens, it's empty at the moment," she said, reaching for Colt's hand, causing him to rise to his feet. "I'm spending my nights with Colt anyway."

"You're living with him?"

She shrugged. "Unofficially."

"Or officially," Colt said, kissing the side of her neck.

Leaving his side, she went to her purse and retrieved a set of spare keys, then handed them over to Archie. "Clean up after yourself. You're responsible for all maintenance. And when I say out, you leave, no questions. I will be moving my practice back there as soon as I can."

"Why did you move it away?"

"That's none of your business," she said. "If you'll excuse us…" He lowered to kiss her cheek to spite Colt, his motivation was obvious. After that he did leave quietly, then she spun around. "Now what's your deal?"

"Why did you do that?" Colt asked. "Why give him a break?"

"It makes no difference to me if he's at my place. I've been at yours. And I'll feel better knowing that someone is there rather than the house sitting empty. If he's occupying it, it's less of a lure for burglars and such. In addition, I know Archie, if he's coming to me then he's exhausted his luck with his first wife, so he's desperate. When Archie's desperate, he'll do whatever he wants anyway."

"If you want me to deal with him—"

"I want you to tell me where you've been and why I

slept alone last night."

"I was installing security at your place last night," he said. "Hoping that if we monitored it, we might catch this guy in the act."

"That's very clever," she said, crossing to take both of his hands to guide him onto the couch with her. "Now you can keep an eye on Archie if you want to, and hopefully we'll be able to identify exactly who is behind this."

"I know who is behind it."

She had been about to lean in and kiss him, but the statement had her drawing back. "You know?" He nodded. "You know who the stalker is? You know who murdered Bobby?" Again, he nodded, and she waited. "Well?"

"Well, what?"

"Who is it?" she asked, exasperated.

"I'm not going to tell you that."

"You're not going to…" Lyssa hit his chest. "Don't be ridiculous, of course you're going to tell me."

"I'm not."

"Why not?" she asked, becoming shriller with every word.

"Because I don't want you to change your behavior."

"A few weeks ago, that was exactly what you wanted. Why the change of heart now?"

"I wanted you to change your behavior because I hoped we could draw him out. Things didn't go exactly to plan, but that doesn't matter because I know who it is now, so we move onto the next stage of the plan."

"Which is what?"

"Compiling an evidence portfolio. I know the identity of our stalker but have no evidence. I don't want the police to stomp in and spook our perp. I plan to get as much evidence as I can and then when I know the case is solid enough to bring the culprit in, I'll hand it over to the cops."

"And in the meantime, I just sit here, a walking target?"

Colt ran his fingers through her hair, but she withdrew. "Come on, you know I'm not going to let you get hurt."

"Accidents happen, you know."

"Yes, but if I tell the cops now and they start doing their thing, you could be in more danger. Right now, the cops don't have enough to do anything, they can't act. I'm going to give them what they need. I'm keeping Chavez in the loop unofficially."

"Why would you do that if you don't trust the cops?" she asked.

"Because if something happens to me—"

She gasped and flew off the couch to head for the desk. "This is crazy!"

"What are you doing?" he asked, watching her snatch her phone from her purse to scroll through the contacts.

Lyssa didn't answer him, she just dialed the phone and waited. When her call was answered, she put it on speakerphone and laid it on the desk. "I need you to kick the shit out of somebody for me."

"Okay," Ruger's voice came down the line. It sounded like his mouth was full of something… potato chips, maybe. "Text me the address. I'll finish eating and get over there."

He didn't ask questions. That Ruger trusted her so implicitly put a smile of satisfaction on her face that she aimed at his brother.

"Are you at Blaser's?" she asked.

"Yeah," Ruger said, swallowing his food, then taking a long, gulping drink. "Right where you left me this morning."

"I can send him to you."

"Wow, victims delivered," Ruger said. "You're a pro, sis. How roughed up do you want him?"

"Roughed up enough that he'll think twice about being an idiot, and maybe can't walk for a couple of days. But not roughed up enough that he'll be incapable of having sex with me."

A brief silence was followed by a laugh. "Colt? You want me to beat up my brother?"

"She's being dramatic," Colt said. Joining the conversation, he came to stand at the opposite side of the desk. "She doesn't like what I said."

"You wouldn't like it either, Ruger. He's being unreasonable."

"Okay, kids, if you can't play nice, I'll have to separate you. What's going on?"

"He knows who the stalker is and won't tell me. He plans to get himself killed just to prove a point."

"That's not what I said," Colt said. "But now that you've got the baby involved you've put him in danger too."

"I don't agree with any of this," Lyssa said, overwhelmed by the depth of her concern for Colt.

"No shit," Colt said, heading for the door. "I'm coming over, Ruge. Stay where you are."

He glared at her as he slammed out of the room. She sighed, hoping Ruger would talk some sense into him. It didn't matter if he was pissed, she'd rather Colt be pissed at her than he act without appropriate back up. He'd tried that once before and someone ended up dead.

TWENTY-NINE

ALTHOUGH THE BROTHERS didn't get in touch for the rest of the day, meaning she was eager to get home, Lyssa made a deliberate effort to focus on Suzette, who had just arrived at her office.

"I feel like we're drifting apart," Suzette said. "That our lives are becoming so different. We're losing each other."

"This is a difficult time, that's all."

They'd settled on her patient couch after Lyssa poured coffee, but the mugs remained on the end table untouched. Suzette had come to talk. It was obvious that she wanted to get her thoughts out, to put them into words, maybe before she lost her nerve. Though it was possible that she'd been thinking and analyzing to such a degree that there was a build-up of pressure. That, perhaps, forced the words out before they were fully formed coherent concepts.

"It's not just that," Suzette said, shaking her head, swiping tears from her cheeks. "I didn't realize how much I depended on you until I didn't have you anymore."

"I've neglected you this week," Lyssa said. "I'm sorry about that, but—"

"I didn't even know about Bobby, I had to hear it from someone else."

"Who did you hear about it from?"

"A detective came to ask about you. He said that you'd been one of the last people to see Bobby alive. It must have been so upsetting, it's just terrible, and I couldn't even be there for you."

"What did the detective want to know about me?"

"Just about your practice, and about Archie, and Colt, and—"

"Personal information," Lyssa said. "Did you tell him anything?"

"Some stuff," Suzette said. "I didn't think there was any harm, he's a cop, a detective."

A detective who had a bone to pick with Colt.

Covering her speculation as to Hoburn's motives, Lyssa sipped her coffee then took Suzette's hand. "How are things going with the wedding plans?"

"It's crazy, I thought I was busy before, but I have everything to confirm. We tried a bunch of cake samples a couple of nights ago."

"I thought you decided on a cake," Lyssa said.

"We did, but we decided we wanted something more special."

"It is going to be the most special day of your life."

"Your wedding was beautiful. I don't think we'll match that… Keith has asked about you. I think he's still holding out hope that you'll change your mind about him."

"That's sweet, but unlikely. Colt's coming to the wedding with me."

"Oh," Suzette said, taking her hand away. "He is?"

"Is that a problem?"

"I just… I didn't think he'd want to come. You know, it's going to be fancy, it won't be fun for him."

"I'll make sure he wears a tux and eats with a fork," Lyssa said, unsure as to where her friend's attitude came from. "You've never been a snob, Suzette, and Colt is a good guy, what's going on?"

"He's snooping into your life and that's… it's weird, don't you think? He's your boyfriend."

"He's also a professional in this field, he's going all

out to help me. He's dedicating all his time and resources to this. I'm grateful. Why don't you like him?"

"He made you beg," Suzette said, shedding her meekness.

"He didn't," Lyssa said. "We struck a deal on that first night. One of his requests was that I didn't tell anyone about it."

"Including me. Don't you think that it's weird he didn't want anyone to know? What possible reason could there be for that?"

"To do what he does, anonymity is necessary. It's as simple as that. I understand why he made the request."

"So you were fine with lying to me?" Suzette asked, her anger breaking out.

"It wasn't a comfortable experience," Lyssa said, putting her coffee cup down. "But it was necessary. I had to respect his wishes in order to get him to help me."

"Something about him doesn't sit right. What kind of person tries to isolate you from your friends? From your support network?"

"Isn't that what Pete is doing when he asks you not to talk to me?"

"That's a completely different thing," Suzette said, offended by the accusation. "You said so yourself, he's worried about my safety. He wants to look after me."

"And that's all Colt wants to do as well. He cares about me. Everything he's done has been in pursuit of the identity of the person who is targeting me."

"But he hasn't, has he?"

Her cellphone rang.

Lyssa got it from her purse on the floor by her feet. She read the screen and frowned. "Hello?"

"It's Crystal."

"Hey, is everything okay?" Lyssa asked.

With the name of the club on her screen, she'd expected Blaser to be the caller. Though her opinion remained that he shouldn't be at the club without medical supervision, she knew he didn't like to be tethered on a leash.

"There are flowers here for you," Crystal said.

Chills speckled through her; the hair on her neck stood up. "There? At the club?"

"They were at the back door," Crystal said. "There's a card."

"What does it say?"

"It says your name and then…"

"What?"

"It says, 'him zero, me one,' someone is keeping score," Crystal said. "What do you want me to do with them? Should I call Blaser and Colt? Is it a perv?"

"No," Lyssa said, though she didn't know that for sure. "Keep them there, I'm coming over."

"Okay. See you soon."

She hung up and grabbed her purse. "I'm sorry, Suzette, but I have to go."

"I'm coming with you," Suzette said, springing to her feet. "We need to have this conversation and I'm tired of us always running out on it."

"You have the rest of your shift to finish."

"I'll tell them I'm ill," Suzette said, retrieving her phone from her purse. "Our friendship is more important than work… and Pete's gone home already, he'll never know I left early."

"Okay," Lyssa said, nodding. "I have something to deal with and then we'll talk, Colt's office should be empty."

The women left the hospital together and got a cab to Risqué. She should phone Colt. If he'd been at the club already, he'd have called, not Crystal. If Blaser or Ruger were there, they'd have called her or Colt first.

The taxi driver talked the whole journey, not that she wanted to have a private conversation with Suzette in front of him, but it did limit what they said to each other.

Crystal was running the bar when they arrived. Though it was quiet, there were enough patrons that she ducked around to the far corner of the bar, which was sort of the family zone, and deliberately less illuminated for that reason.

When Crystal came to them, she curled her lip at Suzette. "What's she doing here?"

"She and I have things to talk about," Lyssa said. "Where are they?"

"Your locker."

"Thanks." Lyssa dived behind the bar to retrieve Colt's office key from the secret floor compartment. When she stood up again, Crystal was headed for Destiny, who had an order to fill. "Is Blase coming in later?" Lyssa called to Crystal who planted a grin on her and twisted to walk backward.

"He said he'd have to get his doctor's approval."

The women laughed. Lyssa rolled her eyes, and left the bar to cross to backstage, with Suzette glued to her heels.

"Why is that funny?" Suzette asked.

"I'm his doctor," Lyssa said. Right on cue, her phone rang, and her ex-boss's name came up on the screen. "I was just talking about you, boss."

"All good?"

"Obviously," she said. "How are you feeling?"

"I'm fucking fine and my brothers are driving me crazy. I need to get out of here. Where are you?"

He was giving her the respect of her profession and her new position in the family. She'd bailed him out, which had forged some kind of bond between them.

"If I tell you that," she said, "you might worry."

"I don't give a fuck if you're in danger," Blaser said, though she knew it wasn't true.

Colt shouted something in the background that she couldn't make out.

"I'm not in danger," she said. "I'm in your club."

"You are?" Blaser said, his voice decidedly lighter. "You're re-hired."

"I am?" she said and laughed. "What brought on the change of heart?"

"If you're there, I can be there," he said. "I'm on my way."

"I don't know if my boyfriend will approve of me working for you."

"Screw him," Blaser said. "I need you on the premises until I get back to normal. I'm short-staffed anyway. I promise no clean-up. You can leave early. My brother will approve of that."

"Okay. I have something to do, then I'll get changed."

"For real?" he asked, as though he hadn't expected her to agree.

"I loved working here," she admitted. "Even if I did suck at it."

"You provided entertainment," Blaser said. "I'll see you in ten minutes."

They hung up.

Lyssa pushed into the locker room and went over to unlock her locker. She never had returned her key to Blaser.

"You really fit in here now," Suzette said. "You've made friends with everyone."

"They're a welcoming bunch," Lyssa said, though she'd never struggled to make friends.

"What's it like working in a place like this? You just waitressed? You didn't have to take off your clothes?"

"There's a sample of the wardrobe back there," Lyssa said, retrieving the flowers from her locker. She tossed the stems into the trash after retrieving the card. Frowning at what it could mean, she took out her phone to text Colt asking if he was coming in with Blaser. He replied in the affirmative; she wasn't surprised. They had their own issues to discuss, and he was probably going stir crazy in the apartment as well.

Putting the note back in her locker, she sought out Suzette who was examining the rails of clothes with wide eyes.

"I'm going with the purple tonight," Lyssa said, pulling out a hanger. "Do you want to try the red?"

"What?"

"How long has it been since we did something crazy together? Call it one last fling before you're married and respectable?"

Suzette laughed. Her best friend was up for the challenge. "Your boss won't mind?"

"If he does, I'll just up his meds and he'll agree to anything," she said, and her smile became a laugh. "It's your call."

"One last fling," Suzette said, snatching an outfit.

Together, they went into the restroom to change while Lyssa gave Suzette the lowdown on the setup.

"I DON'T AGREE WITH THIS," Colt said, scrutinizing Lyssa as she tottered toward him on very high heels.

When close enough, she collapsed into his arms.

"Live a little," she said, planting her mouth on his. In their kiss, they both apologized, but she still snuggled her face in close to whisper in his ear. "I don't like it when we fight."

"Then start behaving yourself," he said and squeezed her ass, pulling her into the vee of his thighs, pressing her into the bulge of his arousal.

"Behave myself?" she said, wriggling against him. "You're the one being naughty."

"The pair of you behave yourselves," Blaser said, appearing at the other side of the bar. "Honestly, what is this place? A playground for the lot of you?" Something caught his eye and he frowned. "I don't recognize that one, when did I hire her?"

He nodded at Suzette giggling with customers and taking orders at a table a few feet from the bar.

"She's having some fun before she gets hitched."

Blaser shook his head. "I give up, really, I do. You all just do what the hell you want, don't you?"

"You don't have to pay her," Lyssa said. "What's wrong with people exploring life experiences especially when it doesn't cost you a dime?"

"And if she falls and breaks her neck or gets sexually assaulted? Who covers my attorney's fees, huh?"

"You're actually insured for stuff like that?" Lyssa asked, finding her feet and her doctor's face.

"This place is legit," Blaser said slowly, then looked at Colt. "What does she think we're running?"

"I told her that all of the girls were required to pick a financial backer and screw his brains out," Colt said. "Don't mess with what I've got going on."

"Really," Blaser said, unamused by his brother's joke.

"I give up on all of you."

"What's his problem?" Ruger asked when he came over to join them.

"He doesn't want to have sex with girls," Lyssa said.

"Who does he want to have sex with?" Ruger asked. "Mom might like a gay son; she needs help with the window dressings in the dining room."

"Come on, guys, this isn't fair," Colt said. "We shouldn't pick on the cripple… wait until he's back to full strength, then we can question his sexuality."

"It's about time someone else took a turn," Ruger said, zeroing in on Lyssa who projected as much innocence as she could muster.

"I still say that you need a session on my couch."

"When's my turn?" Blaser asked.

"You are welcome on my couch anytime," Lyssa said, proud to have someone confess such faith in her skills.

"I'm missing something, aren't I?" Blaser asked, eying them all.

"She's a sex therapist," Ruger said. "She wants to deconstruct every sexual experience you've ever had and somehow use it to prove you're a momma's boy who still secretly wets his bed."

"That is not what I do!" Lyssa asserted.

Only when Colt tightened his embrace did she click that she was the focus of this particular Warner ribbing. She growled at the smiling brothers on the other side of the bar.

Suzette came over waving a sheet of paper. "This is so much fun, and everyone is so nice."

Ruger took the paper and began to fill the order.

"Might have something to do with the fact you're carrying thimbles in your bra," Blaser said.

Everyone took note of Suzette's stiff nipples, but she just laughed. "It's cold in here."

"It's not actually," Blaser said.

"What would you know? You're doped up," Suzette said, sticking out her tongue. "You've probably got a fever from the infection Lys will let take up residence in your veins if you piss me off."

"Don't worry, they guarantee you better tips," Lyssa said, indicating her friend's chest. Colt smacked Lyssa's ass so hard that a frisson of pleasure nipped her center. She tilted her smile to her shoulder. "What?"

"You better not do that," he said.

His hands slid up over her breasts, causing her nipples to pebble and his eyebrows to rise.

"What do you expect them to do when you play with them?" she asked, to which everyone except Colt laughed. She nuzzled a kiss on his lips. "You're the only one I want, babe."

Turning in his arms, she pressed herself close and went right on kissing him until he hummed out. "I should discipline you more often."

Without taking her eyes, or her lips, from Colt, Lyssa called out. "Can I take a break, boss?"

"Why are you asking me?" Blaser asked. "Apparently, you're running the place now. Do what the hell you want."

Trying not to make too much fuss of her excitement, she linked her fingers between Colt's and led him through the club and up to his office. When they arrived, she closed the door and before he could speak, she gave him a hard shove, sending him onto his back on the couch. She climbed on top of him and began to unbutton his loose shirt.

"You know, I don't remember consenting to being molested by an employee," Colt said.

She kissed his neck and covered his lips with her fingertips, dismissing his tease. "Shh." The taste of his chest did something to her and the torrent that had begun downstairs grew to fever pitch. "This is different, I need this," she murmured, not requiring a response.

"Always happy to oblige," he said, skimming his hands through her hair to take it away from his torso.

His change of heart may have had something to do with her action of unfastening his jeans and directing her face into his groin. Squashing the head of his dick between her lips, she let vibrations build in her throat. The sensation would drill itself right through him and sure enough, he grunted, and his fingers curled.

"You like that, babe," she said, rolling her tongue

around his shaft.

"No problems to discuss on this couch," he said.

She lifted her eyes so they could share a smile.

Thundering footsteps outside the room grew louder, then there was commotion from beyond; shouting and something that sounded like screaming. She sat up, holding his manhood in both hands. The door burst open. Her scream dissolved to stunned shock when she saw the guns pointed in their direction.

"What the fuck?" Colt said, snatching her backwards and somehow putting his dick back in his pants in the same move.

"Police! Nobody move! Hands where we can see them!"

Colt's jeans were still undone, but they did as told and exchanged a look. From the gang of officers behind the two addressing them, it became obvious that the police were raiding Risqué. She didn't begin to know why, and that wasn't really the best moment to be asking questions.

THIRTY

THE WOMEN AND MEN were separated and divided into separate holding spaces for employees and patrons. The whole time she didn't utter an extraneous word. The melee of people and activity was enough to make even her head spin.

From what she overheard, they'd had a tip about drugs being run through the club. The police did their thing, but there were no drugs found on the premises. Obviously.

Except the bog of bureaucracy meant she had to be transported to the precinct in cuffs so that detectives from the appropriate department could decide if she had done anything wrong. Being found with Colt, in a compromising position, apparently made her criminal number one. They hadn't found anything else. They needed something. As humiliating as the experience was, she wasn't worried about the outcome. She'd done nothing wrong.

Colt apparently wasn't as confident, or at least wasn't as casual about it. When she next saw him, he was growling something fierce at the cops jeering around him when he shoved into the vice bullpen, where she was sitting. His focus zeroed in on her, and he crossed from one corner of the room to the other in record time.

"Lys," he said in a sigh. She lifted her hands when he

crouched to unlock the cuffs. "I'm so sorry."

"No harm done," she said. Yes, the cops had thought she was a hooker peddling her wares in Risqué. But she was more worried about what that kind of reputation could mean for Blaser than what it meant for her. "It was interesting to go through the experience that so many women do."

"They thought I paid you for sex," he said, throwing the cuffs and the keys onto the floor.

"I told them that your check bounced," she joked.

Colt wasn't in the mood. "This isn't funny. Let's get out of here."

This was kind of his area. Exactly his area. The vice guys kept a snickering eye on the couple until Colt took her outside. She wasn't worried. Getting herself in a tizzy about a misunderstanding would be stupid. She'd been spared the humiliation of jail cells and being booked, so, in the end, time was the only thing wasted.

Colt knew the guys in vice and had been brought in too. Probably as soon as they saw him, they started asking questions, especially knowing it was his brother's club. But she doubted they suspected him of a crime.

Ruger was on the sidewalk outside the precinct finishing off a hot dog when Colt brought her out. Where he got a hot dog at that time of the morning, she had no idea.

"Take her home," Colt said, putting her hand into Ruger's to try walking away.

Ruger dropped her hand and grabbed his brother. "No," he said, shaking his head. "No."

"Let go of me," Colt said, trying to throw his brother off.

Ruger snatched Colt's shirt and spun him around to slam him against the car so hard Lyssa jumped.

"You are not going over there," Ruger growled. "You're not going to do it, brother."

"Blaser's not going to do it, is he? He can't. His shoulder is still busted up."

"You'll get yourself fucking killed," Ruger shouted. "What the fuck happened last time we confronted them? We're not starting a gang war here, Colt. Keep your nose clean! Think!"

"This is personal," Colt said. "They can't fuck about—"

"Yes, they fucking can. This is what they want!"

Lyssa didn't know what they were talking about. Whatever it was, was about tonight and it wasn't about her stalker.

"This is related to Blaser," she said. "Isn't it? This is about why he was shot?"

"Stay out of this," Ruger snapped.

Colt shoved him. "Don't talk to her that way!"

"Find your fucking senses then!"

The men began to tussle. Emotions were running high, and she'd never heard either of them curse so much.

Though they both missed the most immediate concern.

"Hey!" she called out to no response.

Ruger swung for Colt who ducked and rushed him back against the wall. Wrestling out of his brother's hold, Ruger shoved him away. Before either could swing again, Lyssa put herself between them and planted a hand on each of their chests.

"We're standing outside a police precinct!" Shouting wasn't her default, but the men were still glaring at each other over her head, their hearts pumping against her palms. Adrenaline would be flooding them, affecting their decision-making. "Both of you get into the car. We're going back to Blaser's, we're going to get to the bottom of this." Neither moved. "So help me, God, the pair of you will do what you're told, or I'll march in there, declare both of you medically insane, and have you incarcerated in an institution!"

The threat worked. They drew their eyes from each other and skulked into the car. Ruger roared away from the curb. When Colt tried to take her hand in the backseat, she removed it from his reach. It wasn't that she was angry at him, as such, but fighting in the street with his brother was uncalled for and she'd tell him that when they were next alone.

Blaser was at his place, pacing, when they got back. He noticed straight away something was wrong. Something more than what had gone down at the club. Staying silent, he examined his brothers.

"You're not going to apologize to her?" Colt demanded of Blaser.

"He doesn't need to apologize to me," Lyssa said. "He didn't phone the tip into the police, and he didn't set you all up for tonight's raid. He also didn't seduce me in your office."

Colt spun on her. "Me seduce you?"

Lifting her hand, she dismissed him and seated herself at Blaser's kitchen table. "Is someone going to tell me what's going on?"

"No," Colt said.

"I'm a part of it," she said. "This is nothing to do with my stalker, is it? You said Blaser being shot wasn't either, so what is this?"

"It's Gary," Blaser said. "He thinks I'm screwing with his sister, and this is his idea of payback."

"Shooting you is his idea of payback?" she asked.

"Shooting me was an accident," Blaser said.

"You think," Ruger murmured and dropped onto the couch.

"Why didn't you call the cops?" she asked. "If you told them that he shot you—"

"Because he's still in love with Gary's little sister," Ruger said.

"It's not like that," Blaser snapped. "I've told you to stay out of it!"

"Except we're all in it," Colt said, maintaining his position beside the front door. "We're all in it, Blaser, and it has to stop."

"What does that mean?" Blaser asked.

"She can't be that good in the sack," Ruger said, folding his hands behind his head. "That's what Colt is saying, brother, end it. Finish it. Stop shtupping the baby sister."

"You think that will end it?" Blaser asked, his vehemence interesting.

"Do you love her?" Lyssa asked.

"No!"

"So it's just about sex," she said. "What is it about the sex that is addictive?"

"It's not addictive. We're not having sex," Blaser said. "I'm not talking about this with any of you."

Blaser tried to walk away, but Colt bounded across the room to get hold of him. "You damn well will talk about it, because you better explain it, or Lyssa's right: I'm going to the cops."

"Oh, typical you," Blaser said. "Run off to your old buddies, keep yourself on the straight and narrow. Screw the rest of us, right?"

"You're screwing us," Colt said. "It's about time we fought back. I'm not going to stand by doing nothing. It was one thing when Ruge and I were in it, but Lys is involved now. I'm not going to let you drag down the woman I love just because you want to get one up on the guy who sent you to prison."

No one reacted to Colt's declaration, not even him. Did he even know he'd made it? Except that wasn't the time to draw attention to his revelation of love, emotions were running too high. And the announcement that Blaser had spent time in jail was both startling and intriguing.

"This isn't about that," Blaser said.

"You keep saying that, but you can't make up for past mistakes by repeating them over and over again," Ruger said, much calmer than he had been on the street.

It seemed that so long as his family, the people he cared about, were safe, then he was a well of calm and control. It was only when those people were threatened that he was a different beast altogether.

Blaser didn't look ready to tell anyone anything. In fact, his whole demeanor suggested a cornered animal. The last thing she wanted him to do was strike out at his brothers. Reaching over, she took Blaser's hand. The action startled him so much that he tried to pull away, but she persisted and moved in close to him.

Offering a smile only made him frown. "You two stay here," she said to Ruger and Colt, then led Blaser to the bedroom.

Inside, she closed the door and sat him on the bed. "Colt will come through that door if he thinks—"

"Your barriers are making this situation worse," she said. Rounding the bed, she climbed onto it and crossed her legs. "All three of you are as bad as each other. Your brothers are frustrated because they want to help, and you won't let them."

"Colt is pissed that you were taken into the precinct," Blaser said. "He was on the phone screaming about murder while I was trying to clear things up at the club. We got Suzette in a cab home by the way."

"I knew you would take care of her. You're a good guy, Blaser. I don't know about your past, I'll admit that, but you're a good guy. It seems to me that you believe everyone will automatically think the worst of you. So you're already rejecting them, chastising them, before they have the chance to reject you."

"Does that psychobabble help anyone?"

"You're doing it right now," she said. "You're attacking me because you think I'm going to judge you, or reject you, if I get too close to the truth. Loving a woman isn't something to be ashamed of."

"No, Colt's sure not, that brother of mine just declared his intentions for you out there."

She tried to subdue a fluttering smile, but it snuck out. "I noticed that."

"He hasn't told you?" She shook her head. "Well, now you know."

"Yes, and I feel better for it. It's a good thing to be loved and that makes me happy. Have you told Gary's sister how you feel about her?"

"I don't love Bri," he said. "You've got it wrong."

"It is causing a lot of upset. Are you maintaining this relationship with her because of sex or is it spite that motivates you?"

"It's not like that either," Blaser said. "You should all just butt out of my business. I'm sorry that you got drawn into it. It won't happen again."

"What do you plan to do?" she asked when he got off

the bed.

"End it," he said.

"With Bri? It's too late to go around there and—"

"Not with her," he said. "She isn't causing this, Gary is. He's the one I have to stop."

"Wait," she said.

Blaser opened the door and stopped. The exit was blocked by Colt, who appeared like he'd just been about to open it. Ruger was right at his back.

"Listening in, were you?"

"No," Colt said, looking past his brother at her.

His solemnity made her shiver. "What?" she asked, closing in behind Blaser. "What is it?"

"I'm sorry," Colt said. "Hoburn just called, there's been another murder."

"Another murder?"

"I saw Hoburn at the precinct tonight," Colt said. "He spoke for you, for us. I was surprised he stepped up. I don't know why the change of heart, but he just called me to say…there's been a homicide."

"And you think it's something to do with me?" she asked. "Why would you think that?"

"The victim is Lee Zucker," Colt said. "He's another patient of yours."

"Lee," she said and staggered back. Blaser lunged out to snatch her, giving some stability. Good thing too, she might have collapsed at the shock. "He's picking off my patients. Why…? Why would…? I can't…"

"Take your time," Blaser said, guiding her back to the bed.

Colt was on her other side, Ruger with him.

Support was good, but… she couldn't form words or coherent thoughts. "Why would he do this?"

"I don't know," Colt said.

Then she remembered what he'd said in her office. "You know who it is," she said, with a burn of anger. "If you know… you could have stopped this. You let this happen!"

"This isn't his fault," Ruger said, jumping to his brother's defense when not too long ago they were trying to knock each other's teeth out.

"No," Colt said. "She's right. I should have watched him tonight instead of going to the club. I should have known this was a possibility."

He stalked out.

Lyssa followed after him. "Where are you going?"

"To talk to Hoburn," Colt said. "I'm telling him everything, and we're going to get this guy."

"You're going to have him arrested?" Lyssa asked.

"We're going to come up with a game plan," Colt said. "And one way or another, yeah, we're getting him off the streets."

Then without further explanation, or revealing the identity of his suspect, Colt disappeared from Blaser's apartment. She'd go the rest of the night without him and with nothing but unanswered questions.

***

RUGER RAN OFF AFTER COLT, which suited her. Someone had to make sure the big lug didn't hurt himself just because he was peeved. Though that didn't discount the possibility that Ruger would be the one to hurt him. For a while, she tried to get Blaser to talk, but he'd dismissed her each time with a grunt. Eventually, he retired to his bedroom after insisting she go to hers.

Given that Archie occupied her house, she took herself up to Colt's bed and tried to rest. She wanted to hear from Colt that they had arrested the person responsible for hurting two of her patients. But when the phone rang the distressed voice on the other end of the line wasn't Colt's.

"Suzie?" Lyssa asked, sitting up in bed.

Daylight penetrated the curtains, but she felt more ready to be going to bed rather than getting up.

Suzette sniffed on the other end of the line and began to sob. "He left me."

"What? What are you talking about?"

"Pete! He left me! He said he doesn't want to be with me!"

Lyssa gasped. "No!"

Her friend had lost the man she loved because that man didn't appreciate their friendship. Yes, there was an argument to be made that a man should accept his partner's friends. The opposing argument would be that those friends shouldn't endanger their friend's life and liberty.

"I'm coming over to your place. I need to talk. My whole life is a mess!"

"No, don't," Lyssa said. "I mean, don't go to mine, I'm not there. I'm at Colt's."

"Colt's?" Suzette said and sniffed. "Is he laughing at me?"

"Why would he laugh at you?" Lyssa asked. "He's not here, he's out with Ruger. Come over and we'll talk."

"Okay."

Lyssa gave Suzette the address and spoke to her friend until she got in a cab. It was obvious that Suzette didn't want to say goodbye. Either she didn't want to engage in small talk with the driver, or she didn't want to be alone. It was still early enough that the cab would miss the morning traffic, and late enough that it would also miss the nightlife breaking up.

The drive took about ten minutes, and the women didn't hang up until Lyssa opened the door to the dejected Suzette.

"Oh, honey," Lyssa said, hanging up to pull her friend into an embrace.

The hug opened Suzette's tear ducts again and the sobbing recommenced full force. Lyssa managed to maneuver her to the couch, holding her as she cried.

When it seemed to be lessening, Lyssa hazarded a question. "What happened?"

"We were arguing, all night, he wanted to know where I'd been, and what was going on. I told him. I told him everything."

"He wasn't happy?"

"To say the least," Suzette said, slumping back on the couch.

Lyssa measured her distress level. Her body was tense, her eyes bloodshot. It was obvious she hadn't slept. "You need to get some rest before we try to process this."

"Do you think that's it? That he's going to dump me for good?"

"What did he say?"

"That he'd been working late again and was looking forward to coming home to me, and… he was really scared when I wasn't there."

"He was worried for your safety, or did he suspect you of something?" Lyssa asked.

"I don't know, he just seemed really… hurt."

Taking both of her hands, Lyssa pulled Suzette off the couch. "Maybe when he calms down, the two of you can talk about this properly and come to some sort of compromise. He wouldn't have asked you to marry him if he didn't love you, would he?"

"Maybe I pushed him too far. I knew he wasn't wild about me hanging out with you, and he doesn't like the idea of Colt and his brothers."

"Why not?" Lyssa asked.

She shrugged. "I don't know. He just thinks they're no good."

"He doesn't know them," Lyssa said, her own defensive impulses kicked in. "He hasn't met any of them, why would he think—"

"Maybe it's the strip joint thing, I don't know."

From the way her friend sighed, it would be unfair of her to pressure Suzette into revealing more about her conversations with Pete. So she walked backward, bringing Suzette forward, and she didn't complain when they went into the bedroom.

"Why don't we lie down here and get some sleep?" Lyssa said, pulling back the comforter to settle Suzette down. "I didn't sleep well either. When we wake up, we'll talk it out. By that time Pete should have calmed down. You can call him and invite him over, or we can go out."

"You could help us," Suzette yawned. "Use your mad psyche skills to bring us together again."

Unwilling to raise false hope, Lyssa smiled and lay on the bed beside Suzette. "We'll see. Don't give up yet. Even if this is the end of your relationship with Pete, there are plenty of other men out there. Men who will appreciate everything about you. But I think that Pete will miss you and he'll realize that he overreacted. He loves you, Suze. He really does."

"I love him too."

Suzette settled quickly. Her friend didn't need much. All Suzette wanted was acceptance. It upset Lyssa that Pete, the man Suzette had chosen to trust, didn't offer that. But it wasn't her place to start shouting and pointing out all of Pete's flaws, Suzette already felt in the middle. So stroking her friend's hair, she closed her eyes telling herself that it would all work out in the end.

THIRTY-ONE

"WOW, WHAT A SHAME. Two babes in your bed and you missed the whole show."

Ruger's voice made Lyssa crack open one eye. Him and Colt stood at the end of the bed. The sun was shining and noises from outside, namely Blaser's garage, betrayed the world was awake and active.

"Hi," she whispered, focusing on Colt. "Are you tired?"

"I'm tired," Ruger said. "Are you going to invite me into that bed?"

"As long as you promise not to touch anything that doesn't belong to you," Lyssa said, shifting away from Suzette. She left her friend sleeping and crept out of bed, taking Colt's hand to lead him out of the bedroom.

"Stay here," Colt commanded Ruger, who sat on the edge of the bed to take off his boots.

Suzette would no doubt sleep for a while yet. She'd had a difficult night and a draining experience. If Ruger wanted to lie down and close his eyes for twenty minutes, she would never know any different. Ruger would never dream of violating a sleeping woman anyway. Lyssa had no worries where that was concerned.

The first thing that she did was take Colt to the couch, sit him down, and crawl into his lap. "You do look tired," she said, stroking his face and kissing him. "I was worried about you."

"I was with Hoburn."

"Did you tell him about your suspicions?"

"Yes," Colt said. "We spent the night trying to put the pieces together. He shared details about last night's crime scene, and it was disturbing."

"What was disturbing about it?" she asked. "It wasn't the same as Bobby? It wasn't a shot from the street?"

"No," Colt said. "The police are going to come over here later. Hoburn is talking to his superiors as we speak. All goes well, they'll try to persuade the DA to let them arrest the suspect."

"You don't sound convinced?"

"Last night's murder, Lee, was setup to look like a suicide. The perpetrator must have been in the room, in Lee's home. But the forensic team haven't turned up anything yet. No fibers or fingerprints. They think it happened fast."

"If there's no evidence that anyone else was there, what makes you think that it wasn't suicide?" she asked.

As his doctor, she would hope to recognize suicidal tendencies in Lee, and she hadn't. But he had just found out his wife was having an affair, and that could have upset him more than she realized.

"The body was moved," Colt said. "Posed to look like suicide, the signs are subtle, but they're there."

"His wife was having an affair," she said. "You'll need to talk to her lover."

"I can do that off the record, but I don't have the authority to take an official statement from anyone anymore. For now, we'll just have to hope that Hoburn can do his job."

"I think a part of me wants this to be a horrible coincidence," she confessed. "I hate the idea that Lee is gone, but if it was suicide then it wasn't my fault. At least it was my fault in a different way… my fault for not recognizing how distressed he was."

"None of this was your fault," he said, cupping her

face to bring their lips together. "Even if we're right and both patients were killed by the person obsessed with you, that doesn't make it your fault. You are a victim in this too. I don't want to hear you blaming yourself."

"Why would he hurt my patients?" she asked. "It makes no sense to me at all. I care about my patients, of course I do, but if he really wanted to hurt me then why doesn't he go after Suzette or you?"

"I don't know," Colt said. "I've been thinking about the note on the flowers he left at the club. I've got some security gear left from Pinch's supply. Most of it is set up at your house, but I can put a camera on the back door of Risqué later. Blaser has spoken about doing it before, but because it's just employees' back there, he didn't like the idea they'd think he was spying on them. But we're dealing with a different ballgame now."

"I don't want anyone else to get hurt," she said. "What do you think the note means?"

"He's talking about me," Colt said. "He somehow thinks that by taking out Bobby, he got one up on me."

"That doesn't make sense."

"Maybe not to us, but…," Colt said. "I think he's trying to clean up for you. He wants to show you how resourceful he is in fixing your problems."

"My problems? Bobby wasn't a problem for me."

"Not by your reckoning, but Hoburn and I talked it out. If he somehow knew about the fight in your office or knew that Bobby was shouting his mouth off about you sleeping with patients… Maybe the stalker was trying to cover for you. He thought he was taking care of a person who could cause problems for you."

"And what about Lee? He didn't accuse me of sleeping with patients."

"Not that we know of," Colt said. "We'll have to wait and find out what Hoburn turns up. If he finds out something about Lee, or about your connection to him, we might be enlightened as to why your stalker chose to fixate on him."

"Who is going to be next?" she asked, shaking her head. "I have to shut down my practice until this is over. It's too much of a risk to have contact with patients when anything they do or say about our sessions could result in them being murdered."

"I don't like to give in to bullies and I don't like to see you surrender," Colt said. "But it might be for the best. I don't have the resources to always watch and protect every one of your patients. Hoburn won't be able to convince his superiors of the need to do it. I know that for sure, trust me, I've been there."

"I know that you're doing all that you can," she said, finger combing his hair. "I'm happy that you're back home safely."

"I missed you as well," he said, kissing the edge of her lips.

Tucking her head under his chin, she let her body loosen and appreciated just being in his arms. "I love you too, by the way," she said, with a burgeoning smile.

"What?"

"You said you loved me last night and I'm telling you that I love you too." Lifting her head, she looked him in the eye. "I don't believe in withholding my emotions and want to be honest with you. I love you."

"I didn't realize that I'd said it."

"I'm glad that you did," she said.

Relaxing forward, their mouths met again. With a deep inhale his hands came up into her hair to cradle her head.

Given what was going on, it maybe wasn't right that she was so aroused by his proximity and by their declaration. But there was also a part of her that wanted to recognize the value in what they shared. Lee had his life stolen from him before he had the chance to fix his relationship with the woman that he loved. Bobby's life was taken from him before he could appreciate what it was to be loved and to accept that love without suspicion.

Sliding her hands under her tee-shirt, she retreated enough to pull it off over her head. The only thing she wore was her lace panties. The sight of her nakedness had Colt glancing over the back of the couch toward the bedroom.

"There's not a chance I'm letting him see this," Colt

said, encompassing her in his arms and flipping her onto her back on the couch to cover her form with his.

Their position gave him the advantage, which he proved by linking their fingers and pinning her hands by her head so he could lick and suckle at her chest. Want and need swirled inside her. She couldn't manage to keep the wanton pleasure from bubbling and sparking at the contact. Breathing out his name at the same time he tugged off his own tee-shirt, the warmth of his flesh landing on hers changed her exhale to a moan. He kissed her to conceal this mischievous union.

His regard for sanity seemed to be gone when the crackle of shredding fabric split the air. When he stopped kissing her, a length of cotton went over her mouth. He tied it in a tight knot at the side of her head.

"You better be damn quiet," he said, dragging his lips over her jaw and down to her throat. "I don't want any interruptions this time. I need to fuck you more than I need my next breath." His fingertips ran all over her body. He kissed each breast and rubbed his face against each mound, growling out his own appreciation of the form he was going to take advantage of. "Any objections?" This was the first time his eyes met hers. As soon as she shook her head, they went back to admiring her body. "Good, because it's fucking time I took ownership of what's mine."

His jeans were gone in a flash then he tore the lace from her pussy and threw it over the back of the couch. The gag erased her ability to question him, but when his head disappeared between her thighs, she lost all desire to second guess him.

The spikes of pleasure buried deep into her with every tickle of his tongue. The pace of the tip sped up on her clit, then his fingers sunk into her, two of them, fucking her slowly with his digits. All the writing in the world couldn't shake him from his task. He was a man determined. The cascade of orgasm ripped through her with such power that the spasm clamped her gut until she thought she'd never move again.

Cries of her gratification were muffled by the gag. She was grateful for it, staying silent would've been impossible otherwise. Pleasure still rippled over her. Her head was still thrown back when the length of his shaft penetrated her without any invitation, not that he needed one. He slid back and forth, fondling her breasts, stroking her body. Each of his murmured pleasures was accompanied by a sharp thrust that buried him deeper.

Rising up to meet his motion, they settled into a rhythm, their eyes locked. His satisfaction was so obvious that the fire of pride stoked her own yearning. He wanted her and valued her, and she returned those feelings tenfold. He was right that she was owned by him. It was what she wanted because while she was owned by him, she was safe, he'd make sure of that.

Their rhythm increased and he snatched her hips to drive in with a bruising force. She whimpered, but he was somewhere else, his mind was gone, and gritting his teeth, he hissed to hide his own climax, then shoved into her one last time.

Both of them exhaled when he pulled off her gag. He switched up their positions, putting himself beneath her to hold her.

Their bliss was short-lived. A scream came from the bedroom, and it wasn't one of desire.

"I think Suzette just woke up," she whispered and kissed his chest.

"Good guess," he said, reaching over her to the floor to give her the intact tee-shirt. "We should go and make sure she doesn't beat on Ruger."

"We should."

Donning the tee-shirt, she got up to go through and diffuse the situation. Colt snatched her wrist and tugged her down at his side again, she looked at him with a silent question.

"We don't have to run through," he said, taking his time in putting on his jeans. "She can beat on him a little bit. He probably deserves it."

They were still kissing when Ruger came through with a jabbering Suzette running in behind him.

"This pervert was in bed with me!" she screeched and

picked up a side lamp, holding it up as though to protect herself.

"Just for a minute," Ruger said, running his hands through his hair and rubbing his eyes. "Do I look like a man with intentions of screwing you? I just woke up."

"I don't know what your intentions were," Suzette said, her face red with either rage or embarrassment. "I am an engaged woman, I'm taken. You keep your mitts off!"

"Your mitts were the ones on me," he said.

The amused smile that warped his lips would likely set Suzette off again.

Lyssa pounced up and rounded the couch to take the lamp from her friend. "Ruger wasn't going to hurt you," she said, putting the lamp back on the table. "The guys were out all night. They're ready for bed."

"He sure is," Ruger said.

Lyssa led Suzette into the light of the window, to open it and let some fresh air in. She glanced back at Colt who was admiring her naked legs, not listening to a word. There was no time for her to comment, or be flattered, because Suzette spoke.

"Who are they?"

Suzette was looking out of the window. Lyssa followed her line of vision. Colt came in behind them to do the same. He'd obviously been snapped out of his trance by Suzette's tone of wonder.

"I don't know," Lyssa said.

A broad man made of muscle skirted a black Camaro to take the arm of the tiny woman who got out the passenger side. The woman's lips were working fast, but the man didn't say a word. He snatched her other arm and slammed her against the side of the car.

Lyssa tensed. "Should we go out there?" she asked. "They're arguing about something."

"I think he's got control of her," Colt said. "They're fine."

"I think it was the woman Lys was worried about," Suzette said, distracted by the show.

The man did look mean. With a strong brow pulled

down in a scowl that made fear shiver through her, he wasn't the type to be messed with. That teeny-tiny woman wouldn't last long if he turned on her. But the woman continued to speak. When he tried to open the car door, the female pushed her ass back to close it again. She stopped talking and plumped her lips.

Digging her hands into the front pockets of the guy's jeans, the female pouted and said a few short words. The male bared his teeth at her, and she smiled in triumph. His hand came up and he grabbed her jaw to yank her head higher.

Suzette gasped. "Is he going to hurt her?"

"No," Lyssa muttered.

The male hauled the little woman to the tips of her toes and devoured her mouth with such a flaying power that Lyssa's own core began to tingle again.

Suzette whimpered. "Wow."

"No, he's going to fuck her," Colt said and grinned. "Maybe we should get the popcorn."

"What the hell are you guys perving on?" Ruger asked. She was nudged aside to make way for him to peer out of the window too. "Fuck."

"What?" Colt asked.

Lyssa didn't like the tone of Ruger's curse. "Do you know them?"

"You two go into the bedroom," Ruger said, shoving both Suzette and Lyssa away from the window. "Do either of you know how to use a weapon?"

"Why would we need a weapon?" Suzette asked.

"Ruge?" Colt asked.

"He's a great guy, the best in the business," Ruger said. "Last time I saw him, he took me for everything I had at the poker table."

"You're afraid of a poker buddy?" Suzette asked. "Do you owe him money?"

It wasn't fear Lyssa read in Ruger, just concerned wariness. "He's nobody's buddy. When he shows up on your doorstep, especially when you don't know why, there's a fifty percent chance you'll never see daylight, or breathe oxygen, ever again."

"He brought a woman," Lyssa said, moving toward the front door. "If he was going to hurt anyone, why would he bring a woman that he's intimate with to—"

"No, you don't understand," Ruger said, snatching her arm to draw her back. "She's as bad. I mean, she's a sweetheart, but she doesn't need a reason. If she snaps her fingers, he'll pounce. I guarantee it."

"You're afraid of her?" Suzette asked. "And I thought you were a big, tough guy."

"She kidnapped a woman who upset her," Ruger said. "Got her trussed up in some abandoned warehouse, he came in and gutted her."

The eyes of the women flared.

"That has to be exaggerated," Colt said. "She doesn't look like the brutal type."

Deadpan, Ruger turned to his brother. "Some guy hit on her… she cut off his dick."

Colt's throat bobbed, and he took Lyssa's hand. "You two go to the bedroom and lock the door."

"It doesn't lock," Lyssa said, withdrawing her hand from his. "And I like your dick so if there's a chance anyone will try to hurt it—"

"I won't be hitting on her," Colt said. "Please, just—"

The knock on the door interrupted them. She and Colt were still in a state of semi-undress, but she wasn't backing down. Going to the door, she opened it despite both men hissing words of discouragement.

There, on the threshold, was the couple from the parking lot. The man was in front with the woman at his back, peeking around his bulging arm. From their position, it looked like the female had her hand in the back pocket of the guy's jeans.

The male examined them, saying nothing. From where his attention eventually fixed, Lyssa would say he'd stopped on Ruger.

"Ruger," the male growled in a tone so deep she shivered again.

The guy's lips hadn't moved at all, but the word was

clear.

"Rushe," Ruger said, coming in closer to Lyssa's back. "Is this a friendly visit or should I start saying my prayers?"

"You're scaring them," the female said from behind Rushe.

"What was the condition for you coming up here?" Rushe grumbled over his shoulder.

The female drew her lips into her mouth then shifted in closer to press it to the back of his arm. Rushe fixated on Lyssa. She didn't want to shrink back, but that gaze chilled through to the muscle of her hammering heart.

"If you're here to cause trouble," Colt said, joining her and Ruger at the door. "Let us excuse the women."

"Lyssa Cutler," Rushe said, much to their collective surprise.

"Yes."

"Doctor Lyssa Cutler."

"Yes," she said. "What is this about?"

"My woman has beef with you."

"Hey now," Colt said. His hand curled around her arm, and he pulled her back with such force she couldn't oppose it. Only when her body was secreted behind him and Ruger did Colt let go. "If you have a problem with her, it's me you deal with."

"Wow," the voice of the female behind Rushe carried past all the men to Lyssa's ears. "With all of this testosterone flying around, it's a wonder us women can keep our panties dry. Move."

A manicured hand came between Colt and Ruger. They both shifted, and the female came through the parted men without fear for her own safety. Though with a man like Rushe watching her back, it was unlikely this woman ever had to worry about safety.

"I'm Flick," the woman said. "You're Lyssa. You and I have a mutual interest and concern."

"We do?" Lyssa asked.

"Martin Schifford, he's my brother-in-law."

"Oh," Lyssa said, recognizing the name of her

patient. The details of his case came flooding back. She blinked at Rushe over Flick's head. "Oh."

"Yes," Flick said, wearing a broad smile showing shiny white teeth. "We're that couple."

"You know what he discussed with me?" Lyssa asked, unable to take her bulging eyes from Rushe.

"No," Flick said. "But it's difficult to believe that anyone can have a conversation without mentioning that." Nodding backward she indicated Rushe, who was completely unmoved. "He came to me in confidence, he's been visiting you while he travels for business. He didn't want anyone in the family, or in his social circle, to know that he was seeing you."

"Given your specialty," Rushe muttered.

Flick carried on without acknowledging him. "It seems you're having some trouble… trouble that might visit my family, and that's a problem for me."

"Which makes it a problem for him?" Lyssa asked, still looking at Rushe.

"Don't worry about him. He's happy on his leash for now. Providing you're cooperative, that shouldn't change."

"And if we don't cooperate?" Colt asked.

His question attracted the 0glittering yet determined eyes of the tiny female. "Then you better update your will, because we're happy to sacrifice any, and every, person in this room to protect what's ours."

"You've heard about my patients," Lyssa said. "About what's happening to them?"

"Yes," Flick said. "And if my brother is on your stalker's list, we want to know about it. It's in our interest, as well as yours, that this man be stopped."

"We might have already seen to that," Colt said. "The police are on the case now. They're closing in on a suspect as we speak."

"You have a suspect?" Flick asked, her demeanor lighting with pleasure. "Give me his name and address."

"I don't think so," Ruger said.

Rushe growled and stepped forward, his torso came up against Flick's back, and it was only when Flick spread her arms to prevent him that he stopped. "You're protecting him? The suspect?" Her head tilted. "You are protecting the man who is hurting your brother's woman? Why would you do that?"

"If we tell you who he is, he'll magically disappear," Ruger said. "I know what you two are capable of."

"Then you should know that upsetting us isn't a smart move," Flick said.

"Is it true that you cut off the dick of a guy who hit on you?" Suzette asked.

"Not exactly," Flick said. "He was my fiancé. Intimacy between us was forbidden, he knew that I belonged to Rushe."

"You were engaged to one man, but belonged to another?" Suzette said. "I don't understand that."

"And there's no requirement for you to," Flick said. "Now, the suspect, how did you come to the conclusion that this was the man we're looking for?"

"You can come in and we'll talk," Colt said. "Let Suzette get out of here and I'll consult with my brother first."

"That's acceptable," Flick said. "You have five minutes."

She retreated behind Rushe who came into the space with entitlement, Flick's hand was already in the rear pocket of Rushe's jeans again. He led her to the dining table where she sat, but he remained standing behind her chair, looming over her.

Flick was unaffected by his intimidating form. All she did was rest her head back against the buckle of Rushe's belt. When her head shifted a little, Lyssa wondered if there was something more intimate about that move.

"Come on," Colt said, taking her hand.

She, he, Ruger, and Suzette went to his bedroom to come up with a plan of attack... or maybe one of defense would be better with Rushe and Flick on the scene.

THIRTY-TWO

NO ONE GOT THE CHANCE to do much talking. By the time they convinced Suzette to go to her sister's, there was no time left for debate.

Ruger's silence was a red flag underlined by his scowl. Gone was the fun-loving, easy-going Ruger Warner. In his place was an edgy man on alert.

Lyssa and Colt got dressed. Given the reputation of their visitors, it seemed prudent. It wasn't civilized to have a conversation of this magnitude with no underwear on.

Eager not to leave Rushe and his cohort alone for too long, Ruger was either worried about appearing rude, or their guests gathering intelligence while no one was watching.

The three of them returned to the kitchen. Rushe was in the seat that Flick had occupied earlier. The little woman was in his lap with her arms looped around him, wearing something of a saucy smile. The smile was odd and out of place. Rushe appeared as severe as ever and unaffected by whatever amused the woman sitting on him.

"You've got some nerve showing up here," Colt said. Such a hard line was a surprise. Flick appeared as dumbfounded as she felt. "That's your woman, right?" Rushe nodded once. "And if you were trying to protect her from a maniac, would you be happy some random couple showed up demanding answers because some guy you don't give a fuck about might be in danger?"

"I give a fuck about him," Lyssa said, facing her lover. "You know how I feel about my patients and any of them being hurt. I'm pleased that these people care about Martin enough to—"

"Actually…" Flick said, drawing the spotlight. "Rushe couldn't care less about Martin. He thinks leaving the guy to fix this mess on his own might toughen him up. He doesn't know him as well as I do; I can tell you that's never going to happen."

"You and your brother-in-law were never particularly close," Lyssa said, pulling up a chair next to the couple. "And yet you're here in support of him, bringing with you a lover who has cleaned up your family messes before."

"He told you about that?" Flick asked, glancing at Rushe who fixed narrow eyes on her.

"No specifics," Lyssa said, "and you're covered by doctor-patient confidentiality. He didn't talk in explicit terms about any criminal acts that may, or may not, have taken place. So I'm certainly not compelled to report anything that he might have mentioned."

"He got one thing right then," Ruger muttered.

Rushe's focus moved to him. "Silver was looking for you," he said, somehow conveying a semi-veiled threat.

Ruger lifted a hand. "I don't want to talk about that in current company."

"Ah…" Flick said. With a burst of elation, she tightened her grip around Rushe. "Did you hear that, lover? The brother and the good doctor don't know Ruger's dirty little secret."

"Yeah," Ruger said, propping a hand on the fridge to relax his weight on it. Others may be intimidated by the thought of having their secrets spilled, apparently Ruger wasn't one of those people. "Who helped you clean up your little mess with the King Club? And hooked Eric up with the pharmacist? If you want to find yourself another supplier…? I heard a whisper that Scott was back in the country, either of you want to comment on that?"

"Are you threatening us?" Flick demanded and moved as though to leave Rushe's lap, but the brute took hold of her hips.

"Kitten," he growled in an implied warning that didn't require his lips to move.

The woman went limp, dropping her arms from his neck to fold them under her generous breasts. "We came here to help because we have a shared interest. I thought they'd be receptive," Flick said to Rushe. "I should've let you do it your way."

"Which was what?" Ruger asked. "To come in all guns blazing?"

Lyssa had no idea at the complexity of the relationship between these three, but she was seeing even more layers to Ruger than she could have imagined. She reconsidered her assessment of his need to wear women's clothing. Ruger was a guy in charge and seemed to have sway in circles that she didn't know existed.

"He was going to swipe the doc," Flick said, her demeanor becoming more satisfied. "Draw out the crazy fucker."

Colt approached. Lyssa could feel the tension radiating from him. Reaching out, she laid a hand on his abdomen, silently pleading with him to calm down.

"They can swipe all they want," Ruger said from behind her. "Is Tawny still living with that computer geek?"

Rushe shot out of his seat, forcing Flick up, so Lyssa felt compelled to stand too. The burst of testosterone fired her adrenaline. They'd never resolve anything while these three men circled each other vying for the dominant position.

"They didn't do that, did they? No one touched me," Lyssa soothed, holding up restraining hands to the Warners. They were the only two she could hope to have any influence on. "And their intention was never to hurt me."

"Lover," Flick whispered in her own attempt at placation.

The chest of the man at her back swelled with silent panting breaths. Tension crackled, but he did eventually sit again, snatching Flick's hips to yank her down onto him.

"He doesn't watch her directly," Colt said, ready to be the bigger man. Thank God. "You wouldn't have caught him by snatching Lys, hoping to lure him out. He taps into the city's video surveillance network, picks up her image, and follows her through the system."

Lyssa didn't know that. She didn't know Colt knew that either. "You never told me that."

"Because I didn't want you to be paranoid every time you walked down the street," he said. "I told you that the angle of the shots was interesting. They were taken from above because that is where the cameras are located. From there it didn't take much investigation to figure out who would have access to those systems."

His phone rang and he went to answer it. The first few words were normal, but he became more deadpan. That couldn't be a good sign. When he turned his back on the group and lowered his volume, Lyssa moved closer to Ruger. He took her hand in a comforting gesture, betraying he must have assessed Colt's actions in the same way.

Colt hung up and didn't turn for a few seconds. Was he composing himself before returning to the group? When he did turn, he was all aloof determination.

"I have to take you home," Colt said to her.

"What? But—"

"Is Archie still there?" Colt asked.

"Well… I… yeah, I think so."

"Does he know how to use a gun?"

"What?" Her shock came out as a shout. The man standing in front of her couldn't be the one who'd just made love to her on the couch. The hardened look in his eye was unamused. In fact, it was downright pissed off. "Colt—"

"Answer the question," he said. "Does he know how to use a gun?"

"What's going on?" Flick asked, apparently not as shocked. "We have weapons in the car if—"

"We have supplies," Ruger said.

"Supplies are not the problem," Colt said. "Manpower is the issue. Lyssa doesn't know how to use a gun."

"They learn fast," Rushe muttered.

Flick pinched him.

"My girlfriend won't have to," Colt said, taking her shoulders to shake her focus back to him. "Lys, does he know—"

"But… yes," she said. "Yes, he does, but—"

"Good," Colt said. "I'm going to call Blaser to come and take you home. Stay there until you hear from me. Blaser will talk to Archie, he'll make sure you'll be safe."

"Talk?" Lyssa said, disliking the idea of her boyfriend's brother talking to her ex-husband. "Archie doesn't know anything about what's going on. To be frank, I don't want to include him in my business. I wouldn't trust him to look after my houseplant… if I had one."

"Blaser will make it clear there will be consequences if anything happens to you," Colt said. "You'll be safe."

"Who is Archie?" Flick asked.

"Her ex-husband," Rushe answered.

Just how many people were checking her out these days?

"I'm not going anywhere until you tell me what is going on," Lyssa said to Colt.

"The DA issued the arrest warrant, but they can't find the suspect," Colt said. "That was Hoburn on the phone. I'm going to meet him and find out what's going on. We'll do everything we can to help."

"We can stay with the doctor," Flick said.

Colt was already on his way to grab his jacket while Ruger disappeared into the back of the apartment.

"You go wherever you want, sweetheart," Colt said. "Are you really here to stop this guy doing any more harm? If you are, I need your boyfriend's help… Can he play nice with others and get the job done?"

Rushe and Flick were on their way to the door. "Seems to me that you're the one who can't play nice," Flick said. "You can't have him, unless—"

"He needs people who can track this guy, unofficially," Rushe said. "Without following the rules."

"Oh," Flick said. "In that case, you can have him. You can have us both, we stay together."

"Always?" Lyssa asked, letting Colt help her on with her jacket. "You're always together?"

"Unless he ties me to something and leaves me there, yeah," Flick said, smiling and hooking a hand into Rushe's back pocket.

"Does that happen often?" Lyssa asked, guessing that Colt was taken aback by the declaration too.

"Not as often as it used to," Flick said.

"Not as often as I'd like," Rushe muttered.

Lyssa had no time to continue her questioning. Ruger came back with a small sports bag over his shoulder. From the determination on his face and in his gait, she didn't need to ask what was in the bag.

"Everybody ready to bail out?" Ruger asked.

Colt was already on the phone to Blaser. If he was in the garage, which he would be, he'd be able to meet them out front in a matter of seconds. She was being railroaded onto the safe route. She wanted to be involved but didn't want to be petulant. These capable men were doing what needed to be done. So when she was taken outside with the group and swept down the stairs, she went with it. But that didn't quell the sense of impending catastrophe. Her psyche-senses were in overdrive.

AFTER COLT PUT HER INTO A TRUCK, Blaser had showed up in the parking lot. The brothers talked while Rushe locked Flick in his own car. He went to join the Warners. The introduction of Blaser and Rushe was so uneventful her interest was piqued.

When the men were finished talking, they got into their respective vehicles. Blaser with her, Rushe with Flick, and Colt shared a vehicle with Ruger. She assumed the others were going to join the police for the manhunt.

On the drive to her house, she tried to open a dialogue with Blaser, but he wasn't interested in small talk and didn't say much. Blaser wasn't one for gossiping. Given his work at Risqué, she assumed he'd be used to it.

Archie was in her townhouse when they arrived. He was surprised to see not only her, but yet another intimidating man at her side. Colt was difficult enough for him to take, she wasn't going to explain her relationship with Blaser.

The lack of explanation worked in their favor; he was suitably intimidated when Blaser took him aside. Although she didn't hear the specifics, Archie was considerably paler when the men came back to her.

"I'm out," Blaser said. "Going to hook up with the guys."

He was already running down the stairs, so she left Archie in the living room and ran down after him. "Wait, Blaser," she said. He paused at the front door. "I want to… I mean thanks for helping with this."

"It's family," he said and shrugged, then stretched his injured shoulder.

"I'm sorry about that too," she said. "I can't believe that you got a hole in you because of this, because of me."

"This was nothing to do with you, we told you that," he said, indicating his shoulder. "Not everything in our lives started post-Lyssa."

"I haven't been told what it is about," she said. "Until I know, I'll assume you're both covering for Colt."

"For Colt? Do you think he shot me?"

"No, but he knows I feel guilty about people being injured because of—"

"I got this because I deserved it," Blaser said. "I got this because I let down a woman who meant a lot to me."

"Gary's sister?"

"Yeah," he said. "She… she went through a hard time, and I could've prevented it. I was supposed to meet her, but I was late… I wasn't there when she needed me."

"And Gary blames you for that?"

"Gary blames everyone for everything, he thinks the world is against him," Blaser said. "He doesn't think about what happened to Bri in terms of how it hurt her, he only sees how it affected him."

"How did it affect him?"

"He wasn't there for her either," Blaser said. "We both let her down."

"But she's okay now?"

"I think okay is a relative term," he said, grasping the door handle. "I didn't get shot because of you. I got shot because Gary needs to blame someone for what happened to his sister. I'm the only one he can lay his hands on."

"If you know it was him, why don't you tell the police and have him arrested?"

"Because in a sort of weird, roundabout way, Gary is family too."

He would never rat out Colt or Ruger for hurting him. Not that either of them would go around shooting people. If Blaser had been physically intimate with this woman, Bri, Blaser and Gary couldn't be blood, which left only one thing…

"You still care about her."

An uncomfortable half-smile formed on his lips as his gaze dropped. "Care doesn't begin to cover it, Lyssa. But what I did to her, what she went through because of me… no one gets over that."

"Have you asked her?" Lyssa asked, moving in closer to take his hand. "Have you talked to her about what she went through and how you feel about it?"

Snatching his hand away, he pulled open the door. "There isn't a single person in her life who gives a fuck about what she went through. Gary is the only family she has left and all he does is make it about him. I'm not going to do the same thing to her."

"Maybe letting her talk, giving her a safe place to share her experiences is what she needs."

"I wouldn't know how to coach her through that," Blaser said. "I wouldn't know how to help her forget what happened and everything associated with it. That's what she needs to do, and I'm a part of it."

"A part," Lyssa said. "Maybe there's a reason she holds onto you, a reason that she keeps you in her life."

"Yeah," Blaser said. "Because Gary can't stand it."

"Do you really believe she's that callous?"

"Bri? No. But standing up to her brother is her way of taking control."

"And she feels like control has been taken from her?" Lyssa asked, wishing she could move this into her office and get him sitting down.

"Yeah," Blaser said. "Isn't that what they say about rape victims?"

The poor woman had endured a traumatic experience. Talking about that experience and venting the emotion associated with it was important. Helping victims process was part of her training.

"This might not be the time or…" Lyssa said. "I'd like to meet her, if you'd consider letting me do that."

He frowned and backed up. "You want to work your hocus pocus on her?"

"It's medicine," Lyssa said. "But if she's uncomfortable, or isn't interested, that's fine. I want you to know that the offer is there, for both of you, together or apart… We're all family, right?"

The question relaxed him a little, but he didn't look any more eager to take her up on it. "I'll think about it," he said. She nodded. "I better get going."

Letting go of his hand she let him retreat, hoping he would take the time to process her offer. It could help both parties. If Blaser and this Bri woman had been close, or in some kind of relationship, before she went through her trauma, that relationship had been interrupted by the event. Now Bri lived with her ex and her brother, two of the most important men in her life, at each other's throats, blaming each other for something that was the fault of the attacker's.

Knowing that in intellectual terms wouldn't help Bri. She would have to be taken through the experience and have her emotions broken down into simple terms to process them. Blaser cared about Bri, and he was right, that did make them family.

Learning about Blaser gave her a distraction from her life, and what her love might be going through. If she couldn't be of use to Colt, then she would be of use to his brother.

Going into her office she began to work, putting

together information and reading material for Blaser, and for Bri. She hoped it would encourage both of them to seek help. Unless someone wanted it, there was no way to force a person into facing their past, and that was the only way to move into the future happy.

IF THIS WAS A MANHUNT, it could take days to track their suspect. As the hours passed, she got increasingly eager to speak to Colt.

After working for as long as she could, and arranging for flowers for the patients she'd lost, Lyssa went upstairs. It didn't take long for Archie to get on her nerves. His bombardment of questions gave her a new respect for those who were reluctant to answer hers. Despite busying herself with chores, Archie still followed her around giving a lecture about her choice of partner.

This, of course, led to her bringing up how stupid it was of him to get mixed up in defrauding the IRS. That was a smokescreen for her own attack on his relationship. The young woman was clearly only interested in the money Archie accrued through his surgical practice. Their argument quickly descended into the old days. It actually helped to relieve some of her tension but led to them agreeing to remain in separate rooms, which suited her just fine.

She had cooked but wasn't looking forward to sitting at the dinner table with Archie… alone. It would be immature to take her food to the bedroom or office. After setting the table for two, she intended to go into the spare room, where he was residing. A knock at the front door interrupted her journey.

Relief flooded her. Colt. It had to be him. If he had news and was in proximity to her home, there would be no reason for him not to come over.

But when she opened the door, Suzette stood in front of her, not her lover. "Suzette?"

"I went to Colt's, but you weren't back yet," Suzette said, moving past her into the hall. "Some guy called Gus said you'd come home."

"What are you doing here?" Lyssa asked, taking Suzette's jacket to hang it in the hall closet. "I thought you were going to stay with your sister."

"She was driving me nuts and her kids were running around. I just needed to be somewhere I could clear my head. You don't mind, do you?"

"No," Lyssa said. "We never got the chance to talk earlier. Archie is still upstairs. Do you want to talk in the office? I have coffee."

Suzette nodded. Lyssa let her into the office to brew the coffee while she went upstairs to turn off the stove and tell Archie there was food available. She might be missing out, but that was no reason for the meal to go to waste.

Instead of sitting on her doctor's chair, she sat with Suzette on the couch.

"How are you feeling?" Lyssa asked her friend.

"Alone, scared, confused," Suzette said.

"You're going to be fine," Lyssa said. "This will blow over. I know that Pete will come to his senses."

"I…" Her voice cracked. Lyssa put her coffee aside and slid closer to take Suzette's hand. "I'm just so in love with him and I was sure that this was it. Everything seemed to be so perfect. I don't know how it fell apart so quickly. A few weeks ago, we were fine and now… this. I mean… I can't even… I don't…"

"It's okay," Lyssa said, taking Suzette's cup to put it on the table to hug her. "This is a shock. Your emotions are perfectly normal and it's good to express them." Suzette cried for a while, but eventually sat back enough to blink her watery eyes. Another hug could be needed any minute and Lyssa was happy to oblige. Coaching a friend was so different to coaching a patient. It was funny how easily she slid between the roles. "Have you spoken to Pete today?"

"Not since before I came to Colt's this morning… I wanted to call him, but I'm too scared. What if he hangs up or sends me to voicemail or something? I've taken all the rejection I can today."

"I'm going to get wine from upstairs, okay? Then we can either talk about how to fix this, or we'll curse men and everything they stand for. Sound good?"

With a blubbery sniff, Suzette nodded and wiped her nose on her sleeve, prompting Lyssa to retrieve the tissue box from the end table.

"Thank you," Suzette said, blowing her nose. "I don't know what I'd do without you."

Lyssa gave her hand a squeeze and went upstairs. Pouring away the coffee, she got a bottle of wine and a couple of glasses. Archie was happily eating the dinner she had made while sitting in front of the television. He didn't acknowledge her. Didn't that just epitomize their relationship? It was funny how quickly they slid back into their old ways.

Nostalgia over the similarity of the set up put a smile on her face. There wasn't anything in the world that would persuade her to go back, especially not now that she had her Colt to rely on.

THIRTY-THREE

SUZETTE SPENT THE NIGHT in bed with her, but they didn't wake up to Colt or Ruger watching over them. The friends and Archie had breakfast together and spent the longest time talking about absolutely nothing. It was amazing how skilled they were at small talk. All of them avoided the elephant in the room: none of them wanted to be in each other's company at all. They'd each rather be somewhere with their respective partners.

Going through the motions of the day, they were preoccupied with their own messes. Archie attempted to call the receptionist who had thrown him out, but she was refusing to take his calls. Lyssa tried to call Colt, but it went to voicemail. He had to be busy. He was pulling out all the stops to ensure her safety, but she longed to hear his voice.

Suzette tried to call Pete too, but his phone was diverting to voicemail as well.

"It must mean he's over me," Suzette wailed.

Archie tsked and turned up the volume on the television. The man had never had any patience for Suzette. He rarely had patience for anyone.

For a man with a successful business, he didn't have many ends to tie up or explanations to make. He had a staff to take care of that for him. All he had to do was show up for surgery and there was none of that going on this weekend. Had he clued his staff into the fact there may be no wages for them at the end of the month? Probably not.

"It doesn't mean that he's over you," Lyssa said. The women sat together drinking coffee in the kitchen, where they'd been contemplating making lunch. They'd yet to work up the required motivation. "It could mean anything. Maybe he's busy or got called into work. There's a chance he's devastated and is at home right now pining."

"Do you think that I should go over there?"

"You don't want to pressure him," Lyssa said. "Remember you have genuine grievances too. You should be able to air those with him and come to a compromise. This relationship can't only be about him; it has to be about both of you."

"Can you counsel us?" Suzette asked. "Maybe if you're there to play mediator... he'll see reason, you know? He'll see how good you are at what you do and how special you are, and he won't feel the need to... push you out or protect me from you."

Lyssa nudged her coffee mug out of the way to reach over and take Suzette's hand. "You know that I will always be available to you as a friend. But Pete isn't comfortable with me, and it would be unfair to put him in a room with both of us. A patient has to be able to trust their doctor and he's going to think that I am biased."

"But you're not! You're always fair."

"I would be biased," Lyssa said, smiling. "I appreciate your compliment, but I know about things in your relationship that he doesn't know I know. You're also my oldest and dearest friend, how could I look at your relationship without a skewed view? If it came to the crunch in any situation, can you see yourself siding with Colt over me?"

"No." Suzette sighed and dropped an elbow to the tabletop. "But I can't not get married, Lys. I can't believe how quickly this fell apart. Everything is planned, it's all booked and paid for. I thought I'd be walking down the aisle toward him, and now..."

"He doesn't want you spending time with me while he feels that I create an unsafe environment. That's reasonable. Colt is working right now to remove the threat. Once he does, Pete will have no reason to prevent our friendship from going back to how it was. Maybe once that happens, he'll begin to see just how special you are to me. He'll learn that I would never knowingly endanger you."

"What if Colt can't do it? What if he can't remove the threat?"

If Colt was unsuccessful, Lyssa would have all kinds of problems. The least of which would be her best friend's fiancé, or former fiancé, depending on what he was by then.

"He'll be successful," she said. "These things just take time."

"How can you be so optimistic?" Suzette whined. "You're always so optimistic."

Misery did love company and right now Lyssa wasn't providing that company.

"I won't let this person have power over me," Lyssa said. "I have more faith in Colt than I do in the stalker. If one of them is going to triumph, it's going to be my Colt."

"So once the stalker is caught and put in jail, do you think Pete will forget everything else? About Risqué, and me going there even though I knew he wouldn't be happy with me doing it?"

"The lying is harder to get over," Lyssa said, being honest with her friend. "But I do believe it was the shock of the police raid that provoked such a strong reaction in him. Did you tell him that you'd been out with your sister?"

"Yes, but he didn't believe me."

"So you ended up telling him the truth?"

"Yes, and that's when he exploded," Suzette said.

"Like I said, it was a shocking story, and we already know how concerned he is for your safety. Imagine hearing such a story from him, knowing that the person you love has been in danger while you weren't there for them."

"Do you really think that this is about that?" Suzette asked, completely unconvinced. "He knew that I wasn't in any danger, not real danger. I mean it was the cops, right? They wouldn't have done anything to hurt me."

"Yes, but you went to a potentially dangerous place. We know that Risqué is safe. Pete doesn't. All he knows is you visited a strip club in a seedy part of town, alone. If he doesn't frequent these places, he doesn't know what they're like. His mind went to the worst-case scenario. Before I knew Colt and Risqué, I would have assumed it was a dangerous place. In fact, I did. I took you that first night because I wasn't sure that it was safe to go there alone. It's only my experience of the place, and the people there, that has taught me otherwise."

Suzette perked up, coddling her cup in both hands, sliding it toward her chest. "So maybe if I take Pete there and introduce him to some of the people, he will learn that—"

"I don't think Pete will be open to visiting the club, not right off the bat. Maybe in time you can build up to taking him there and introducing him to the people that we know. Fundamentally, this is about trust. He feels betrayed. You put yourself in danger to help me when he asked you to take no part in the situation."

"But I wasn't in danger!" Suzette asserted. "We went to that place together. It was recommended by a cop! Nothing bad happened to me when we went together before."

"No, but it was a risk. Pete probably realizes now just how important this friendship is to you and how far you are willing to go to help me."

"That's a bad thing? That I'm loyal to my friends and willing to support them?"

"No," Lyssa smiled. "But you didn't go to Pete and ask him to help you. You went behind his back to seek out another man."

"Who happens to have experience in this area."

"You could have explained your worries to Pete and asked him to accompany you to Risqué," Lyssa said. "Did you consider that?"

"No. We both know how he would have reacted. He'd already banned me from seeing you. He was never going to help me, help you. If I had asked him and he had said no, I would've gone alone anyway, without his support. Isn't it worse to do something you've already been forbidden from doing than to do it without asking?"

She smiled. "It's easier to ask forgiveness than permission? That's what you're relying on? Arguing your way out of this on a technicality isn't going to happen. Pete needs to know that you trust him and value him. He wants to see you put your relationship with him before everything else. As far as he's concerned, you're going to get married and spend your lives growing old together. You are the mother of his future children."

"And that's all great," Suzette said. "I feel the same way."

"His dream is to be with you, but how long will that dream last if you get yourself hurt, or worse, because of me?"

"This is so messed up. I want to be with him. But I have to be myself too, and I have to be allowed to have friendships. I don't forbid him from spending time with his friends and colleagues."

"He doesn't have a friendship like this though, does he?"

"Keith is the closest thing that he has to a best friend. I've never known him to associate with anyone else to be honest, even at work."

Lyssa couldn't judge Pete. She worked alone. Most of her contact was with patients. Colleagues made referrals by email; she rarely spoke to them on the phone. Suzette was her best friend, and all that she needed.

"Would he do what you did?" Lyssa asked. "Would Pete take a possibly grave risk to ensure Keith's safety?"

"I'm not sure he'd take that kind of risk to ensure mine."

Seeing her best friend depressed was upsetting. The more they discussed the relationship, the more her concern grew. "If you're not sure of that then you shouldn't be marrying him."

Being blunt wasn't typically her course. They weren't in her doctor's office and sometimes the truth just had to be told.

Stunned, it took Suzette the longest time to respond. "I know our relationship is not perfect. And I know Pete has flaws, just like I do, but… I love him."

If she had a nickel… Lyssa had made it a point to take on mostly male patients. They tended to be more direct and not so caught up in the messy mire of emotions. Emotions were the one thing that couldn't be reasoned away. Men were engaged enough to take practical advice. But in the majority of cases, women acted with their hearts and not their heads. That very line, "*I love him*" seemed to be an answer and explanation for everything. She didn't fault the women. She herself had been bogged down by a heavy heart that knew her partner's actions were wrong, but still couldn't bring itself to reject them.

She and Archie had a deep connection when they met. Falling in love with him had been inevitable. Their relationship had cooled quickly. Their "deep" connection ended up being mostly sexual. Her naïve mind and body made it into something else. They should have split up long before they did, but Lyssa had told herself the same thing. That she loved Archie and it would all work out. For a while, she believed things would go back to the way they were, in time. That all they had to do was find each other again. How wrong she had been.

If Suzette loved Pete, and the depth of feeling was returned, the couple should fight to be together. But if forging on was obligation because the church was already booked, it fell to her to stop her friend from making such a permanent mistake. Marriages may be able to end, but divorce stayed with a person for life. Suzette was so full of promise and energy, it would be heartbreaking if she became jaded or bitter.

Readying herself to ask some difficult questions, Lyssa was interrupted by the drone of the doorbell. Few people used that. Both women sat straighter. Their optimism reflected back on itself.

Leaving Archie in front of the television, the women went downstairs to answer the door without either saying a word. Hiding disappointment was as difficult for her as it was for Suzette to disguise her elation.

"Pete," Suzette said with a twitching grin.

"I thought you would be here," Pete said, glancing at

Lyssa. "We should talk."

Suzette was nodding furiously, and shoved Lyssa out of the way to grant Pete entry. "Come in. We can talk upstairs."

Pete passed the women and headed upstairs.

Suzette was close behind him until Lyssa caught her arm to hold her back. "Be careful," she said. "Try to be calm."

"He came here, for me," Suzette hissed, letting her grin loose. "That must mean he loves me."

"He didn't say he was here for you, he said he was here to talk."

The grin vanished and her complexion greyed. "Do you think he's here to talk about cancelling the wedding?"

"I don't know why he's here," Lyssa said, hating to be the bearer of bad news. "I'm just telling you not to get your hopes up. Archie and I will leave—"

A sharp crack from upstairs startled them. After a moment agape, they ran upstairs to see what caused the noise. At first, there was nothing to see. Pete wasn't anywhere around and although the television was still on, she couldn't see Archie either.

Maybe Archie had gone to the bedroom and… She came around the couch and saw him slumped on the floor, blood on the back of his head.

"Oh my God," she said, running around the couch to lie him down and assess his injury. But the hole in his forehead was larger, an exit wound. "He's been shot."

Suzette stood at the back of the couch, deathly white and visibly shaking. "How did…? I don't understand how…?"

Although futile, she checked Archie's airway and tried to find a pulse. There was none; his pupils were fixed.

"He's dead."

"Which was exactly the point."

Both women turned toward the kitchen, and Lyssa struggled to get back onto her feet. Pete was there on the threshold, a gun hanging loose in his hand.

"What are you doing?" Suzette asked. "Are you…? Did you…?"

"It's long overdue," Pete said, ignoring his fiancée.

"Wouldn't you agree?"

"The death of my ex-husband? Why would I want Archie dead?"

"He hurt you," Pete said. "Isn't that what you tell your patients? To get rid of anyone who hurts you?"

"What I tell my patients?" Lyssa asked. Examining the scene, everything slotted into place. Her wide eyes fixed on Pete; she gasped. "It's you."

"I'm at three and Warner hasn't managed one," Pete said with a smile on his face that was completely inappropriate. "You should pick your men more carefully. Find one that is willing to go to any lengths for you."

"What is going on?" Suzette asked. "I don't understand what's happening."

"It's him," Lyssa said. "He's the one… the nut, the crazy, the stalker!"

Still Suzette didn't seem to get it and stood there dumb as Pete approached, retrieving something from his pocket. The grating snick of handcuffs was impossible to mistake.

"What are you going to do?" Lyssa asked. "What's the plan?"

Suzette kicked into gear, gasping and struggling. Pete got hold of her and tied fabric around her head, imprisoning the desperate scream fighting for release.

"You and I have things to discuss, doctor," Pete said, shoving Suzette over the couch, sending her rolling forward onto Archie's body.

Her friend screamed behind the gag again and tried to scramble away, but Pete came around and got hold of her cuffs.

"Don't hurt her!"

"She won't be hurt," Pete said, forcing Suzette to her feet, he caressed her face. "My future wife and I discussed spicing things up in the bedroom. Maybe now is the time to explore that." Bringing the gun to Suzette's forehead, he glared at Lyssa. "Walk."

"Where?"

"Your bedroom. We're all going in there together."

The bedroom wasn't the most conventional choice for a conversation, so she had to wonder at his ulterior motive.

"Okay," Lyssa said. "We'll go through there together and talk."

"I'm the one who gives the orders and makes the plans!" he said, shoving Suzette forward to get closer to Lyssa, kicking Archie's body in the process.

"Yes." Lyssa nodded. "You are the one in control."

"Good," Pete sneered. "I'm glad you understand that. Now move!"

With no other option, Lyssa did what he asked. Suzette was crying. Despite the gag, she was managing to blubber. Lyssa wanted to keep her wits about her and wasn't ready to lose hope yet.

When they got to the bedroom, she paused at the end of the bed. Pete tied Suzette's cuffed hands to the headboard. All Lyssa could do was watch. When he was done and stood up, they made eye contact.

"Now what?" she asked.

"You're going to call off Warner."

"I'm what?"

"You heard me," Pete said, waving the gun at her.

Her concern narrowed on Suzette. In that position, on her back with her arms pulled up, Suzette's chest was constricted... she was hyperventilating. Moving toward her friend, she only got a few steps when Pete jumped forward. She didn't want him getting nervous; his trigger finger was twitchy.

"I'm just going to check that she's okay," Lyssa said. "She's uncomfortable."

"She wouldn't be here if she'd listened to me," Pete said in a hiss, then turned his attention to Suzette. "You should have listened to me. I was looking after you. But you just wouldn't listen, would you?"

"Is this why you wanted to keep us separate?" Lyssa asked, slowly completing her journey to Suzette, one careful side-step at a time.

"I didn't want her involved," Pete said. "She didn't need to be involved. But now that she is... it's her own fault."

"What is her own fault?" Lyssa asked, trying to help Suzette to sit in a more upright position.

"If only she had listened…"

The barrel of the gun swung from her to the sobbing Suzette.

"No," Lyssa said, bouncing up the bed to put her body between Suzette and the gun. "You don't want to hurt her. You don't want to hurt anyone. Please, Pete, tell me what this is about. How could you do this? I don't understand why—"

"You just don't get it," he said.

His gun arm relaxed to his side. Good. There it was aimed at the floor, not her friend. The only way they'd make it out of this was getting through each second, one at a time.

"No," she said. "I don't. Please explain it to me. Did I hurt you in some way or do you want to have a relationship with me? Please, tell me why you would—"

"He left me!"

The blatant rage startled her, but she kept fear away from her expression. Bonding with him may be the only way to break through the pathology. If they had rapport, maybe she could break down the reasons for his behavior.

"A person you cared about," she said.

"The man I was supposed to be with," he said and raised the gun again. "Don't pretend that you don't know. I showed you what it took to help someone. I've protected you so that you could help me, and you're going to help me."

"How would you like me to do that?"

"First, you're going to call off Warner. Tell him to get the cops off my tail."

Colt wasn't all-powerful. That was beside the point. She wouldn't refuse a chance to talk to him. On the phone, maybe she could tell him what was going on, or at least hint at it. So she nodded. For now, at least, that placated Pete, but she had no idea what he'd want her to do next.

THIRTY-FOUR

COLT WAS TIRED but wasn't at the end of his rope yet. He wanted to hear Lyssa's consoling voice; except he'd promised himself he wouldn't call until he had good news. Unofficially, Hoburn had been keeping him in the loop through the night. Colt had his brothers, Chavez, and this Rushe guy with his chick doing all they could all night. So far, Pete Harding had evaded them.

"The guy isn't that smart," Colt said when Ruger swung into the central, circular booth of the diner they'd all agreed to meet in at lunchtime.

"He's obsessed," Ruger said. "That makes the difference. It doesn't matter how smart he is. This is all he's thought about, all day, every day, for God knows how long."

"So he's considered all the contingencies," Colt muttered.

"Planned for them," Blaser said, coming up behind Colt then sliding into the booth beside him. "If he thought about going on the run, planned for it, he could be half a world away."

"What he wants is your woman."

The female voice came from behind them. He turned as Flick approached, her hand tucked into Rushe's jeans pocket.

"Lyssa is safe," Colt said. "I left her with her ex-husband. If anything goes wrong, he'll look after her."

"Sure about that?" Flick asked. Colt didn't immediately answer. "Rushe wouldn't leave me with anyone he wasn't sure would stand in front of a bullet for me… The list of who he'd trust to look after me is rather short. You should have that same conviction… if you love her."

"Lyssa is strong," Blaser said. "She's the type of girl who can look after herself."

"You remember the stories I told you about that one?" Ruger asked, indicating Flick with a shift of his chin before he tried to seek out a waitress.

Rushe sat down opposite Blaser, taking Flick onto his lap, like the two couldn't be physically separated. Maybe he was trying to put his mark on the woman in front of the group of males. Except there was no doubting who she belonged to. The adoration in her eyes whenever she looked at Rushe was enough to prove that.

"The stories are almost always exaggerated," Flick said.

"Not by much," Rushe muttered, taking a laminated menu from the center of the table.

Blaser worked his shoulder in a circle, pushing a hand to it and working out the kinks. Colt was about to ask if he was taking his meds, because Lyssa would, but Flick spoke first.

"What happened to your arm?" she asked.

"We don't care," Rushe grumbled.

"I'm guessing that no one here has any updates," Colt said. "I'm waiting for Hoburn to call me. I left him a voicemail."

"How long do we wait?" Ruger asked. "Have you checked in with Lyssa?"

"She'll want to hear progress, and right now we haven't made any."

His phone rang and he was glad to see the detective's name flash up on the screen. "Hoburn?" he answered.

"Got news."

"Great," Colt said, trying not to whoop with joy in present company, maintaining his cool was better for his street cred. "Where did you find him?"

"No," Hoburn said. "We haven't found Harding yet. We're trying to locate his fiancée too. You said she came to yours 'cause her and Harding broke up? But she left your place yesterday morning and went to her sister's?"

"That's right."

"According to the sister, she left there yesterday. No one has seen her since last night," Hoburn said. "She went back over to your place looking for Doctor Cutler."

"My place?" Colt said. "How did you—"

"Spoke to Gus," Hoburn said, though the two weren't best of friends he did know the Warner family. They were related to a lot of people in the neighborhood, so it was hardly unusual. "He said he told her that you'd sent Lyssa home to hang out with her ex-husband."

"That's the news you have?" Colt asked, wondering why Suzette was seeking out Lyssa when she was supposed to be staying with her sister.

"No," Hoburn said, his voice taking a harder line. "I just heard through the grapevine that a guy was arrested, thought it might interest you."

"Connected to Lyssa's stalker?"

"No, connected to your brother being shot," Hoburn said. His focus leaped to Blaser who was sharing a menu with Ruger. "Would you know anything about that?"

"The arrest?" Colt asked, being deliberately evasive. "I don't know anything about that. I've been hunting down Harding all night."

"Whatever. Apparently, the guy was ranting about shooting your brother and phoning the tip in about drugs at Risqué."

"Ranting?"

"Yeah, boasting, 'cept the guy he was talking to happened to be an undercover cop."

Discretion wasn't one of Gary's qualities. He'd be happy to run his mouth, telling people how tough he was, reputation was important to him. Not that his credibility would improve by ratting on himself to an undercover cop. That was as good as turning himself in.

"He's at the precinct now. Waiting for his lawyer… The detective is trying to track Blaser down. You wouldn't know where he is, would you?"

The question was asked with full knowledge that even if Colt didn't know his twin's location, he could track him down. Just so happened that he currently had an eyeball on the person the cops were looking for.

"You want a statement?" Colt asked. "I can pass the message along, but I don't know how cooperative he will be."

"Blaser Warner? Cooperative?" Hoburn laughed. "I don't think there's a cop in the county who would ever make the mistake of believing Blaser would cooperate with an investigation."

"He's straightened out," Colt said, filled with the need to defend his brother, despite often jumping to similar conclusions himself. "I'm sure he'll let you know what happened."

"The question is, why wouldn't Blaser report a shooting? And if he was busted up, who treated him? Do you know any doctors, Colt? Anyone who would be able to patch up a gunshot wound without taking the victim to the emergency room?"

Yeah. Yeah. He got the message.

"I'll let him know," Colt said. "What is Gary looking at?"

His brothers stopped talking to pay attention.

"They've got him on at least wasting police time and knowingly providing false information. With his priors…"

"So why do you care about my brother?"

"You don't have to ask that," Hoburn said. "You're not that long out of the job."

They would want to throw the book at Gary. His record was longer than the state was wide, but most of it was petty. The shooting gave them the chance to get him on something big, especially if they tried to sell it as attempted murder.

"I'm going to call Lys," Colt said. "Ask if Suzette

found her."

"We're heading over that way soon. We were tracking down another lead with the best friend, Keith. Thought it would pan out, but it fell through. We'll have to question Suzette, see if she can provide us with any further ideas. Keep me updated if you get anything?"

"Sure," Colt said and hung up the phone.

"What was that about?" Blaser asked. "You were talking about Gary?"

"He's been arrested."

"For what?"

"Shooting you and calling in the false tip."

Blaser was out of the booth in a heartbeat. "I've got to find Bri."

"Who's Bri?" Flick asked, pushing down the menu that she and Rushe had been hiding behind.

"We don't care," Rushe said.

"Bri will already know he's been arrested," Ruger said to Blaser.

"Yeah, but she won't know what to do about it. I have to go to her or she'll…"

"Think the arrest was your fault," Colt said. "Okay, go, just get in touch when you've seen her, okay?"

"Yeah," Blaser said, shuffling toward the door. "Call me if… you know!"

And he was gone. As much as Blaser wanted to help Lyssa, Colt knew that Bri meant more to him than he was ready to confess. If the situation was reversed and Lyssa was the one in need, he would want to be freed from other responsibilities too. Colt had Ruger, Rushe, and the police department on his side; Blaser and Bri only had each other.

"I'm going outside to call Lyssa," Colt said, shoving Ruger to get him out of the way.

"Are you going to ditch us?" Flick asked.

"He won't ditch," Ruger said, sliding back into the booth once Colt was out of it. "I'll stay here and keep you guys company. We have things to catch up on."

"Yeah," Rushe said, locking eyes with Ruger. "We do."

Colt never worried too much about what Ruger did when he left them. His baby brother could handle himself. He knew more than anyone else about how Ruger made his money, but he hadn't known he dealt with people like Rushe. Finding that out made him question if he should have been paying more attention to his little brother, and if Ruger should be out there on his own without back up.

THE PHONE RANG. Lyssa got up from the bed, showing Pete both hands in surrender.

"I should check who that is," she said.

"If it's Warner, you tell him that you're fine and that you want him to call off the cops," Pete ordered.

"Okay," she said, edging to the handset on her nightstand.

Glancing down, Colt's name flashed up.

"Put it on speaker," Pete demanded, still waving the gun around.

Lyssa nodded once and reached down to press the speaker button. Colt would know he was on speaker; the echoing tone would be impossible to miss. That would be his first clue something was wrong. If she was alone in the house with Archie, she would never put a call between her and her lover on loudspeaker for everyone to hear.

"Hello," she said, remaining calm.

"Hey," Colt said, his tone concise, suggesting there was no good news. Though with the stalker there in front of her, she could be sure that the police hadn't caught him. "How are you doing?"

"I'm okay," she said, just as Pete had instructed her to do.

Their eyes burned into each other. If Pete needed her help, he wouldn't shoot her. At least, not first. Suzette was still on the bed, crying. Her vulnerable friend could be a target.

"Just okay?" he asked. "I'm sorry I haven't called. We've been busy. I want to get this whack-job off the streets."

"I know," Lyssa said, hoping that Pete wouldn't be offended. "But you don't have to."

"Excuse me?"

She wasn't entirely sure how to call off the cops without alerting them that the stalker was there. Obviously, she wanted them to know, but Pete didn't. When he shook the gun at her, she nodded.

"You need to call off the cops. I mean, I don't think that it's necessary to go to all of this effort for one little stalker."

"One little stalker?" Colt repeated. "Are you forgetting what this guy did to Bobby and Lee?"

"No, but I mean, there's no evidence he was involved with the murders at all. It's possible that he was just trying to protect me, or that he's a man in need, a man who just needs a little help from a doctor. That's not a crime. If a patient comes to me for treatment, if he comes here to my home, I need to treat him, don't I?

Colt didn't speak.

The line was still connected. The breeze was still there, as was the occasional sound of passing traffic.

"Okay," Colt said. "I understand. I'll see what I can do."

"Okay, thank you, babe," she said. "I love you."

"I love you too," he said. "Okay? Everything's going to be okay."

"I know."

Pete marched over and prodded the base unit to disconnect the line. "He better get them off my tail," he said, backing away from her again. "This will be over soon, and I don't want them on me forever."

"You said that you needed help, what do you need me to do?"

"You have to apologize, apologize to me for what you did… then you're going to call him."

"Who?"

"Brett! Brett Wilkes!"

It took her a few seconds to process the name. "He was a patient," she said. "I haven't seen him for months."

"No, because you ordered him to leave me and then he moved away. He moved away from me!"

Brett's partner was closeted and didn't want the wider world to know about their relationship. Brett had never revealed his partner's identity, even with their doctor-patient confidentiality. Concealing the truth of who they were took a toll on Brett. As such her advice had been communication, she would never tell a patient to leave a partner in explicit terms. Doing so would often alienate them if they weren't ready to hear that a relationship may be toxic.

"Brett made his own decision about your relationship," Lyssa said. "He loved you, but he believed that you weren't ready to be with him. Brett was comfortable with who he was—"

"So was I! I was comfortable."

"I haven't seen Brett for several months," Lyssa said. "I don't know where he is. I know that he left his partner because he couldn't live the lie anymore. He wanted to be free of the deception and let the world know how he loved you. By denying him that right, he felt that he was suppressing a part of himself. You weren't comfortable with who you were, with being in a same sex relationship, and he felt that you didn't love him like he loved you. Your unwillingness to be open hurt—"

"It wasn't like that!"

"Forgive me," Lyssa said, seating herself on the bed in front of Suzette, whose volume was increasing. "But you have been in a relationship with a woman, a relationship that was supposed to culminate in marriage. How do you identify your sexuality?"

"I heard what Brett said when he left me. I heard it when he told me he didn't believe I was ready to be with him… I thought maybe he was right and I… I knew that being gay would hurt everyone in my life and…"

Now that the shouting had stopped, she was getting through to him. "Being in that position must have been very difficult."

"I knew that if I couldn't be with Brett that I couldn't be with any man…"

"So you sought out Suzette?"

Shaking his head, he maintained his aim with the gun,

but lowered his focus. "No, I didn't look for her."

"If you were conflicted, you could have sought professional help yourself. Losing someone you love is a—"

"I did! I… I went to a pastor."

"A pastor," she repeated, that hadn't been the kind of help that she had meant.

"Yes, he gave me advice and he… I went to a doctor that he recommended. The pastor promised that this doctor could cure me, and I did everything that he told me to."

"Cure you," she said. "You thought that if you couldn't work out your relationship with Brett, if you couldn't have him, then you couldn't be gay? Is that what you thought?"

"I did everything the doctor said," Pete murmured, his shoulders sagged but when he lifted his attention, there were tears in his eyes. "He gave me drugs, they made me really sick, and he gave me injections. I had to watch movies…"

Rubbing his eyes with a free hand, she didn't know if he was trying to erase the tears or the images the so-called doctor had put in his mind.

Her limited research on these conversion camps hadn't turned up anything positive. In fact, everything she learned of them only made her sick. These places should be outlawed as far as she was concerned; here was no use in a person denying who they were. Often the camps did severe, long-term psychological damage to people who had no pre-existing conditions other than their aversion, or anxiety, about admitting who they really were.

"What you went through must have been traumatic," she said, leaving the bed to take half a step toward him. "Denying who you are is never the answer."

"I know that now! I know that!

"Okay," she said, holding her hands up again. "Good. I'm glad that you are ready to move past that experience."

"I met Keith at the camp, we were supposed to… to support each other, and make sure that we didn't… revert."

"Keith knows that you are here today?"

"No, I couldn't admit to him that I… that I failed."

"You haven't failed," she said. "This is a victory. You

should be proud of yourself for recognizing your true self. You have nothing to be ashamed of. If being with a man, in a relationship with a man, makes you happy, you should embrace that."

"How can I? The only man I want is Brett and I already lost him. You made sure of that!"

"Maybe it's not too late," she said. "Maybe you can get in touch with him and—"

"I can't find him! He left me and he took everything with him! The man I love is gone! That's why I'm here."

"Why you're here?" she asked, unsure what resolution he sought.

"You're going to undo this. You're going to find him. You must be able to find him."

"I… I don't think that I have a phone number or an address for him. We could go downstairs and check for—"

"No! I don't want your lies and your manipulation! Fix it! All I want you to do is to fix it."

A tear skittered down his face.

"Why don't we start by making sure that when you do find Brett, you can be with him and never find yourself in this situation again."

From the way his brow shifted, he hadn't considered that. "What…? What do you mean?"

"Well, Brett wanted to be with you. It was your reluctance to be open about your relationship that caused it to end."

"No! No, it was you! Brett loved me but you told him to leave me!"

"Is that why you've been doing all of this?" she asked. "You blame me for losing Brett?"

Reversing until his back hit the wall, he strengthened the arm that was holding the gun. Holding it aloft for so long would be tiring. "I came to find you. I wanted to talk to you. I… I called your office. As soon as I told you I was the partner of a patient, you refused to see me. I didn't get to explain. I didn't even mention Brett and you cut me off."

It was her policy not to treat both sides of a relationship without the express consent and knowledge of the other party. Even that was rare. Usually, she'd see both partners as a couple, with only the occasional complementary solo session, if required.

"It can create a conflict," she explained. "If you told me that you were the partner of a patient, and that the patient didn't know you were contacting me, I would have been against treating you. It's only fair that my existing patient takes priority."

"But he wasn't your patient, he had already left me! You didn't let me explain."

Either she had been busy, or his erratic nature had come across on the call. "I'm sorry," she said.

"I started to watch you, to see if you'd been telling the truth, and if Brett was still coming to you. I thought he might still be in the city."

"You watched me through the city network of cameras," she said. "That was inappropriate."

"It's no big deal to get into that system," he said. "If they really wanted to keep people out then they would protect it and they don't."

After the truth of Pete's crimes came out in the press, the city would no doubt be more particular about the security of that system. Of course, that would be too late to help her and Suzette.

"It's very intrusive," she said.

"The cameras are there to watch people who need to be watched. You were going around telling people to break hearts, to devastate lives, that makes you dangerous. I wanted to know how you could live with yourself, and what made you so special that you get to decide who should have love and who shouldn't. So I just tapped in to see how you lived your life after you had ruined mine."

"But your need to see me grew?"

"I saw you with your friend, happy and laughing. I couldn't understand how you could be happy when you'd torn my world apart."

"You wanted to hurt those I cared about? Was that your goal?"

"No," he said, his gun slipped lower.

Suzette was beginning to quiet.

Worried about her friend's wellbeing, Lyssa glanced back to see Suzette was listening. "Why get involved with Suzette? Were you trying to convince yourself that you were straight?"

"I wanted to get closer, to talk to you, to make you see what you were doing was wrong. I wanted to be around, in your life, in case Brett made contact with you. I even thought about getting into your office to find out if you knew where Brett was. But I couldn't approach you directly, so I got a job at the hospital where you had privileges and sought Suzie then."

"To seduce her? I don't—"

"How she could be friends with such a callous person was beyond me," he carried on as though Lyssa hadn't spoken, further displaying his narcissism. "Suzie gave me the chance to get close to you; she made it clear that she was interested in me. When she started to lose interest, or noticed my lack of interest rather, I proposed. Maintaining interest in her when I knew my heart was Brett's was difficult; after the proposal I didn't have to, she just ran with it."

"You used her," Lyssa said. Did he see the callousness of his own actions? "But I don't understand the rest, the flowers, the notes, the rock through the window?"

"You told Brett that I wasn't a good person to have a relationship with. I proved you wrong, I sent flowers, and was attentive in watching you everywhere, just like I would watch over Brett. You should've been impressed I was so thoughtful… you took it all the wrong way."

The first note saying, *"I see you"* creeped her out. Apparently, it was supposed to make her feel watched over, that was probably his reasoning behind the photographs and the video too.

"You were filming me."

"To protect you," he said. "I showed you what it was to protect someone. I've done more for you than your own supposed boyfriend. You told Brett to get rid of me because I hurt him, and I wanted to prove to you that I wouldn't hurt him, that I could be the best boyfriend there was."

"Is that why you killed Bobby?"

"He was telling people that you were sleeping with patients. If you lost your license, then Brett would never come back. Lee was pissed at you too after Archie showed up in his session. I protected you. I am a good partner and you're going to tell Brett that."

"I can't, I don't know where he is."

"You'll find him," Pete said. "You will find him. You'll make him come back to me and tell him all the nice things I've done for you, how I'll do anything it takes to protect someone important to me."

Even if she found Brett, she doubted he'd be tempted to come back just because Pete sent her some pretty flowers and murdered people who were mean about her. But it was clear that Pete wasn't in his right mind. Perhaps he had always struggled with mental illness, or the conversion camp may have tipped him over the edge. Whichever it was, his rational mind was long gone now.

"What about the brick?"

"You took all my good deeds the wrong way. Suzie told me everything. You were calling me some kind of crazy stalker set on scaring you," he said, his weight sagging deeper against the wall.

His focus was slipping, like maybe it was all too much.

"You were angry at me?" That started at witnessing what he dubbed her interference in Brett and Pete's relationship. "You wanted me to be scared?"

"I wanted you to think twice about what you were saying to patients. I had no idea how many happy couples you were breaking up."

"That doesn't explain the brick through the window or the shooting outside Risqué."

His smile inched up. "The brick was fun; I wanted to see you scared. Like I was scared… when I lost Brett. Paying some kid to throw the brick through the window was easy. I wanted to be there to see your face when it happened."

"No wonder you wanted to run away so fast afterwards," she said. "You didn't want to talk to the cops. You wanted to get out of there."

Finding sympathy for him was getting more difficult by the second.

"It was my chance to get you and Suzette apart. Like I said, I didn't want her involved. I wanted her to stay away from your poison and I didn't want her to be here now, for this."

"You didn't want anyone looking for you," she said. "You didn't want Suzette to support me because you didn't want to be caught. But, surely, you wouldn't have married her? She would have been hurt when you dumped her."

"I planned to be gentle," he proclaimed. "By then, you would have ensured Brett and I were back together. Suzette would understand where my heart lay. Brett and I would have left quietly, and none of this would have happened… then Warner got involved."

"Colt? What has he got to do with…?"

Sirens outside broke her concentration. Pete grabbed hold of her to drag her through the house into the living room. Holding her body in front of him, he peeked past the edge of the curtain. Outside a dozen police cars, and twice as many officers, all pointed at her house.

"What have you done?" Pete shouted, throwing Lyssa back.

She stumbled on the edge of the rug and collapsed next to Archie's body but kept her eyes on the gun. "I think they're here for you."

"You were supposed to call them off! What am I supposed to do now?"

Panic lit his alert eyes and edgy movements. Questions piled up, but those would have to wait until his surprise waned.

Suzette was in the bedroom, crying again, screaming so loud they heard it at the opposite end of the house. It didn't matter. The police knew they were there. They just didn't know who would come out alive, and right now, neither did she.

THIRTY-FIVE

HOBURN WAS JUST A FEW feet inside the cordon.

"What's going on in there?" Colt hollered at him.

"We don't know yet," Hoburn said. "They're not picking up the phone."

Within a minute of his call with Lyssa, he'd known something was wrong. Calling the cops was instinct, was it a mistake? All this activity could freak the fucker out.

"Who is in there?" Colt asked. "Have your guys got a line of sight—"

"We're still getting set up," Hoburn said, walking away.

Damn. Goddamn, mother—he was powerless. On the outside looking in. A bystander.

He'd get in there if he could, but with all these witnesses, how far would he get?

"What's going on?" Ruger asked, coming up next to Colt with Flick at his side.

"I don't know," Colt said. "They'll try to get a line of sight… I don't know where Harding is, there's a lot of dark corners in there, hard to see places, from out here anyway." Flick nodded and rolled her eyes toward the building. The way she loitered behind Ruger was suspicious. "Are you worried that someone will see you?"

"The police?" Flick asked. "No… not around here anyway. Now if we were in New Jersey and all of these cops were here…"

Her attempt at a joke increased his mistrust.

"Where's Rushe?" he asked.

"Rushe does have an aversion to cops," Ruger said. "He's probably wanted in every state… and maybe Canada too."

"He is not," Flick said. "He's helping. Standing around on the side-lines isn't Rushe's style."

Rushe had vanished almost as soon as he gave them the news that Pete was at Lyssa's. He'd been in the midst of dialing Hoburn when Rushe kissed the face off Flick, turned and took off. Would he ever know the guy's intention? Probably not.

New Jersey was an interesting reference. No way well-spoken Flick was from there originally. It had to be where she and her lover were based. Taking their double act on the road was a good indicator of how serious they were about helping the brother-in-law, Lyssa's patient. Schifford had been so serious about concealing his therapy that he only visited Lyssa when he was in the area on business. So many people led such complicated lives.

"Where does Schifford live?"

"Not far from my parents," Flick said.

"Which is where?"

"What do you care?"

Had she always been cagey with details or had Rushe changed her? "Does he know that this is going on?"

"We don't talk much," Flick said. "He only comes down here once a month or so to deal with clients; that's when he saw Doctor Cutler. He's at home with my sister right now. We would rather if this little problem went away without him being directly involved."

Like having to give a statement to the police or standing up in court against the suspect. Narrowing his eyes, Colt turned to examine the house. They wanted a dead suspect, not one who would be able to plead innocent or insanity in order to go to trial. With that clarity, he figured out Rushe's location.

HER FATE WAS PREDICTABLE when Harding tied Suzette to the end of the living room radiator. The other end was reserved for her. At least being on the floor gave them clearance from anything the cops might do to end the standoff. Whatever outcome Pete anticipated, the police surrounding the property wasn't part of it.

"You have to talk to them," Lyssa said. The phone had just stopped ringing for the tenth time or so. "They'll want to know what you want."

"You know what I want!" he snapped.

The shouting wasn't pleasant, but it was an improvement over the stony silence he'd displayed since discovering the police outside.

"If Brett is what you want, tell them that," she said. "They are the police. They should be able to find him."

Sitting on the floor, at the back of the couch, Pete paused like maybe he was considering it. "Do you think they could?" he asked eventually.

"Yes," she said. "Tell them that you want to talk to him. Maybe he'll want to come back."

That could buy some time for Colt and the police to come up with other options.

"It will take him time to get here," Pete said, shaking his head.

"What choice do you have?" she asked. "You have to talk to them, or we'll never get out of here and you'll never see Brett again."

Again, he paused. A range of emotions flickered across his face. The situation was terrifying, no doubt about that, but Pete did offer an interesting professional conundrum. Often those so far gone in their psychosis struggled to maintain any sort of normal life.

Pete's insanity had extended to rationalizing murder. That put him at the peak of the scale. The rest of his days would be spent in an institution. Even if medication and counselling helped, there would be little hope of him returning to society.

"You talk to them," he said, crawling across the floor toward her.

Keeping low suggested a fear of snipers. Smart. Her large windows provided an excellent, open view. Good for this situation. Not so good when he was using street cameras to peer inside.

He began to loosen her bounds. The gun rested beside his thigh. Was she brave enough to grab it?

Suzette squeaked, attracting her and Pete's attention. Before she could blink, another figure appeared.

Pete scrambled for the gun, but it was already gone.

Free of her bonds, Lyssa scrambled toward Suzette, using her body as a shield while trying to loosen her friend's restraints.

Bang.

One single sound put the world on pause.

Her back was turned, she hadn't seen the kill shot, but she didn't need to. When she peeked over her shoulder, there was no doubting Pete was dead. Only moments ago, he'd been threatening their lives. Now he was a lifeless corpse. Thanks to the looming form in the shadow of the hall doorway.

"Rushe," she said, having just enough breath left in her body to form the word.

"I was never here," he said. "You guys got the gun yourselves."

"I...I..."

Suzette must have been free enough to finish untying herself because she pulled down the gag and got to her feet. Her limbs were shaking, her face tear stained, but determination glowed in her. Suzette passed Lyssa and held an open palm to Rushe.

"Give it to me," Suzette said.

"What?" Lyssa said.

"I'll tell them I did it," Suzette said, her eyes fixed on Rushe. "Thank you for saving our lives."

The situation had come to a quick end. After shock

subsided, only relief remained in its place. The phone rang again. For a few blurred moments, no one moved.

Colt.

Lyssa got up and ran over to grab the phone.

"He's dead," she said, whipping around to seek out Suzette. Rushe was already gone. "It's safe to come in. Pete is dead. Archie is dead too… and I really need to speak to Colt Warner."

"We're coming in," Hoburn's voice came down the line. "You did good."

The line died.

Suzette stood gazing down at Pete.

"Honey…" Lyssa started, moving toward her. "Are you okay?"

"All this time," Suzette said.

"I'm so sorry."

Noise of police entering the front door echoed up the stairs.

Suzette shook off her confusion to look at Lyssa and whisper. "He put the gun down to free you so that you could talk to them, just like what happened. I'd managed to loosen the rope; I grabbed the gun."

Lyssa nodded once just as the SWAT team came in with their guns high. Both women raised their hands.

NO ONE ELSE TRIED TO SHOOT at them. The activity was focused first on the two static bodies in the living room. It was quickly established that they were in fact deceased. Colt came in with Hoburn after SWAT. Before the detective had a chance to ask anything, Colt demanded that both women were checked out by the paramedics.

Activity remained constant. Both were cleared by the EMT's, and then Hoburn started in on his questioning. Her statement was taken, but she would be called into the precinct at a later date to confirm the details and sign off on it. As promised, neither she nor Suzette mentioned Rushe to the cops. Only after Colt came back to her side did she have a chance to breathe and absorb the melee of people surrounding them, each with their own purpose.

With her lover, the truth would out. If he started in on his questioning first, she'd have no chance to ask anything. "Where is everyone?"

"Ruger is with Suzette," he said. "Shooting someone can shake a person up. Especially when you kill them. I asked him to sit with her for a while.

"And Blaser?"

"With Bri, her brother was arrested today. She's going through a difficult time. I called to let him know what was going on while you were giving your statement."

Blaser was showing Bri he could be there for her in a time of need, that was good. Did Bri know that Gary had shot Blaser? Did she suspect her brother's motives were linked to her trauma, as Blaser did?

The crowd of cops and other professionals thinned. A crime scene crew were in her house documenting everything. That left her on the opposite sidewalk, unable to do anything but watch troupes of people going in and out of her house.

"Rushe shot him," she murmured, still staring at her home.

"What?" Colt asked.

His strong hands curled around the back of her neck to pull her close. She needed his strength. Valued it.

"Rushe, he appeared from nowhere. Pete untied me to talk to the police, to negotiate. Then Rushe came in, one shot, Pete was dead. It was over that quickly."

"These situations can drag on, but the end? It's usually quick."

"Rushe asked us to say he wasn't there. Suzette jumped at the chance to take responsibility."

Her eyes wandered to his, reading his concern and surprise at her confession.

"She probably feels responsible… for trusting Pete," Colt said.

"How did you know it was him?" she asked. "Why didn't you tell me?"

"I couldn't tell you," he said. "If I had, your actions

and body language would have clued him in that we knew. You and Suzette were going through enough, this way you didn't have to lie to her."

"But how did you know?"

"The pictures were taken from above. Only someone with tech skills could've accessed the city cameras that have those angles. After ruling out employees with access, the list of possible suspects dropped. You remember the morning after the shooting? When I called you a genius and ran out on you?"

"Yes."

"That was when I realized the pictures were taken from above, from the city's camera network. Figuring out who had access to that system was harder. Tracking down the details of people with the skills to access the network illegally meant calling in a favor from an old friend."

"And that told you it was Pete?"

Shaking his head, he took her hand to lead her to the furthest point from the house within the cordon, far away from listening ears. "Pinch tracked down who purchased the camera we found in your bedroom, and where the feed transmitted to," he said. "I didn't know for sure until I cross-referenced both sets of data. Once I did, I got our guy."

"The night you were installing security?"

"Ruger and I went into Harding's place and found evidence," Colt said. "The only thing I hadn't established was why. I don't know his motive."

"He was gay and in love with one of my patients. When they split, he went to a conversion camp that promised to straighten him out. Whatever chemicals they gave him, coupled with the brainwashing and counselling… he lost his mind. No doubt there was a pre-existing mental illness, one that probably made it difficult for him to come to terms with who he was. In a lot of ways, he was a victim too."

"Yeah?" Colt said. "Please don't tell me that you feel sorry for the guy?"

Suzette and Ruger appeared from the muddle of professionals doing their job up ahead. Ruger supported her teary best friend under his arm, bringing her across the sidewalk. As soon as they were close enough, she left Colt's hands and gave Suzette a hug.

"Oh honey, how are you doing?" Lyssa asked. They hadn't seen each other since they were side by side in the ambulance. The cops had taken their statements separately; there had been no time to offer her support. "I'm so sorry about all of this."

"I should be apologizing to you," Suzette said, mustering a smile when they broke their hug. "All of this time, and everything that you went through and… I gave him access to you, I… I told him things that he must have used against you, or to get close to you. I told him about that guy being unhappy, Lee. I was the one who told Pete about Archie ending your session and… now both of those men are dead."

"This is not your fault," Lyssa said. "I'm just so pleased that it's over and no one got hurt… Well… I mean except…"

Suzette's fiancé was gone. The wedding plans loomed over them. Just a few hours ago, Suzette had hopes she'd be walking down the aisle. In the duration of the ordeal, she learned her groom was gay and never really interested in marrying her. Suzette had been through a lot and would probably need some counselling of her own.

"I've told Suze that she can stay at my place," Ruger said.

"You move fast," Colt said.

Ruger's lips curled and he draped an arm around Suzette again. No doubt her friend took comfort in the consoling gesture. "I'm heading out of town for a while. She can stay in my place while she gets back on her feet."

"It's not like I want to go back to Pete's," Suzette said. "I really do appreciate the offer."

"That's perfect," Lyssa said, slipping an arm around Colt's waist. "I'll probably be spending a lot of time over there."

"Doubt it," Colt said, countering her arm with his own, lowering a cheek onto her head. "Being I'll be living in your house with you."

Stepping back, Lyssa looked up at him. "You will?"

"No reason not to," he said. "We'll end up moving in together anyway. Why shouldn't we? I love you."

Eloquent. Her man made a good point and proved he was open to being communicative. Good. Wow. He was incredible. "We'll have to stay at yours until all of these guys are out of my place."

"A night or two at most," he said. "It'll give me time to pack."

"What will Blaser say?"

"Good riddance," Ruger interjected.

"What happened to Rushe and his girlfriend?" Suzette asked.

Everyone took time to look around, but there was no sign of the couple.

"It's typical of them to do their work and disappear," Ruger said. "Which I should do too."

"You be careful," Colt said to his brother. "Call me when you get where you're going."

Ruger nodded then sighed down at Suzette. "I'll take you to pick up your crap from Harding's and give you a ride to my place."

"Thanks," she said.

The women hugged and made plans to see each other at Colt's after Suzette was settled in. The brothers did a complicated handshake and shared a man hug, then Ruger took Suzette away.

"I hope that Blaser is okay," Lyssa said, watching Ruger and Suzette disappear around the corner.

"He'll be fine as long as he gets things straightened out with Bri."

"And if he doesn't?"

"Are you kidding? Now that we have you in the family, the Warners won't have relationship troubles, or secrets."

He took her away from the house, probably to find a cab somewhere away from the hubbub. All she wanted to do was get back to his place to sleep in the arms of the man she loved... maybe after a little quiet—or not so quiet—private bonding time.

"I don't know your parents very well yet, but your mom worries about Ruger the most. I don't think she'd ever say it because he's proud of acting so capable."

"We all worry about Ruger the most," Colt said. "But he's a smart kid and he knows what he's doing."

They got away from the scene and were walking toward a busy street, somewhere they would be sure to get a taxi.

"I can't believe it's over."

"I'm just sorry you had to go through it at all," he said, pressing a kiss to her head.

"I had to go through it," she said.

"Had to?"

"If I hadn't, I would never have found you," she said. "The chances of me wandering into Risqué on my own were pretty slim."

"We should buy Miguel a gift," Colt said, pulling her closer. "Something to say thanks for hooking us up."

"About that," she said. "How about instead of seeing the damsels you intend to save at Risqué, you start seeing them at the house?"

"Your house?"

"Our house," she said. "We can finally get around to remodeling the top floor."

"I thought that was for when you planned to have kids," he said.

"Which will work out perfectly."

"It will?"

"You can babysit during the day while I see patients, and I'll take over the responsibilities at night when you're prowling… They have two uncles and an aunt who will be more than happy to take their turn looking after them."

"You think?"

"Suzette will be like an aunt. Ruger can babysit while he's in town, and Blaser will enjoy spending time with them as well."

"Blaser? With kids?" Colt said as though he'd never considered it.

"He'll have time to warm up to the idea," she said.

"We'll have to practice while the renovation work is going on. I don't want to be pregnant in a house full of dust and construction workers."

They continued walking to the end of the block. Had her presumptuousness freaked him out? He'd gotten away with being bold about the moving in, why should they abide by two different rules?

"You want to have kids?" he asked after a long silence. "With me?"

"I want to have kids with you."

"Man…" he said and sighed, linking his fingers between hers. "Mom's going to love you."

"If you're not sure about us, you should—"

"I'm sure," he said, pulling her to a stop at the edge of the sidewalk to wrap his arms around her. "I plan to get down on one knee, I think I started considering it the night we met."

She laughed. "I plan to say yes."

"Good," he said, unable to contain his smile. "You took a helluva risk coming to me in Risqué that first night. But I'm glad you did."

"You," she said, pressing herself close. "Were definitely a risk worth taking."

Pushing onto her tiptoes, she traced her lips on his. He didn't want anything soft or sweet and pressed harder, demanding more. A craving to be ensconced in his apartment, alone with him, burst within her. Grabbing his hand, she broke the kiss and ran into the street to stop the first cab that passed.

Practicing baby-making was an excuse to get naked with him. One she'd take full advantage of. Being with this man, now that the drama was over, would bring her peace. Her life had a new direction. Now that she had Colt, she would never be alone on her journey again.

TO BE CONTINUED...

Thank you for reading this tale!
If you can, please take the time to review.

~

Ask your local library for more Scarlett Finn novels!

~

For all things Scarlett Finn
check out:

www.scarlettfinn.com

BOOK TWO

SCARLETT FINN

OUT NOW!

www.ingramcontent.com/pod-product-compliance
Lightning Source LLC
Chambersburg PA
CBHW060754190726
48285CB00002B/426